ABOUT TH

Susan Rollinson has worked for most of her life as a teacher in secondary, further and higher education, teaching English and Philosophy as well as delivering Teacher Training and MSc programmes. Her writing is inspired both by her literary passion and by her strong interest in history. She has lived in rural Hertfordshire and Buckinghamshire for most of her life and is widely travelled.

www.susanrollinson.com

VOICES PAST

06.10.18

To Timmy

Enjoy!

Best wishes,

Susan Rollinson

SUSAN ROLLINSON

Copyright © 2009 Susan Rollinson

The moral right of the author has been asserted.

Apart from any fair dealing for the purposes of research or private study, or criticism or review, as permitted under the Copyright, Designs and Patents Act 1988, this publication may only be reproduced, stored or transmitted, in any form or by any means, with the prior permission in writing of the publishers, or in the case of reprographic reproduction in accordance with the terms of licences issued by the Copyright Licensing Agency. Enquiries concerning reproduction outside those terms should be sent to the publishers.

Matador
5 Weir Road
Kibworth Beauchamp
Leicester LE8 0LQ, UK
Tel: (+44) 116 279 2299
Fax: 0116 279 2277
Email: books@troubador.co.uk
Web: www.troubador.co.uk/matador

ISBN 978 1848762 664

British Library Cataloguing in Publication Data.
A catalogue record for this book is available from the British Library.

Typeset in 11pt Bembo by Troubador Publishing Ltd, Leicester, UK
Printed in the UK by TJ International, Padstow, Cornwall

Matador is an imprint of Troubador Publishing Ltd

For Keith Doughty who provided constant inspiration

ACKNOWLEDGEMENTS

Grateful thanks to the following people who helped me in so many ways to write and research my book. Everyone gave of their time freely and all of them offered me much needed support at the various stages of my writing. *Voices Past* would not have been written without them.

Judith Furse, my good friend
Brett Thorn, Keeper of Archaeology at Bucks County Museum
David Jenkins, Superintendent Minister of Aylesbury Vale Methodist Circuit
Richard Carter, Builder
David Grubb, Fee Chandler, Carole Laskin, Natasha Stevens, Julie Austin
Tim Drinkall, Cover Design

Thanks also to Boscastle Museum of Witchcraft for their kind permission to use images from their collection.

VOICES PAST

Susan Rollinson

A deep, dark, dreadful secret
Lies hereunder, beneath our very feet.
We, the living, solemnly swear
We owe it to the dead,
To unbury past deeds and question why,
To unleash their secrets, open wide
The chasms long forgot, ring out
The desperate tales of hidden death.

1740 Anon

CHAPTER 1

As I stand looking out of the kitchen window a grey haired man emerges from the chapel next door pushing an antiquated black trolley with a coffin perched on top. The trolley moves reluctantly across the bumpy stone surface as the man thrusts it towards the pavement, seemingly intent on going in another direction. Wearing a black suit and top hat the man looks like something out of a film. Perhaps he's an actor. I glance up and down the road.

The man jostles the trolley onto the pavement and turns his head back towards the chapel as a line of darkly clad mourners materialises in his wake. Nodding to them to follow he trudges off along the pavement past my house heading in the direction of the church. Maybe it's real after all. There's no sign of a film crew.

I dart to follow his trundling progress past the line of windows fronting the house, the coffin so close I could reach out and touch it. The elderly pall bearer bends forward as he pushes his load with the funeral procession filing past the windows behind him and I wonder fleetingly what will happen if the coffin falls off. Will the body roll out or is the lid fixed down in some way? I have images of a white shrouded body toppling into the road, the black suited man looking suitably aghast. What a bizarre burial custom.

The recalcitrant trolley and trail of mourners disappear from view at the end of the house only to reappear again several moments later as they cross the road, the traffic drawn to a halt. The procession reaches the other side and moves slowly up the lane to the church and then is abruptly gone from sight.

As the afternoon lengthens Barnie my Labrador cross sidles up to me and I realise it's time for his afternoon walk. Taking up his lead I fasten his collar and put on anorak and boots and making my way out of the house I cross the road, drawn to the burial scene.

Hesitantly I approach the group of mourners gathered at the graveside at the far end of the churchyard, Barnie a pale shadow at my side. Standing in the background I watch whilst each of the figures silhouetted in the darkening afternoon takes a handful of earth in turn and throws it gently on top of the coffin, the stony earth making a sharp clattering sound as it lands on the shiny wood.

The cameo seems etched in time as I draw back into the long grass. And then as the darkness wraps itself around them the mourners move silently round the grave peering down at the coffin and murmuring softly to one another. The procession moves slowly away, back round the side of the church towards the lane and I notice a small boy clutching a cuddly toy to his chest as he struggles to keep up with his mother.

Am I imagining it or is there someone over behind the chestnut trees? I sense someone watching me. Turning I catch a glimpse of a shadowy figure in the clump of trees, is it a lingering mourner I wonder? The figure moves behind the trees and is gone.

Cutting briskly across the churchyard I reach the footpath leading to the cricket pitch, I can see the gravedigger through the fence now moving to centre stage and taking final charge of the coffin. He shovels the mound of rocky earth back into the grave mechanically, the clatter of the soil breaking the silence, the increasingly earthy odour of disturbed soil reaching my nostrils. I can hear his hoarse breathing in the chill air as I call to Barnie and set off across the field.

Next day I return to the graveyard. The freshly filled grave is covered with brightly coloured autumn flowers laid in remembrance of one Chloe Ward. Resplendent in the sunshine with wreaths of red and yellow chrysanthemums, orange and yellow gerberas, red and white carnations and crimson roses with sprays of indigo flowers trimmed with gypsophila, the riot of colours enlivening the surrounding graves.

And who is Chloe Ward I wonder? The tiny brass-coloured plaque gives her name but no age, no details and I can only imagine what she was like, how she came to die; whether it was a timely death or a death too soon.

As I move away through the old part of the graveyard I notice the centuries old gravestones sticking up like old teeth now worn and weather-beaten into strange and unusual shapes, some lying askew, some propped from behind by a stone. No-one to tend these graves nor to think of the departed, no enduring words engraved on them.

The dead are now anonymous.

CHAPTER 2

Surprising the number of people who pass by the house I thought as I sat over coffee the next morning. Must be going to get their papers I thought abstractedly as I finished the last of my toast. During the week there were fewer villagers about.

I returned to my book, a light novel which made for uncomplicated reading. Just what I needed at the moment. Finishing my coffee and pouring myself another cup I stood up, a long lonely Saturday ahead. Bury yourself in work and you'll get by I told myself, that and take Barnie for a long walk.

Teaching at the nearby university there was always plenty of marking and preparation to do and it helped make the weekends pass quickly. Now on my own and new to the village I had few friends in the area and it would inevitably take time to get to know people. Widowed suddenly three years ago at the age of twenty eight, I'd made the move to the house several months ago.

The house was immediately absorbing and had captivated my imagination. From the moment I stepped inside to look at it that spring day six months ago it had me fixated.

Middle House

Why Middle House had been my first thought. I was still no nearer to finding an answer to that question. It wasn't in the middle of the village and it wasn't in the middle of a row of houses, the chapel being on one side and a detached house on the other. So middle of what?

The house had been completely bare when I first viewed it, the previous occupants having already moved out so there was nothing in it to take my eye from the intriguing nooks and crannies, the old beams and open grates, the low ceilings and uneven walls. I remembered reaching up and being able to touch the ceiling in the dining room without even standing on my toes. Although it was a cottage the rooms were quite large and airy with good sized windows. The kitchen would need a fair amount of work but I could see beyond that and picture a new cottage style kitchen with a comforting Aga in the inglenook.

And then I'd gone upstairs. After looking at the bedrooms with their sloping ceilings and small windows set into the roof like eyes I had looked out of the back at the rolling landscape and the line of trees beyond the garden fence. The garden was large, too large for me really I thought. But there was something about the place. This is my house I'd whispered to myself, it's for me and I knew right away that I had to buy it.

I never even met the previous owners who had accepted my offer via their solicitor. As soon as the offer was accepted I had pushed through the sale of my own house and hastened the move as fast as I could. Now established in the house with my new kitchen and maroon-coloured Aga I felt settled and had a sense of belonging within the village even though I hardly knew anyone.

When Mark died I stayed put in our house for a while and then keen to make a fresh life for myself I applied for several teaching posts outside London and had landed a job in Buckinghamshire. Hence the move to Whittlesham, just on the outskirts of Milton Keynes.

I moved over to the sink and looked through the delicately patterned frosted glass window. The sun shone brightly on the grassy bank opposite belying the chilly feel in the air and I could see the line of horse chestnuts beginning to shed their copper and gold coloured tresses, the leaves piling in swathes beside the wooden bench beneath them. I took a deep breath.

My first autumn, my fresh start.

❦

A couple of days later whilst painting the wooden gates at the side of the house I was interrupted by Harry Furlong. Harry, a retired villager, seemed to fill his time wandering around the village chatting to all and sundry.

Lost in thought I realised with a start that Harry was saying something to me. "What did you say? Dead bodies. Bodies under the house!" I said abruptly.

"Mm, yeah, that's right. Yer've got dead bodies under yer house. Down in yer cellars," Harry repeated deliberately. He fixed me with a knowing look and nodded as he spoke, his pipe gripped firmly between his yellow stained teeth.

I had a sudden vision of something awful being discovered beneath the house, piled up bodies buried in earth and cement. All too often these things were in the news. Or was he talking about bodies buried long ago?

"What kind of dead bodies?" I asked. "No-one told me about any cellars or anything about dead bodies," but I was talking to myself. Harry was trudging off down the street, puffing steadily on his pipe. He was dressed as usual in a pair of faded brown trousers and an old check jacket, his tweed cap pulled down hard on his forehead.

Putting Harry's unexpected comments deliberately to one side I decided to concentrate on finishing the gate before it rained, and worked steadily on until the gates were finished.

A bit later on I called in on my neighbour Bernard in the hopes of finding something out about the cellars under the house and also to shed light on Harry Furlong's disquieting mention of dead bodies. Bernard was a broad-shouldered ex-boxer with a somewhat battered nose. He and his elderly wife had been very friendly ever since I'd moved into the village. He'd lived in the village all his life and it seemed to me that if anyone was going to know about the house and its past it was him.

"As far as I can recollect," he said thoughtfully in reply to my question, "the cellars under your house were quite extensive. Three or four of them I think." He paused, scratching his head. "But I don't think there's any way into them now," he continued. "As I remember my parents bought this house around the 1930s. The original house had been demolished before their time as it was falling into disrepair. It would've been similar to yours as far as I know."

"Oh," I said. "That's a surprise. Your house is quite different to mine now. So it would have originally been the same?"

"So it was but it had to be pulled down as I heard it. It had become almost derelict. But we've got the old cellars under here same as before."

"Maybe I can have a look at them some time?" I asked.

"Course you can m' dear," said Bernard. "They're jammed full of rubbish like most cellars. One day I must turn them out."

"Now I come to think of it," he added, "I remember hearing something about the entrance to your cellars having been blocked off a long time ago on the Methodist's land."

"How strange," I said. "I wonder why the entrance was outside the house. Doesn't make sense to me. So where would the entrance have been, do you know?"

"Just by your kitchen window if I recall right," said Bernard. "I can't remember how I heard about it. Must've been ages back, when I was a child."

"Very odd."

"Yep, it is odd. I've no idea why that was the case. I suppose there must've been a reason for it."

"Yes I'm sure. Anyway Bernard," I asked cautiously, "are you aware of anything to do with dead bodies connected to my house? Harry Furlong dropped it into the conversation this morning when I was painting the gates."

"Nothing that I know of," said Bernard shrugging his shoulders. "And you know I've lived here all my life. Except when I was away in the war of course."

7

"Well Harry said something like 'You've got dead bodies under the house'. What could he mean by that?" I asked.

"Oh you know what Harry Furlong's like," said Bernard with a smile. "He's always on the gossip and much of it is just tittle tattle. He means no harm."

"Oh no, I'm sure he's not malicious," I said uncertainly. "But there must be something in what he said. He had no reason to just come out with something like that."

"Best forget about it. I certainly don't know anything about any dead bodies," said Bernard. "Come on. Let's go and take Doris a coffee. She's in the garden."

CHAPTER 3

"Yes Fee, your house does date back a long way. Probably to medieval times," said Michael, nodding.

Bernard had pointed me in the direction of Michael Baines as someone who could help me find out more about the house and its cellars.

Michael, a local teacher and historian, was a tall and somewhat rumpled looking figure in his forties. He had welcomed me cheerily into his sprawling house just up the road. Now we were seated opposite one another in a pair of rose coloured settees in his sitting room, a large room with double French windows leading into an overgrown cottage garden.

"Your house was probably built around the mid-1500s," he said thoughtfully, "going by the structure and the brick and stone construction."

"As old as that," I said. "How on earth can you tell?"

"Well," replied Michael, "it's the quality of the materials that's the clue. Often the oldest surviving houses were built from stone and materials taken from other buildings. For example, during the Dissolution of the Monasteries many of the Abbeys were deconstructed and the materials used to build houses and suchlike."

"Remind me," I said, "why the monasteries were dissolved can you? I'm afraid my history is very rusty. I didn't take much notice when I was at school."

"Briefly it was what happened from 1536–1541 when Henry VIII disbanded the monastic communities across England, Wales and Ireland and confiscated their property. He first banished the monks from their Abbeys and Priories. Then he had their treasures removed and sold off the infrastructure, all the beams, stones, roof tiles, the furniture and so on. All these were bought by the gentry and local tradesmen who were then in a position to build very substantial houses. The monks used only the finest materials you see."

"And you think my house was one of those houses?"

"Yes, I do. Looking at its construction and the way it has survived, I'm almost certain. And you are just opposite the site of the old abbey," said Michael. "Thinking about it I'm sure of it."

"I didn't know the house opposite to mine used to be an abbey."

"Well it was but most of has been demolished as I say and the materials recycled," said Michael. "An early example of recycling. Most people think it's a new concept."

"I suppose that explains why some houses built all that time ago still exist today," I said. "The houses of everyday folk would have fallen down or been demolished long ago."

"Correct," said Michael.

"That's interesting," I said. "The estate agent said it was probably around three hundred years old. So they were way out."

"Oh estate agents are often wrong about these things," said Michael. "Anyway properties built before the Land Registration Act in the 1860s are invariably hard to date. Estate agents are likely to err on the side of caution when dating a property."

"Possibly," I said. "Anyway the house must have seen a lot that's for sure."

"Quite so, what with generations over time," said Michael, leaning over to turn on the gas fire. "Well how can I help you?" he asked as he returned to his seat. "You said you had some questions you wanted to ask me when you rang yesterday."

"Yes. As you know I'm new to the village and I'm really interested in finding out more about my house and in particular about my cellars. What would they have been like and what would they have been used for? I do know they've been closed up for a while and I'm not sure if there's any way into them now."

"Well I don't know much about your house specifically but most houses built at that time would have had cellars. Probably built at the same time as the house," replied Michael. "They would've been used mainly for storage."

"What would they have been made of?"

"I expect cellars would have brick walls in a village like this. There used to be quite a few brick quarries around here you know. And they would probably have a stone floor."

"Right," I said feeling relieved that Michael might be able to help me. "It seems there's no access to the cellars now," I added. "Is it possible they were filled in?"

"Oh yes, quite possible. Large numbers of cellars were filled in during the early and middle part of the last century because of dampness and mould and so on. Also the expense of making them serviceable, doing them up. Many people thought it just wasn't worth it."

"So they may or may not have been filled in."

"That's right. But there are people in the village who might be able to remember things about your house and maybe the cellars as well. People like Harry Furlong for example or maybe Bernard, your neighbour. They're both of an age."

"Oh yes," I said with a wry smile. "I've met Harry. He and Bernard are a great pair of characters. Actually I did speak to Bernard before and he didn't know much except that he thought they'd been closed up quite a while back, long before his time. That was when he put me on to you."

"I see. Well what Harry doesn't know about the village is probably not worth knowing," said Michael with a chuckle. "He's lived here for seventy odd years. I should speak to him. I'm sure he'll be able to help you." He moved over to turn the gas fire down.

"Anyway what brought you to the village?" he continued. "You say you're interested in your house. Are you particularly interested in old places?"

"I suppose I am. The house I lived in before I moved here was about a hundred and fifty years old and that seemed old to me at the time. Before that I'd lived largely in modern properties so this is quite a change. Also living in a village. I've always been a townie."

"Whittlesham is certainly a lovely place. Plenty of charm," said Michael.

"Oh yes, it's a lovely village. Anyway, my last house didn't have a cellar as far as I know but I've always been interested in underground rooms and passages, ever since I was a child."

"You're right," said Michael. "There is something inherently intriguing about them. Always makes you think of the past and you never know what you're going to find, what people will have left behind."

"Yes I find I'm becoming fascinated by the past," I said meditatively. "Not that I was ever inspired by history when I was at school. I had the most awful teachers who made everything so tedious. I just rebelled and never listened."

"It's appalling what some teachers are responsible for," said Michael. "I know I'm biased being a history teacher but you can learn so much from it. It's so exciting, that is if you get the right teacher."

"Absolutely. I really wish I'd had somebody like that."

"Well it seems you're finding things out now," said Michael.

"Yes, living in an old house certainly gives you the pull of history. So you definitely think there would have been cellars under my house?"

"Almost certainly."

"Well that's something. I'm going to have to check them out. Get someone to help me find out whether they've been closed up or not, whether there's a way into them. Anyway," I continued, "you asked me why Whittlesham? Well I used to live in Watford and teach in London but for various reasons I wanted a change in my life and I wanted to be more in the country. So I applied for a number of teaching jobs around the edges of London and was lucky enough to land one in Milton Keynes. That's then I began to look at villages out this way. And when I viewed houses here in the village something told me I must buy Middle House."

I paused, "It was like some kind of inner voice almost. Compelling really. I just felt I had to buy the house. I felt as if I was coming home. I suppose it sounds strange when you put it like that."

"Not really," said Michael. "Houses do have vibes, especially old houses. They're bound to have an ambience or feelings connecting with the past and the people who've lived there throughout the ages. I don't think it's strange at all. The past can talk to us you know, if we're prepared to listen."

"There is just one more thing," I said slowly. "You probably won't be able to help me but Harry Furlong said something to me about dead bodies. Dead bodies under my house. What did he mean do you think?"

"Don't know," said Michael, "not specifically what he means. I've lived in the village for years and never heard mention of anything like that. But when you think of it most houses will be places where people have died, either in the house or on the site before it was built. So essentially death is all around us, every one of us. People will have died where we stand in the garden, in the street, on motorways, in shops, everywhere."

"Weird thought," I said. "So what you're saying is that death or its aftermath is everywhere."

CHAPTER 4

The village was peaceful and I could sometimes hear the silence when there were no cars. The house hung around me at times like that and I could sense its ownership of me. At other times the passers by just outside the windows gave me a feeling of being in the centre of things, the hub of village life. Perhaps that's what Middle House means I thought.

I spent time painting the walls throughout in traditional colours, deep reds and pinks and softer buttermilk and creams inspired by the Kashmir rugs I had bought. I also searched for furniture that reflected the charm of the house. And I enjoyed the quiet way of village life, a far cry from the bustle of Watford and London.

The historic roots of the village were all too evident. With its castle mound, the now demolished abbey and what had been a courthouse, the village had evidently been noteworthy in the past. It must have been more like a small town than the village it was now. Michael Baines had told me that the population one hundred years ago had been more than double what it was now, with far more abundant shops and local businesses. Now it was more of a backwater, quite off the main route and largely left alone to its own charm apart from a few passing tourists drawn by the historic buildings and old thatched cottages.

As I got to know the village the house continued to embrace and engross me. I was intrigued about its past. What about the cellars? And what about those rumoured dead bodies? I speculated about how I could find a way into the cellars and when and why they had been closed up. I wondered also about what Michael had said about death being everywhere. Were there ghosts in the house? Were there ghosts in the cellars?

I was anxious to talk to Harry Furlong and see what he really knew or didn't know. Whether he was just elaborating or bending the truth or even making the whole thing up. However he didn't seem to be around.

Then one day I was surprised to receive an invoice for 10p from the chapel treasurer 'For right to light or window use.' Was it something to do with past window taxes I wondered.

A couple of days later I approached Dan Ellis, the treasurer, who was often to be seen doing odd maintenance jobs at the chapel and asked him why the bill had been sent and why the amount. He was sitting on a small stool halfway along the passage at the side of the church, painstakingly weeding the path and throwing the weeds into a bucket at the side of him.

"Oh that," he said slowly, rubbing his hands down his yellow and grey paint-splattered shirt and then involuntarily running a hand through his grey hair. "I thought you'd be surprised to receive my invoice." He picked up the large mug of tea placed carefully by his feet and took a gulp.

"Well what's it for?" I queried. "It's rather an inconsequential amount."

"Right," said Dan straightening his back on the stool. "Let me explain. It's a 10p tax per year payable by you in return for window rights."

"What window rights?" I asked.

"It's the right to have a window in your kitchen. To do with the right to light laws," Dan said deliberately. "In general terms the minimum amount of light is equivalent to the light from one candle, one foot away. And the glass must be kept opaque, you can't change that."

"Opaque? Why must the window glass be opaque?" I queried thinking of the frosted glass which I had thought to be very charming. This was bizarre.

"Well let me put it in plain words. You have the right to that amount of light and that amount of light only. Should the chapel site be redeveloped nobody can build anything next door to you if by doing so it impedes the amount of light you have now. That's why the chapel was built back from the road, to afford the house owner their light entitlement."

"I see," I said still somewhat baffled by the eccentricity of the whole thing.

Dan continued in full flow. "Under the Prescription Act 1832 just over half the room should be lit by natural light equivalent to the light of a candle. So you don't have the entitlement to a plain glass window. It's called a 'nuisance law' in legal terms. If you don't pay the money we shall block up your window."

"And would you really do that?" I asked.

"Of course," he said with a glimmer of a smile. That explained a lot I thought. Anyway it sounded as if I had to pay up.

"Here," I said passing Dan a ten pound note. "Keep the change. I have a feeling that I'm here to stay."

"And by the way," I added as I turned to go back up the path. "If I move and someone else buys the house, does that mean you'd put the 10p amount up?"

"Nope," said Dan moving his stool further along the path and sliding the bucket towards him. "It's set in perpetuity."

I looked obliquely at the chapel door as I made my way back up the side passage picturing the ancient black and gilt trolley and the unstable coffin wobbling towards the pavement. It seemed that living next door to the Methodists was going to be an education in itself, what with their strange burial customs and now their right to light laws. I wondered what would happen next.

⁂

The next day, taking Barnie with me, I pay a visit to the churchyard, drawn by the row of tombstone teeth which remain emblazoned in my mind's eye. It's a bright, crisp day. The sun speckling through the wizened lime trees lining the pathway and the delicate chestnut trees shedding leaves to gather in rusty piles at their feet. The grass is heavy with dew and I can feel the damp beginning to seep through my trainers, the autumn leaves scrunching beneath my feet.

Today is Sunday and I can hear the sound of a guitar spilling from the church along with raised voices singing:

> Lord, Now I see
> You only want me to believe
> Not to change
> In all my failure and defeats
> To believe what You have done
> And not in what I see
> Yes I believe. I believe in you ….

I stand and listen to the hymn. The music is vibrant, the guitar a modern-day backdrop replacing the traditional church organ.

Remembering an article I read about crosses being cut into church walls by crusaders about to leave for the Holy Land I scrutinise the surround of a small door set into the north side of the church where crosses of this kind have often been found. Where there is only a vertical line it seems the crusader did not return home. Where both lines of the cross are scored it is said to be evidence that the crusader did indeed return home to thankfully make the horizontal incision. No luck. There is nothing to be seen.

Dwarfed by the towering church I walk away from the heavy shadows and venture across the damp uneven grass to stand in the speckled sunlight. I find myself beside the grave of a couple, Louisa and William Makepeace. Both died in the late 1880s, both around eighty five years old. And then Elizabeth Dickens, remembered by loved ones through the placing of an unusual tubular metal cross, arced across the top and inscribed 'Blessed are the dead when they lie with the Lord'. Ninety years old, 19 October 1881.

Moving on from the isolated patch of ground where there are only three remaining gravestones I make my way past a line of five uniformly arched tombstones standing abruptly in a line like aged sentinels or protectors. And then a bit further along I come across the grave of Rhoda Beasley, who died aged one on 19 October 1881.

What a coincidence. The old lady of ninety and the one year old baby both dying on the same October day all those years ago. What I wonder did baby Rhoda die of? She survived her infancy only to die suddenly at one year old. And buried with her much later on are her parents Freda and Thomas Beasley.

That is why we have tombstones I murmur to myself, to ensure that we do remember the dead. The dead who are here in the churchyard.

Crossing with Barnie to the far side of the graveyard I am wandering along the grassy path where the stones look to be more recent when my gaze is drawn by an unusual shaped gravestone in the corner. A long, flat, greyish stone mottled with yellowing lichen, quite overgrown with weeds. Down the centre is a raised cross and as I bend down close I can just read the inscription.

Eric Linnell
Died and Departed 13 April 1952

Strange, I sat to myself, straightening up because Linnell is my maiden name. And my father, I can somehow remember him talking way back of a brother called Eric. Eric Linnell he would have been. The very same. What does this mean? Is it just a coincidence, someone with the same name. Or is it the tombstone of a relative. How very peculiar. I'm not aware of any family connections with the village.

As I ponder on this curious discovery I become aware of voices behind me. "That's the grave you know. That one there. That's where he's buried."

"Well, that's a right fine remembrance stone you've got him isn't it?" Turning I see two old ladies stop alongside a grave in the newer part of the graveyard, near to where Chloe Ward is buried.

"Will you be going in there with him when you go?" the friend asks.

"Ah, well, yes I expect so. If it's good enough for him, it's good enough for me," replies the widow as they move on down the uneven grass-tufted path to fetch an old metal watering can hanging on a hook on the church wall.

Carefully filling the can from a small tap set in the wall, the widow returns to the grave and fills the coloured glass vase with water before plunging in a bunch of bright red chrysanthemums.

Pulling on Barnie's lead I am about to leave the graveyard when a tall slanting tombstone to my left suddenly looks as if it's falling sideways and about to crash to the ground on top of me. I feel myself sway momentarily and catch my breath, putting my hands out to steady myself. Then moving sharply away I realise that it is a trick of the intense sunlight caused by the shimmering shadows of the chestnut trees behind me.

Later that day sitting in the garden the autumnal sun is bright all about me, shadows sharply defining the trees and bushes sloping down the bank. I sit on the curved iron bench, sun filtering through the seat to form elongated swirls on the grass below. The line of choisia bushes curves down towards the pampas grasses as they move delicately in the light breeze, the pointed frond-like flowers silhouetted against the dipping sun. Autumn is definitely here, my first autumn in the house. The first in my new life. How will things be this time next year I wonder. So much has happened in the last few years, such momentous things I could never have foreseen. Life is so unpredictable, what with the good and the bad.

I sit relaxing, my thoughts shifting towards the agreeable thought of soon being able to sit by an open fire. The soft sound of the acer leaves shifting and blowing in the wind, the crackly pop as crispy leaves drop softly to the ground to rest in heaps with the gathering swirls of purple brown leaves. Sounds of the early evening traffic deepening, swishing through the village homeward bound as the sun abruptly drops behind the trees. Instantly the last vestiges of warmth from the sun disappear and I watch the shadows in the garden lengthening as they creep towards my feet.

Suddenly I feel the cold. It is getting dark, less hospitable, less welcoming. The garden takes on an atmosphere of its own chilled and expectant, waiting for the night to envelop and wrap itself round the trees and plants. Waiting for night animals, birds and insects to emerge. It is they who own the garden at night and I who am the intruder, the interloper.

I realise that Barnie is digging ferociously beside me at the end of the garage, scrabbling excitedly in the earth behind the bushes. He digs furiously flinging clods of mud aside wildly, paws scrabbling in the soft earth oblivious to my entreaties for him to stop.

And as I watch he turns up a bone, a long narrow bone about twenty centimetres in length. It's dry, pale and blotchy in colour and it looks old and brittle. I eye it warily. Human or animal?

I need to find out more about the house and its cellars and after a couple of weeks I manage to catch up with Harry Furlong as he saunters past the house. He tells me he's been to stay with his sister in Buckingham hence his elusiveness.

As we stand on the narrow pavement by the chapel I discover that the house originally extended a further two metres or so onto the land where the chapel now stands. "So what happened?" I ask feeling as if I am getting somewhere at last.

"Well," Harry says sucking habitually at his pipe and pushing his cap down firmly over his forehead as the story unfolds at some length.

It seems that in 1844 the chapel was located in a small building further down the road. The village was growing in importance, the congregation was swelling rapidly and the chapel was consequently becoming far too small.

And so it was that a wealthy local benefactor purchased a vacant piece of land to the right of my house. However although the plot of land was of a considerable length it did not front to the road, so the then treasurer approached the owner of my house and after lengthy negotiation was able to purchase a small portion of their land.

The Methodists then knocked the end part of the house down and built the chapel that stands today. "So," adds Harry, "your cellars they had'ter be shut up as the entrance was in that there part of the house. The end bit of yer kitchen."

"Seems a bit drastic, demolishing part of the house."

"Well that was what they did as I heard it tell," Harry says. "And that's how the trap door to yer cellar was bolted down and sealed. Then it were covered with huge flat stones and layers of earth. After that they built that stone wall round the front garden of the chapel," he continues theatrically, flourishing his pipe in his right hand as he indicates the chapel rose bed beside us. And then pulling out a worn green and gold pack of Virginia flake tobacco from his pocket he methodically refills his pipe, tamping it down with his forefinger.

"So that's what happened. What a thing to do!"

"Well that ain't the only entrance," Harry goes on. "There's bound to be some other way inter them. You mark my words."

"You don't happen to know where that other entrance might have been?" I ask quickly before Harry disappears off down the road in his usual abrupt way. I am thinking this must be a record length conversation for him.

"No, I don't rightly know but it might have been at the stair end," he replies. "That's where you often find 'em."

"Anyways," he adds tamping his pipe tobacco down further, "you knows you've got some of the castle stones set right in the middle of yer house."

"How come?"

"It were built at the time the castle fell into disuse. You can see them big ol' stones above your kitchen range running right through ter the next room. You'll see what I mean if you goes and looks," and with that Harry set off heading in the direction of his house.

So the house is probably built with stones from the castle as well as from the old abbey, quite a revelation. This is a house with a past for sure. Reflecting on what Harry has just said I step sideways on to the spot in the flowerbed where the sealed trapdoor to the cellar lies. The sun shines on the soft yellow brick of the chapel as I stand in the shadows. The delicately patterned frosted glass of the kitchen window catches my eye and I notice for the first time the different bricks on the end of the house, quite unlike those along the front. I see too that the brick wall dividing my garden from the chapel extends up into the sloping lower part of the house and it's evident that this was built at the time the end of the house was demolished.

Interesting how a snippet of information can lead one to see things in a completely different light and I wonder again what stories the house could tell, what scenes the stones from the castle and abbey have witnessed.

※

There is something different as I enter the kitchen. It's large, larger than I remember and evidently the hub of the house. The walls are rough whitewash, not like the smooth cream walls of my kitchen. There is a cast iron open range with inglenook seats set into the stonework beneath the broad chimney breast. Copious bunches of dried herbs and garlands of yellowing hops drape from hooks above the lintel and there is a carved stone coat of arms set above the fireplace.

The rectangular table over by the far wall is covered with a rough cloth and ladder-backed chairs with skimpy red cushions ranged round it, sparse curtains barely covering the window behind. The window which is no longer there in my kitchen. A couple of brightly coloured rag rugs lie strewn on the floor and there is a waft of freshly baked bread and simmering stew. Hanging on a hook in the corner some dark-coloured working clothes, a pair of oil lamps placed either side of the fireplace together with the fire itself lighting the scene with a soft glow.

I move hesitantly over to the open range and stand warming my hands. There is no-one here, all is silent but I somehow sense that suddenly all will become bustle and clamour as the stew is ready and the bread done to a turn.

Slowly I turn away from the fire and as I do so I notice for the first time that there is a curtained front door which must open onto the street, unlike my house where the front door is strangely at the back.

Taking a last lingering look at the room I see my kitchen and yet not my kitchen. I am aware that other people live here, that I am somehow a usurper, that I am trespassing in the past. I stand soaking up the images, the smell of bubbling stew and baking bread filling my nostrils realising at the same time that I am hungry and also that I must leave.

The past should not be allowed to catch up with the present.

Pulling the curtain carefully to one side I open the front door and step outside. It's different here too.

I turn cautiously towards the chapel and as I approach the end of the house I see the outline of a willowy young man bent over digging in the flowerbed with a spade. As I watch he begins to remove the rose bushes one by one as he works steadily on, piling the earth systematically to one side, the heap growing progressively in size. The pile of spindly rose bushes thrust in a heap on the side.

And then the man carefully scrapes back the trampled earth beneath his feet exposing several pale-coloured stone slabs. He stoops to brush away the scattered remnants of soil and struggling with first one and then the other manages to prise the heavy stones to one side using a thickset pickaxe. He straightens his back and stands aside, revealing a trap door covered in soft earth, a rusty padlock holding the flaps together.

The trapdoor is open after some pulling and shoving and forcing of the padlock and then I am descending into the cellar, the man just in front of me leads the way with a wide-beamed torch.

Shadowy cobwebs dance on the floor and walls as I move warily down. The wooden steps are steep and I venture cautiously behind him. I find myself in a low-ceilinged cellar with whitewashed walls. The air is chill and in the torchlight I can see my breath spiralling in the air . . . . .

CHAPTER 5

Judith and her mother took the decision to move when her father died. He had been ill for quite some time. The house was far too large, expensive to heat and the life had gone out of it. It had been home for a long time but she welcomed the thought of leaving and was eager to get on with it.

They moved to a cottage in a village called Whittlesham. She had heard of the village before and had often been driven through it and as far as she knew it was just one long straight road. But when she moved into the cottage she found there was a lot more to the village than she had thought. The cottage was small but very cosy and immediately she felt at home. This was the first old house she had lived in and already she could feel the vibes, the memories, the presence of others who had lived there.

It smelt different too. She could smell the beams, the fireplace and the old stones which formed part of the house. She had heard that some of the stones had come from the nearby castle when it fell into disrepair. Several of the houses in the village, the estate agent said, had a part of the castle within them. What stories these houses could tell she thought. They must have seen so much change, so much happiness and excitement, so much trauma and grief. Even tragedy, violence, war and death. She smiled to herself. Maybe they should start taking DNA from houses of the past to try and find out what they had been party to.

Judith couldn't see the house in the same way as others having being blind since birth, but she could see it in her own way. She could imagine what it looked like. She could feel the surfaces, the irregular cast walls and the rough-hewn beams and she could put all these together as images in her mind. She had felt her way completely round the house when she first moved in with her mother and had done this several times since.

Now she knew almost every inch of the house, all the odd little nooks and crannies, the strange shaped holes in the beams with their oddly angled notches, the wide kitchen range and the inglenook seats on either side. Feeling her way round the house she was aware that the doors were misshapen and cut askew in some places and quite straight fitting in others. Her mother had told her that she could actually reach up and touch the ceiling in her bare feet in some of the rooms so she was aware how very low they were in parts of the house. She loved the smell of the wood burning stove in the sitting room and the cosy jingling sound of the curtains being drawn at night.

Her bedroom was a particular delight to her with its sloping irregular walls and curved alcove in the corner with a huge beam running through the middle. She used this as a shelf for some of her books and other favourite bits and pieces. Her bed fitted neatly into the opposite corner which gave it the feel of an enclosed bunk bed with its fitted drawers underneath, the soft rolled pillows and cushions giving it a luxurious silky feel.

She was glad that there was a spare bedroom so she was able to have this for her workspace. Now she had had all her equipment set up and knew exactly where everything was placed. She was beginning to be able to work at speed again on her PC and had expertly stored everything round her within easy reach.

Her mother Audrey, keen to get to know more about the village and her neighbours was often out and about. But Judith was much quieter and more placid, content to be within the house, enjoying it and settling in. She was busy too. Working for herself she transcribed documents and magazines into Braille using specialist Braille transcription software and her Tiresias embosser which was her special form of printer.

The name Tiresias always made her think of the Greek myth about a man called Tiresias who was blinded by the jealous god Hera, wife of Zeus. Zeus looking on took pity on him and gave him wisdom and the ability to see the future. This she felt was very much the case with a lot of blind people she had known and also in many ways herself. She could feel things other people could not and she had an uncanny knack of being able to predict things at times. Knowing she had this aptitude she always listened to her inner self and was often proved right about her presentiment.

Her business had been built up from very small beginnings when she found she could not get a job using her law degree. Frustrated and angry at being rebuffed at interview after interview, "I'm afraid we've given the job to someone else," yet again and again, she had started her Braille business about three years before. Now she was employing her mother part-time. She had more than enough work and was able to pay herself and her mother a reasonable salary. She had helped other sight-impaired friends to get going with their businesses too and was pleased to have been able to help.

In many ways her degree had given her a number of the tools she needed. She was well organised, an incisive thinker, could understand and interpret the scripts she transcribed into Braille whatever their subject matter and she enjoyed her work. Her underlying feelings of the unfairness of a society who would not give her a chance in the outside world of work had subsided and she felt pleased with the way she had developed and grown her business.

She knew she should get out more and she would do so in time. First she had to get immersed in the house, refocus her thoughts on work after the move which had caused considerable disruption to her and get herself back into her own methodical work pattern.

Some days later she ventured out using her stick cautiously as the house was on a hill and the path sloped downwards quite steeply. She had refused her mother's offer of help to find her way about on this initial sortie and set off down the hill, tapping her stick as she went. She came to the bottom of the hill and listening carefully crossed the small side street, turning right into what she knew was the High Street, the long main road she had been driven through so many times in the past.

The pathway was not as even as the pavements she was used to in Milton Keynes and she knew she had to be careful. She decided to walk for about another ten minutes and then return, having taken some air and also gained a feel for the village and its sounds, smells and atmosphere.

She passed a few people and one or two said "Hi," or "Good afternoon." She replied in similar vein and moved on, habitually tapping her stick to the left and right. The air smelt somewhat dusty but one expected that. It was everywhere, roads in particular. There was also the scent of certain shrubs as she moved past the houses, not that she was good on garden smells. When it came to flowers and in particular roses she had a good idea of scents and names but not with shrubs.

She heard the cars and lorries swoosh by her only feet from the pavement and felt the occasional rush of air and noise made by the larger vehicles. Buses made an altogether different noise and air movement, being taller as well as longer. They also made a kind of gliding and hissing noise, something to do with the brakes she supposed. Strange, she thought, the buses seem to be double-deckers round here, not low like the small run-around buses in Milton Keynes. Are they full, she wondered, and where are all the people going?

Feeling her watch to check the time she decided to turn round and make her way back. Next time I will come with someone who can describe things she thought, but being fiercely proud and determined she had wanted to go out on her own alone first just to absorb the atmosphere. Easier to take in the ambience and vibes when she was alone and could give her full concentration to what was going on and what she was feeling.

As she tapped her way back along the rather irregular pavement she became aware of someone moving towards her with a dog. She could hear the soft jangle of the lead as well as the regular tap, tap, tap of claws on the pavement as well as the distinctive rubbery sound of Wellingtons.

Being somewhat wary of dogs Judith stood to the side and waited.

A woman stopped beside her and said, "Don't worry, Barnie is fine with people."

"I'm just careful with dogs when I first meet them you know," said Judith. "I'm alright when I know them. What kind of dog is it?"

"He's a Labrador mix. A bit of a barker I'm afraid but great with adults and children, particularly young children. He loves all the attention."

"He feels lovely and soft," said Judith putting out her hand and stroking the dog. "I often wonder whether I should get a guide dog."

"Well I'm sure they give their owners a great sense of confidence and freedom," replied Fee.

"I suppose it's all the looking after them that puts me off," said Judith shyly. "You have to give them so much."

"True but you get so much back. Barnie's a real friend. Anyway do you live in the village?" Fee asked. "I haven't seen you about before."

"Yes," Judith replied. I live up Whinny Hill, near the top on the right with my mother. It's the first time I've lived in a village, quite different from being a 'townie'. I lived in Milton Keynes and London most of my life when I wasn't away at school. So I'm really looking forward to finding out about the village."

"I'm a fairly recent newcomer too," said Fee taking in Judith's shoulder length blond hair, her neat appearance and diminutive size. She looked around five feet. "Hi, I'm Fee. Fee Hunter."

"Hi, I'm Judith Mason. It would be really good to get to know you better," said Judith spontaneously. "I don't know anyone in the village yet."

"Neither do I," said Fee warmly, "apart from a few old men!"

"I know there's a lot of history connected with the place, what with all the old pubs and houses, the castle and everything. Do you know much about the village?" asked Judith.

Fee replied that as she was fairly new to the village too she was also trying to learn about its history. She realised that Judith was blind, maybe completely without sight, and thought how brave she was to be out on her own right by the main road. "I live here just beside the Methodist Chapel," she said.

"My mother and I go to the chapel," said Judith. "I hadn't quite realised that we were outside it."

"It's a lovely old building," Fee said. "Very prestigious actually for a village of this size."

"I know, my mother said. But the congregation is a bit on the low side. They're really looking for new members," said Judith. "They're trying lots of things like coffee afternoons and drop-in groups on Sundays after lunch."

"Well it sounds as if they're doing their bit," Fee said. "Perhaps you'd like to drop round sometime for a coffee?"

Judith and Fee swapped names and telephone numbers and they parted. Judith thought that Fee was probably of similar age to her, late twenties or early thirties, and about the same height or a bit taller. Difficult to imagine what Fee looked like but she seemed very friendly and had an easy manner.

Judith was pleased to have met her. Sometimes she really related to people and could easily fall into conversation with them. At other times she became quite tongue-tied and just completely lost her confidence. At times like that she realised she probably came over as very boring and uninteresting. She needed to feel positive and encouraging vibes from other people before she could let them see her real self.

She suddenly felt the chill in the air as the autumn day closed in and became aware that the traffic flow on the road was increasing. The cars whisked by in quick succession and she felt the air rush grow and smelt the petrol fumes intensify. Pulling her jacket more tightly round her she realised that she should get home. She moved off along the High Street turning up Whinny Hill and tapping her way back home. Fewer cars passed her as she went, she was thankful that this was a much quieter road.

CHAPTER 6

I am standing again in the flowerbed on the spot above the concealed trapdoor in front of the chapel waiting for a local builder Raymond to arrive. It's a landmark day. Raymond is going to try and open up the cellars and at last I should be able to find out what's down there.

In my mind's eye I picture the cellar as I saw it in that dreamlike vision. I can see the steep wooden staircase with whitewashed walls festooned with cobwebs and layers of dust. Is that how they'll be, did I really see them as they are?

Bernard seems to think that there could be four cellars one under each room and I wonder whether we'll be able to access them all. These and other thoughts jumble in my mind as they have done since I discovered the unexpected existence of the cellars. Will I actually be able to find out why they were sealed up in the first place and what about Harry Furlong, what does he really know about supposed bodies under the house?

⁂

I shuffle my feet in the soft earth impatient at having to wait for the builder. He's late. He should have been here half an hour ago. I hear the swish, swish of cars passing and feel the soft warmth of the late autumn sun. I've checked with regard to listed buildings on the internet and there's no need to get consent to open up your own cellars. The only consent needed was from the Methodists to carry out the digging work on what is their property and they were fine about it. They are as interested as I am to know what's under the house and what relics might be found. As usual Dan was full of stories and told me about the Treasure Act 1996 which established a voluntary scheme to record archaeological objects found by members of the public. "You might need to call them in," he'd said with a smile.

At last Raymond pulled to a halt in his old Cherokee van, the open back laden with equipment. "Hi there," he said. "Sorry I'm late. I've 'ad ter move my cows down to Buckingham to my mum's place. Her field's bigger 'an mine for the winter until I sell 'em. Anyway I'm here now. Shall I make a start? I think I've got all the diggin' tools I'm gonna need."

He unloaded various tools as he spoke. A couple of pickaxes, several shovels, a rake and a hoe, forks, trowels, clamps and some iron bars, gloves, a dustpan and brush and finally a couple of large wheelbarrows.

"Fine, yes, let's make a start. I mean yes you make a start. I'll keep out of the way," I replied positioning myself on the wall a few feet away. I watched as Raymond put his tools down neatly within reaching distance of the corner of the house. Next he unloaded the two wheelbarrows and placed them alongside.

He stood back and surveyed the job. First he dug up two of the rose bushes, their crimson flower heads already drooping. He eased the soil round the roots and shook them gently, placing them carefully on the flowerbed on the other side of the path. Then taking a spade he dug the soil over roughly to loosen it. He worked it through for a few minutes and then picked up a shovel and began heaping the soft earth into one of the wheelbarrows. The earth was fine and crumbly and kept infilling back into the hole as Raymond dug but he persevered, throwing the larger stones and flints onto a pile on one side.

After about fifteen minutes the wheelbarrow was piled up and full and Raymond wheeled it carefully out of the way and then positioned the other barrow in its place. Taking his jacket off he threw it across the pavement into the back of his van and wiped his forehead with the sleeve of his shirt.

"This 'ere is hot work," he said.

"I take the hint. I'll get you a cup of tea. Milk and one sugar isn't it?" Raymond nodded.

When I returned with his mug of milky tea the second wheelbarrow was filling up. He worked on, shovelling the soil methodically like a mechanical digger. A slim, strong man with short spiked hair he was always the same, unruffled and unshakable. He took everything in his stride and loved to have a chat and a bit of a laugh.

However today he was keen to finish the task and not in the mood for idle chat. The second barrow was now full and he wheeled it away from the hole to line up beside the first one. "I can jest about see them slabs," he exclaimed. "Right where Harry said by the sound of it."

"Goodness I didn't think you'd get to them so soon," I said excitedly as coffee in hand I went over to have a look. I could just make out a few patches of stone beneath the trampled soil.

Raymond downed his tea in a couple of gulps and then grabbed a trowel and started to scrape away the soil from the top of the emerging stone slabs. Rummaging in his pile of tools I seized another trowel and helped to scrape away the soil until the area exposed was about sixty centimetres square, the stone slabs a dusty yellow.

"I wish I'd bought me Air Spade with me," said Raymond. "It's me latest tool, it air jets the soil and debris away just like that. I've lent it to Mick 'cos he's doing some garden work and excavatin' near some trees. You'd like it, you would. It's an amazin' gadget."

The next part looked as if it would be more difficult. The slabs were rectangular and quite large and they looked heavy. However Raymond soon proved his strength. Using a pointed trowel to score the soil alongside the slabs he deftly loosened the stones round their edges. Next he took a chisel and dug down into the soil to free up the stones.

Working systematically he bent down and worried away at the edges with the chisel gradually freeing up the sides. Wedging a pickaxe in the emerging space, he used his foot to push the pickaxe down at the same time that he raised the stone. Without seeming to feel the weight of the slab he grasped it with both hands and pushed it sharply to one side, knocking one of the remaining rose bushes to the side as he did so. He turned and grasped the other stone slab, shoving and pushing it along until it lay away from the hole beside the first stone. He turned to me wiping the dripping beads of sweat from his forehead against his sleeve.

"Don't know what Dan is going ter say about 'is rose bush," he grinned. "However what's one rose bush when yer havin' fun!"

I smiled. Raymond had a good sense of humour. He'd even threatened to bump off the Methodist's treasurer if he hadn't allowed us to open up the cellar.

"We can just chuck that one away," I suggested "and make out there were only five rose bushes, not six! He won't know."

Now I could see that there was indeed a wooden trapdoor in the cavity created, with rusted metal bars running horizontally across. The rough-hewn timber was greyish and splintery. "Be careful with that wood," I said. "Watch out for the splinters."

"I've had more splinters than 'ot dinners," he retorted. "You should ask me wife, she knows all about that she does. Same as the fact that I'm always cutting meself. I try ter to be careful but then I'm in a rush." As he spoke he picked up his gloves and put them on.

"Don't forget. If we need to call someone to help you just stop right away," I said. "I know you want to get moving with this but you must be careful. After all the entrance might give way or there could be subsidence. Just hurry slowly."

"Will do," said Raymond as he squatted down and pulled at the rusted metal latch in the middle of the trapdoor. He reached into his tool bag and took out some easing oil. "I think it jest needs a bit of this." Pouring a few drops of oil onto the latch he carefully worked it open and then using his chisel teased gently at the edge of the wooden flap, gradually easing the trapdoor open.

We looked at each other in anticipation. "Hello. What are you two up to?" said a voice.

Somewhat startled Raymond and I looked up to see the vicar standing on the pavement beside us. He was peering towards the hole. "What will the Methodists think?" he asked as Raymond dropped the wooden trapdoor back down with a resounding bang trying to look nonchalant.

"Oh they know about this alright. In fact Dan Ellis is coming along later to see how we're getting on," I replied hoping he would lose interest and move on. "We're just checking up on things," I mumbled.

"What kind of things?" queried the vicar. "What do you think you are going to find down there, under the flowerbed?"

"Well to tell you the truth we're just trying to get into my cellars. They were closed up when the Methodists bought this bit of land. This is where the trapdoor is," I said somewhat guiltily.

"You could be opening up all kinds of trouble you know," said the vicar. He held out his hand, "By the way my name's Robert Delforth. I'm the vicar."

"Hi. I'm Fee Hunter and I live here," I said indicating the house. "And this is Raymond."

"I hope you don't think I'm intruding but you really don't know what you're going to find under there," said Robert. "I've had a fair bit of experience of old Rectories and the like. It's very likely to be unsafe. And anyway think about public safety. You'll probably have to get planning permission from the council as you're working outside your own property and so close to the road."

"Oh," I said taken aback. "I hadn't thought of that. I did check about listed building consent but I didn't check about planning permission."

"And how are you going to block the trapdoor off to stop people getting into the cellars? You know what the youngsters are like. They'd be down there as soon as winking," he added.

"Oh goodness. Perhaps he's right," I said disconsolately looking at Raymond.

Raymond was also looking disappointed. "I was jest getting excited about what we might find down there. Do you really want me to stop when we're so very nearly there?"

"I think you'd better," I said. "I think the vicar's probably right about the problems it could cause. We'll have to think of something else, some other way into the cellars."

Reluctantly, Raymond bent down and secured the latch on the

trapdoor and then moved over to fetch one of the wheelbarrows. Slowly he tipped the soil back into the hole, chucking the stones in after it and stamping it down with his feet. I watched feeling deflated after the excitement of being so close to discovering the secrets of the cellars.

"Depressing, isn't it?" I said, "being so near and yet so far as they say. Now I know what the saying means."

CHAPTER 7

It's a blustery day, bright and sunny and the leaves shimmer a golden reddish brown, drifting gently to the ground as we walk down the lane towards the castle mound. Barnie sniffs and moseys along the grass verge enjoying the smells and I, am I on a date?

My 'date' is a historian called James and someone who is an expert on the Normans. I met him through a work colleague, Abbie, who put me in touch with him when I told her I wanted to find out more about the village. She knew him from when she worked previously at the university in Oxford. She had given him my telephone number and we spoke on the telephone a couple of times before he suggested that we pay a visit to the castle mound.

I realise when we meet that there is something very attractive about James and I know from Abbie who was keen to divulge the fact that he is unattached and a possible new 'friend'. He looks around thirty five. He's tall, with close cropped dark hair, slim and casually dressed in charcoal jeans and a beige jacket.

Abbie explained that he works at one of the Oxford Colleges in the history department. He lives just outside Stony Stratford about fifteen miles away. I don't know if he has ever been married. What does he think of me I wonder as we stroll down the lane? No doubt Abbie had given him a pen picture of me. Thirty one, dark reddish auburn hair, petite, a lecturer, widowed, own house, dog, no lodgers, no baggage.

James has obtained a copy of an old line drawing which shows the scarped ringwork of Bernay Castle as it would have looked like circa 1145. The cross hatched markings round the edges show the developments as it expanded and grew in both size and prestige during the thirteenth century.

"Why build a castle here?" I ask James, looking up from the drawing towards the mound on the other side of the fence. "What made it so important?"

"The Normans built their first castles in the south east, at Hastings and at intervals along the south coast as you probably know. Then they moved north, building smaller castles in strategic positions. Bernay Castle was built here because of the hill and the excellent view of the surrounding countryside. There are also a couple of rising springs which would have been essential when choosing the site for a castle."

The scale on the side of the map indicates that the mound is about fifty six metres wide and seventy eight metres long. A sizeable fortress. It is indeed well positioned, high above the valley with views stretching for miles to the south and to the east. "It must have been quite impenetrable from this side," I say intrigued by the early technology of siege warfare. "But what about the north-westerly side? That wouldn't have provided such a good vantage point from which to spot the enemy."

"You're right," James replies. "It would definitely have been the vulnerable side, most likely the side from which Cromwell attacked when it was finally taken. There's far less of a view and, taking out the houses which are there now, even short distance visibility would have been a problem with all the trees and the rise and fall of the landscape."

"But they must have thought that it was a good enough position anyway," I add as we open the wicket gate and walk into the field, "what with the height of the mound, the view on at least two sides and the running water."

"Sure."

Climbing the mound we wander around the perimeter of the castle wall starting by what would have been the main gate at the north east end of the mound. James points to the drawing. "This is probably where they kept their prisoners. A kind of gaol."

"Why didn't they just kill them? What use were they?"

"Oh you can be sure that the Normans wouldn't have bothered to feed anyone for no reason. They would've kept a reasonable number of prisoners alive to carry out heavy building work and maintenance," replies James.

"Who were the prisoners?"

"They would mainly have been the remnants of the defeated army who would regroup every so often and attack the castle in an attempt to drive them out. When these men were captured they were taken as prisoners. They would have been male, able-bodied and strong and they would have been fed just the right amount of food to keep them fit so that they could be of maximum use to the baron and his soldiers. The prisoners would have been kept in this area here and put to work labouring, moving stones and timber and so on."

Looking across at the grassy moat I have a sudden image of swarthy bearded invaders swarming up the hill towards the castle, some being killed in the assault and others being taken prisoner.

"I wonder where they buried the dead, both from the castle and the prisoners?" I ask James thoughtfully. "They wouldn't want them too close to the castle itself for reasons of sanitation but there must be a burial site round here. Just think of all those remains! Now that would be an interesting find. Where would it have been do you think?"

"That's not something I can claim to be an expert on," says James laughing. He looks at the drawing. "Well it wouldn't have been on the western aspect because that's where the springs rise and they wouldn't have wanted to pollute the water. It would either have been somewhere down there to the south or over to the east I should imagine," he says pointing down the valley.

"The dead are everywhere, that's what someone said to me the other day," I say remembering what Michael Baines had said. "And that must be especially true here. So many people must have died. There must be a whole lot of spirits!"

"You're right," James says with a smile. "And of course the

Normans who died would've been buried here too, not in France where they would probably want to have been laid to rest."

"Spirits 'caught' in the wrong place. Strange notion once you begin to think about it. It's surprising there isn't more spirit unrest if you know what I mean."

"Well in some places of course there is considerable unrest. Think about all the stories there are about poltergeists."

"I suppose so. What **is** a poltergeist? Are all spirits poltergeists and vice versa?"

"Not sure," replied James. "A poltergeist is a noisy spirit as far as I know, one that makes their presence known either by sound or by moving objects. I don't know what the quiet ones are called."

"I suppose we should just be grateful that they're not all noisy," I exclaim. "Otherwise we'd never get away from them."

As we walk over to the north west side James points out the now almost non-existent pond. "That was a pond down there called Weir Pond," he says indicating a much larger pond marked on the map. "See, you can just make out a small hollow at the bottom of the slope?"

"Now it's covered with trees and shrubs but back then all that tangle and undergrowth wouldn't have been there. They would have kept the moat and pond completely clear. None of the trees on the mound would have been here either, obviously, so the view would've been unimpeded all round this south end," he says indicating the vale with his forearm. "Just what they needed in terms of defence. And if you look a bit further down there, see, that lower point. That's where they would have had their fishpond. Breeding fish gave them a ready supply of food."

"Very well organised. Amazing. What kind of fish would they have kept?"

"Well it would mainly have been carp and perch and other similar fish. And eels," James replies. "The barons had to be quite self sufficient at times, both with water and food in order to survive being blockaded by the enemy. One of the simplest ways to raid a castle was to poison the water supply, but that wouldn't have been easy here at Bernay as the castle is built above several rising springs. That's probably why the castle survived for over 500 years."

"Here we are at the site of the south tower," he continues as we stop to look at the broad sweep across the valley before us. "This is where the baron, originally Hugh de Bernay, would have had his Great Hall, the soldiers being housed at the other end of the fortress in the Lower Hall. This part of the castle was the motte, probably built on an existing natural hill and shaped by his men into a higher mound surrounded by the moat."

We walk slowly back across the mound to the north end, carefully navigating the sprawling clumps of nettles and James points to a raised escarpment outside the castle walls. "That outer part is the bailey which would have been a protected area outside the fortress where the stables and such like were located along with the chapel, kitchens and workshops. Even weapons could be stored in the bailey which was afforded protection from the castle mound." Suddenly he pauses, looking a bit self conscious. "Oh I am sorry. I'm going on far too much. I'm giving you a right old history lesson. I didn't mean to."

"Oh please don't apologise. I'm absolutely fascinated by all this. I didn't really study history much myself. Anyway this is real history, all around us," I exclaim. "Who wouldn't be interested?"

"As long as you're sure," James adds. "There is something else I've read about the castle which I'm sure you'll be interested in. Apparently there used to be an abbey in the High Street. It was a sister house to the monastery at Woburn Abbey I think. Anyway it's said that there is at least one tunnel running between the castle and the abbey. I read it when I was in one of the libraries in Oxford. They've got the most amazing collection of books there."

"Wow. So there may well have been a tunnel running from here over in that direction. That's the direction of my house," I say glancing towards the shadowy outline of my house just visible through the trees.

"Is that so?" asks James. "I hadn't quite realised the position of your house in relation to the castle. I know it's on the High Street. So you must be somewhere near the site of the old abbey."

"How amazing. I didn't even know there was an abbey in Whittlesham. Anyway why would they have taken the trouble to dig a tunnel, what would it have been used for?"

"Well it was quite common in those days to construct a tunnel between a castle and an abbey. It's well documented in all sort of places like Norwich and Winchester, Hertford and Bristol and so on. I know Whittlesham is only a village now but it used to be a lot larger. Both castle and abbey were a fair size."

"I wonder if there are any signs of a tunnel round here now?" I ask surveying the area. "Or would it have been blocked in – maybe by English Heritage, I think it's them who own it now. They would have been worried about health and safety I expect."

"You're right, they wouldn't want members of the public falling down a hole or tunnel and injuring themselves. Let me see if I can find out anything more about the tunnel for you," says James. Looking at his watch he adds, "Anyway, it's lunchtime. How about retiring to your local for a beer and a bite? You've still got one I presume? This is making me thirsty."

"Yes I'd like that. Fortunately we've still got two pubs, the Black Horse and the Royal Oak. Both are good and they sell real ales." We make our way down the sloping bank across the grassy moat and through the wicket gate leading to the lane. "I'd like to show you something on the way. It won't take long."

"Fine. I think I can just about hold onto my thirst for a few minutes."

Earlier in the week I had found some crusader crosses scored into an old wall just up from the castle, the largest of the crosses being particularly impressive. Cut into a large flat faced stone it was framed by garlands of thick ivy spilling down the wall. The cross was deeply scored and about twenty centimetres in length, fourteen centimetres across and more than half a centimetre deep. Excited by my find I had carefully scrutinised the whole length of the ancient wall and found two more crosses slightly smaller in size and also carved onto the front surface of large flat stones. And then I found several much smaller crosses, around eight by four centimetres lower down in the wall on smaller stones at the bottom. I couldn't believe my luck and I wanted to see what James thought of them.

All of them were distinctively scored both ways so it would seem that these crusaders did return from the holy wars to make their horizontal mark and say their prayers of thanks. There were also some less distinct smallish vertical lines which could be a sign of unfinished crosses but it was hard to be sure as inevitably the marks on the wall only become really noticeable when both lines were scored

I point out one of the larger crosses and James bends down tracing the deep cut with his finger. "Just imagine the crusader standing here all that time ago making this vertical incision with his dagger. He was going into the unknown, didn't know if he would ever return. He would have been one of the most respected soldiers from the castle. One of the most loyal and a proven swordsman. What would his adventures in the holy war have been like?" he says softly. "And then he returned safely and made the horizontal incision. Quite something."

I'm glad that James is suitably impressed by the votive crosses. He thinks it quite likely that were put there by the crusaders. I stand back to take some photos of the wall, uncertain as to whether the marks will come out as the lane is quite dark and shaded beneath the tall trees.

"Right," says James calling to Barnie. "Let's away to that pub of yours."

CHAPTER 8

James has arranged to call for me on Saturday so that he can tell me what he has found out about the village. We're meeting Judith and her friend Tom for lunch at the pub over the road, and decide to go over a bit early so that he can tell me his news before they arrive.

"I'd really like to have a look round your house later," he'd said as I opened the door. "It looks like a fascinating old place. But we'd better get going now so that I can fill you in, we don't want to bore the others. By the way do you know when your house was built?"

"This chap Michael, he's a local historian, told me it was probably around the mid 1500s," I said closing the front door behind us. "It's got some of the old stone from the castle and possibly beams and other parts from the old abbey."

"I hadn't realised how old it was," said James stopping to look at the back of the house.

"Well the foundation as you can see is stone. And the original part of the house, at the far end, has two adjoining fireplaces which are also built from stone taken from the castle."

"I can see what you mean about the old stone," he said bending down to inspect the foundation layer more closely.

"It's really soft, the stone. I've had to have the inside stone work treated with a special spray to stop it crumbling. I suppose it's partly affected by the central heating. Anyway I'll show you round later."

It's another windswept day as we stroll over the road. The pub immediately feels warm and cosy and there is a pleasant aroma of smouldering logs. It's early and there aren't many other customers yet.

"What will you have?" I asked walking over to the bar to check the pumps. "You like Spitfire don't you?"

"Oh yes. One of my favourites. You see it more and more these days thank goodness," said James.

"Pint of Spitfire please and a bottle of Cobra," I said smiling at Barry the landlord.

"How have you been?" I asked James. "It's been a week since we met."

"I've been away at a conference for a couple of days, in Leeds. Very interesting conference called 'Turning Points'."

"What was it about?" I asked moving away from the bar to sit down near the fire.

"Well the focus of the conference was to look at when things change in history and why. For example what distinguishes one era or one century or even one decade from another. And how do we recognise the moment when one period transforms to the next?"

"Sounds interesting and very relevant, what with everything that's been going on since the millennium," I said sipping my beer. "9/11 to name just one thing. And now the credit crunch. What turning points they've been, for everybody."

"Yes the thrust is certainly apposite in today's world, just as it is when it's applied to the past. Essentially it always has been. Every age you can think of has had earth-changing moments." He paused. "We were looking at how individuals in the past used these 'turning points' to understand what was going on. It's a different area for me so very useful."

"Sounds vast. Maybe you'll show me some of the papers?"

"Of course. I'll bring a couple over next time I come," said James. "Great to have Spitfire."

"Good," I said. "I suppose the evolution of the internet is another important contemporary 'turning point'. If you look at the way in which protests, riots and of course acts of terrorism, even the overthrowing of governments, can all be planned and executed without the need for individuals to meet or even know each other."

"You're right, the world will never be the same," James agreed. "And no-one is going to take things back to the way it was before the internet. How would we ever manage our lives without it?"

"Impossible. Same with phones and mobiles. We couldn't exist without them."

"No and yet when mobiles first came out I thought they were completely over the top and unnecessary. I didn't have one for ages," said James putting his glass down. "By the way would you like any crisps or anything?"

"Not for me thanks. Anyway," I settled back in my seat, "tell me what you managed to find out about the village."

"I was able to find out quite a bit actually," replied James. "The old house opposite yours was originally an abbey. It was built by the order of monks at Woburn Abbey in 1400 after they took over the church in 1397. Woburn Abbey was a daughter house of Fountevrault Abbey, one of the French Cistercian houses, so the monks here would also have been Cistercians."

"Oh," I said, "weren't they the monks who wore white habits?"

"Yes that's right. Woburn Abbey was actually built in 1145 and it in turn also established a number of daughter houses, including the abbey at Whittlesham. Sadly it was taken from the monastic order in 1547 by Henry VIII and passed on to John Russell, the first Earl of Bedford."

"So from what you're saying it's likely that none of the existing abbey remains now?"

"Well maybe some of the original walls are still there but I should think that most of it was destroyed during the Dissolution of the Monasteries," said James. "So much went at that time, all those beautiful buildings and monastic artefacts. And all the expertise and knowledge of the monks. It was all dissipated."

"Devasting and such a waste."

"Some historians believe that the closure of the English monasteries may have suppressed what would have been a much earlier industrial revolution," replied James. "It's well documented that the monks at that time were extremely technologically advanced. For example they had already developed specialised furnaces for the production of cast iron. All that and many other innovations were lost as a result of Henry VIII's purge."

"So he had a whole lot to answer for, quite apart from beheading most of his wives!" I said indignantly.

"He certainly did."

"Anyway, going back to the abbey," I said, "I remember now that there's a door in the wall at the far end. It leads from the garden of what was the abbey into the churchyard. It's a very large garden by the looks of it."

"That would most probably have been the kitchen gardens," said James. "The monastery would have owned and worked most of the fields around here. They were self-sufficient in those times of course, very good farmers and agriculturists as well as manufacturing cast iron and other objects. They were also into horse breeding."

"Amazing just how advanced they must've been," I said.

"Yes, unbelievable really," said James glancing round to see if there was any sign of Judith and her friend. "History might have been really very different if the monasteries hadn't been dissolved."

"By the way," he went on, "I also found out more about a supposed subterranean passage running from the castle to the abbey. There was probably a tunnel and maybe other passages which were constructed to provide an escape route from the castle before the abbey was built or even thought of. It would also allow the inhabitants of the castle to surprise the enemy from behind their lines if needed."

"Wow, I suppose that makes sense. I must say I don't really know much about castle warfare."

"It was all very skilful stuff. We think we've got all the technology for war today but they were right on top of the game in those days. They knew exactly what they were doing," said James.

"Sounds like it," I said wrapt by the detail James was providing.

"Oh and one other thing. I read that you can sometimes hear a hollow sound in the High Street at certain points when driving over it with a heavy vehicle. That could be where the tunnel passes under the road."

"Perhaps we should try that. Mind you we'd have to get a pretty heavy vehicle I should think. An ordinary car wouldn't be any good or I'd have heard it before," I said laughing.

"So," I continued, "if you're right about the abbey and the castle my house is actually located almost exactly as the crow flies between the two. And if you're thinking what I'm thinking the tunnel could run right under the house, which wasn't built of course for another hundred years or so. Incredible! I wonder if there's any way into it now."

"I shouldn't get too carried away with the thought of rumoured passageways," said James. "Seriously there's talk of tunnels and passages in towns and villages everywhere and I'm afraid that very few have been found to exist. You can ask any archaeologist. They're always sceptical about these things."

"Okay, I won't really expect to find a tunnel but it sure is fun speculating about it."

"Yeah," said James. "It makes for a good yarn. Anyway, how about another lager?"

"Thanks."

James moved over to the bar and brought back a round of drinks. "Thanks for your research, it's all very interesting," I said as he came and sat down again.

"You said you weren't interested in history," exclaimed James laughing, "but you seem like a proper little historian now."

"Well it's as if things suddenly seem to make sense. The house is part of the fabric of history if you like. It's as if the whole village has been woven together over the years and now we're making sense of it. All the parts fit together, starting with the castle and the crusader crosses, linking in with the abbey and the monks and the large old manor houses round here, and then the building of my house and the village growing into a town with lots of shops and pubs. You'd never know that now would you?"

"No you wouldn't. I think I've only seen about three shops," said James.

"There are actually five shops now. And two pubs, although there were four until not so long ago. At one time there were apparently more than thirty shops, several smithies, umpteen farms and about twenty pubs. Not counting the brick makers and stone quarriers. The village must have been heaving."

"Sounds like it. I'd love to have seen it as it was then," said James. "There's so much social history we could learn from it."

"Sure. I sometimes wish we could travel back in time, go back and see things as they were then. Anyway Judith and Tom will be here any minute. I'll be interested to see what this Tom is like. Judith has told me a lot about him. I think she's keen."

As we sat warming ourselves by the fire Judith and Tom arrived. Tom looked to be over six foot, dwarfing the five foot Judith. He had short, curly blonde hair and an angular face with gaunt cheekbones.

James moved over to the bar and after introductions asked what they wanted to drink. I guided Judith to sit at the table by the fire. "Howse you?" I asked. "I haven't seen you for a couple of weeks. How's business?"

"Fine," Judith replied. "Sometimes I can't believe how much work just keeps coming in. I've been brailling training materials for health workers in mental health services and it's been quite interesting, but there were lots of diagrams. I generally say I can't do them or I ask the customer to write a description for me to Braille. But mum and I thought we'd have a go at describing them ourselves. It was a real challenge! I hope though that the person using the Braille finds them useful."

"Amazing what you get up to," I said. "It sounds really interesting. You'll have to show me how your Braille transcriptor works."

"Love to. That sort of technology has actually been around for some time thank goodness. It's so liberating and of course there are sound activated systems around as well."

"Anyway we're very busy indeed at the moment," said Judith taking a sip of her wine. "I hope I won't need to employ someone else as that would make things rather more complicated. However if it comes to that I will. How about you? What's all this about James that you haven't told me?"

Later I show James round the house, starting with the kitchen and the story about the blocked up cellar entrance in the Methodists' front garden, the ten pence tax on the kitchen window and their curiously antiquated funeral arrangements.

"What a house," he says. "I expect that's just the beginning of it. What else is there that you don't know about I wonder?"

I show him the ammonites above the back to back fireplaces in the kitchen and dining room. Set alongside the stone from the castle they measure about fifteen centimetres in diameter. "They must have been found along with the local stone in this area, possibly also from the castle mound," I explain. "Ever since ammonites were first discovered by man there have been all kinds of beliefs about their magical and medicinal properties. I suppose that's because they are really quite unusual."

"They certainly are. I've seen them in various places of course and read about them, but I've not seen them used in the walls of houses before."

"They actually look like coiled snakes don't they, coiled snakes frozen in time," I say laughing.

James puts his hand up and traces the curved rough contours of one of them.

"Apparently they're quite common in this area. I don't know too much more about their origins. Anyway," I continue, "I know you said I shouldn't speculate but just imagine if the stories were true about the tunnel. If you look out of the back window here in the dining room you can see the castle mound and, if you look out of the front window, there's the old house that was built on the abbey grounds. It would mean that if there was a tunnel it would probably run directly beneath where we're standing now."

CHAPTER 9

I'm lying in bed mulling over and over in my mind how to find a way into the cellar. It's no good trying again at the chapel end of the house. The vicar's right, I can't have everyone taking a look or worse falling down the hole. It's too near the road and anyway I wouldn't be able to stop people going down into my cellar. It's just not feasible. There must be a different entrance, another way in which is not so public.

Mentally I picture the floors of the rooms downstairs. Solid quarry tiles in the kitchen, carpets over cement screed in the dining room and study and oak timbers in the living room. All inaccessible on the face of it and not easy to take up without causing a whole lot of damage.

Okay so what about outside. What about going in from another angle, somewhere else. Again I imagine the external walls in my mind's eye. No good trying from the front pavement, the same will apply as going in beside the chapel and in any case I would need permission from the Council which would probably not be forthcoming. The south end of the house slopes on the outside and would be hard to dig up in the right place and then there's the issue of the fireplace. That leaves the back of the house alongside the sitting room, the study and the dining room. Throwing back the duvet and sitting up I decide to talk to Raymond about the practicalities of accessing the cellars from one of these points.

Still immersed in thought whilst having breakfast I have a brainwave, something which hadn't occurred to me before. The under part of the staircase in the study has been boxed in with wooden panelling to form a cupboard. Could this be a way of getting down into the cellars without causing serious disruption I wonder.

Going hastily through to the study I rummage in the cupboard under the stairs, pushing the tins of paint and other bits and pieces to one side. I can see that the dusty floor is screed cement too which is fine as it can easily be re-laid if we find there's no way into the cellars or they've been closed up.

Excitedly I call Raymond. "So what do you think? Is it worth a go?"

"Sure is. It might jest work and there's no 'arm in it. Not going in through the cupboard floor like that."

"So you'll give it a go?"

"Course. I'll 'av ter bring me long drill with me," he says, "so's I can drill down through the cement ter find out if there's any resistance. If there isn't then we'll know we're through."

"And then we'll know if it's worth digging up the cement and trying to find a way in. Great stuff. Maybe this is the way forward at last."

"Right," says Raymond. "I'll be there termorrow, around 8.30."

"See you then. Bye" and I put down the phone feeling energised. Returning to the study I hurriedly pull everything out of the cupboard and stack it all to one side. The cupboard smells musty and is bigger than I had remembered, running right back under the stairs to the front of the house. I remember what Harry Furlong said to me about cellar entrances often being at the stair end. Maybe he was right.

I climb inside wedging the small wooden door open with a piece of cardboard. Brushing away the dust I crouch on the floor trying to imagine what is there beneath my feet. Images of a dank and smelly void flash through my mind and then in contrast I envision it filled with jumbles of household items and, stashed somewhere in the corner, an old suitcase filled with valuables.

"Don't get carried away girl," I say out loud. "The cellars may have all been filled with rubble. It may all lead nowhere. Just stop getting keyed up and get on with something else."

Climbing out of the cupboard determinedly I try to distract myself by giving James a bell. He's just as exuberant as I am. And then I have the jitters all afternoon as I keep getting up from marking scripts to go and check the cupboard. Is there anything I've missed?

❦

Raymond arrives early next day for once. "This is a big ol' cupboard yer know," he says peering into the cupboard. "Yer could quite easily get two or three people in there without any trouble." He plugs his drill into a socket on the wall and runs the wire across to the cupboard. "I'm just goin' ter drill down 'ere straight as a dye t' see what we can find."

He climbs cautiously into the cupboard. Pulling the drill in behind him he holds the bit steady in the centre of the floor space and drills carefully through the cement floor. Piles of fine dust puff back up from the hole settling in a heap round the edge.

"I'm nearly down ter 200 mm," he says, "and still goin'. Hmh, there's a bit of resistance," he pauses and removes the drill from the hole. Blowing the dust away he begins to drill again.

Then, "Blimey I've broke through. It's definitely 'ollow." He removes the drill bit and examines it. "See there's no dirt coming up, just the cement dust. It's 'ollow otherwise we'd be inter mud coming up on the drill bit. An' see 'ere, that there's wood shavings, that means we're goin' through wood further down. Must be wooden joists down there as yer would expect in a cellar," he observes. Bending down and sniffing at the hole he adds, "I can't smell nothing."

"So that means there is a cellar," I exclaim peering into the cupboard. "It wasn't filled in after all."

"More 'an likely. Have yer got a piece of wire, a long piece or an old wire coat hanger? I'd like ter try shoving it down the 'ole to see how far it goes down."

I hurry and fetch a coat hanger and watch as Raymond untwists it and straightens it out. He feeds the wire down the hole and wiggles it about. "Well that means sumink. It's definitely a void down there."

"Oh Raymond, you're a star. Fantastic. You've cracked it."

"So what do yer want me t'do now?" he asks climbing back out of the cupboard and straightening himself up.

"I think you should carry on and break up the cement with something so that we can see what's under there. We can't leave it now. Oh that's the postman. I'll be back in a minute. I expect you want some tea anyway?"

The postman has a parcel for me and we chat briefly while I sign for it. Then I go through to the kitchen and make Raymond his mug of tea.

By the time I return to the study he's laid out dust sheets and lined up his tools on the floor. Gulping his tea he peers into the cupboard. "Tha's it," he says straightening up. "Tha's the way ter do it. I'll cut a series of joined up 'oles in a square ter make the cement loose. That way I can prise it up and we can see what's underneath."

He climbs inside and starts drilling a number of small holes close together in a line, clouds of fine dust billowing up as he does so. "I'd better put my mask on," he says feeling in his pocket. "You'd best put one on too if yer goin' ter watch. There's some in my van, in the back."

By the time I return to the study he's drilling a second line of holes at right angles to the first. Now I can see little puffs of smoke coming from the hole and the drill bit judders. Raymond stops and removes the drill saying, "Tha's the drill 'itting wood. It's a masonry drill so it won't cut timber. It just gets all hot and tha's what's causin' the smoke. I'll ha' ter be careful not ter go so deep with it."

He carries on drilling until there's a neat square about sixty centimetres in size. There's dust everywhere. He grabs a dustpan and sweeps it into a rubbish sack, then using a couple of chisels he prises the cement loose exposing a piece of dark coloured plastic. Taking a screwdriver he scores the edges of the plastic membrane and rips it to one side.

"Tha's a trap door there," he exclaims. "One of those 'inged ones like you get in pub cellars. They flaps downwards, makes it easier ter open and less weight when it's in two pieces like that."

Climbing excitedly into the cupboard I peer round his shoulder at the trap door. "So what next? Will you have to make the hole bigger?"

"Yup, jest carry on the same and cut a bigger 'ole. I've got ter try and cut it so that we find the edges of the 'atch," Raymond says, carefully clearing the debris from the area so that he can begin again with his drilling.

"Time for another cup of tea, I think," and I move into the kitchen.

As I'm boiling the kettle the electricity blows with a thud and the kitchen lights go out.

"Hey are you alright?" I call running towards the study.

"I wonder why that 'appened?" he says. "Ain't nothing I'm doin'."

Back in the kitchen I climb onto a chair and reaching up turn the electricity back on. There's no sign as to why the fuse blew and it's making me feel jittery. Maybe this is all a bit too ridiculous, cutting holes in the floor like that. Are we going to come to regret it I wonder?

It takes him a while to drill an outer section of cement and I occupy myself with kitchen tasks. "Are yer comin' through?" he calls as I push the button on the washing machine.

By now Raymond is covered in dust, his hair completely white. He picks at the membrane and now we can clearly see the wooden trapdoor with a large wrought iron bolt securing it across the middle. He grasps the bolt and tries to work it loose. "This aint goin' ter be easy, it's all jammed up."

"I'll get some easing oil," I say jumping up and fetching some from the utility room.

Raymond squirts the oil over the catch, rubbing it in painstakingly with a cloth. He repeats this several times and then taking his time he carefully works it loose and eases back the bolt. As he pushes it to one side the two flaps of the trapdoor drop down into the void with a thud. The cellar hole is pitch black and there's a dusty, musty smell. He shines a torch down through the open hatch revealing a wooden staircase angling to the left.

As the dust settles I take my camera from a side table and snap a couple of shots of Raymond covered in a layers of dust peering down the hole. "You can show this to your wife to make her laugh at what you get up to," I say with a smile.

"She's always laughin' at me anyways," he grins. "We'll have ter go careful," he goes on. "No sayin' what condition these steps are in." He puts a foot on the top step and carefully puts a bit of weight on it. "This one 'ere seems okay. I wonder when this entrance was closed up and why? They must've 'ad a reason."

Sitting on the edge of the hatch he reaches down and taps the top few steps with his foot. "These ones seem okay. I'll try sum' more of 'em but I'll keep m' hands on the wood surround ter be on the safe side." He eases himself down through the hatch and taking a deep breath I prepare to follow him.

CHAPTER 10

I gaped in surprise. To my disappointment the cellar was absolutely bare. No rotting old furniture, beer barrels or wine bottles, no old suitcases bursting at the seams, no piles of magazines or newspapers, no rusting paint pots, no rubbish or boxes of old hats, nothing. Nothing except limply hanging festoons of grimy old spiders webs coated with dust, dangling from the whitewashed walls and wooden beams.

I looked at Raymond in bewilderment.

Early the next day Judith arrived to explore the cellars with me. "So what do you think we'll find?" she asked tentatively buttoning her jacket.

"Well we know at least one of the cellars is bare."

"I feel it's all a bit of an adventure," Judith said uncertainly. "Not the kind of thing I've done before. We just don't know what's down there. It could be anything."

"Well I'm a bit nervous myself about what we might find. But I've been waiting for this moment for so long. We've just got to bite the bullet and get down there. Shame James and Tom couldn't be here but what the heck."

"Okay then," said Judith. "I suppose I'm ready. Let's go for it."

Moving the table from in front of the cupboard I cautiously opened the small wooden door under the stairs. The flaps of the trapdoor were left dropped down and there was a large yellow plastic torch to the side of the hatch. The cellar hole was pitch-black and I could smell the slightly musty atmosphere.

Yesterday Raymond had fixed a loft light with a long cable clamped to a rusty metal spur high up on the wall to light the cellar below, but I realised that we'd need the torch to explore the other cellars. I switched on the socket by the top of the stairs and the void was filled with light instantly becoming less forbidding.

I looked down into the cellar warily thinking to myself that we could actually be opening up a whole can of worms. Was I going to regret my obsession with the cellars? I felt the tension in my neck. Consciously putting my uneasiness to one side I said, "The stairs are wooden and they're quite solid. Raymond and I tried them yesterday, right down to the bottom, and they're safe alright."

"What's the best way for me to get down?" Judith asked warily.

"There's quite a sturdy rope handrail on the right-hand side. You can feel it if you put your hand out. I'll go first and you can come down behind me. Probably best to hold onto the rail and bump down in a sitting position. Raymond said there are about eleven or twelve steps."

"Okay then, I'll be fine," Judith said resolutely.

Grasping the torch in one hand I sat on the edge of the hatch and eased my legs down through the hole. I decided to bump down the stairs myself. Although we'd had a quick look at the cellar yesterday Raymond had suddenly been called away by his wife because one of his children was sick and I wasn't going to do any exploration of the unknown on my own. I put out my hand and guided Judith to sit beside me holding her hand out so that she could grasp the handrail.

"There, that's the rail," I said. "Just hold on tightly."

"Thanks."

Bumping down the stairs I could see by the reddish patches that the walls were made of brick beneath the peeling whitewash. They were quite uneven, much more irregular than the brickwork of the house.

At the foot of the stairs there was a heavily worn patch where the floor dipped, indented by footsteps over time. The floor was made of large yellowish stone flags and the cellar was almost square in shape, about three and a half metres long and slightly less in width.

My disappointment from the day before remained as I gazed about the empty space before me. It was all a let down. I had expected to find so many clues, clues about the people before and their way of life. Clues maybe as to why the cellar had been closed up all that time ago, evidence of what went on down here. I felt disillusioned after all the anticipation and my struggle to get the cellar opened. I stood up and put my hand out to guide Judith as she bumped down the last couple of steps.

"You're right," she said, "the steps feel quite solid. Worn in places, but solid. Must be heavy old oak." She reached the bottom and stood up steadying herself with her hand on the wall and I could see her taking in the atmosphere, seeing it in her own way. She stood motionless.

I looked about me hoping to find something, something of interest. And then I noticed two small alcoves set into the wall along the left-hand side of the cellar. They were high up with a slightly pointed arched top. I could see that the stone flags finished and that the floor was just rough earth in the far corner beneath the furthermost alcove.

My gaze moved on and took in the arched doorway set in the middle at the far end of the room and I realised that there was no door between this and the next cellar. I could see rusty hinges swathed in cobwebs fixed to the wooden doorframe but no sign of the door.

The ceiling was low and looking up I could see the dark wooden beams in serried rows above my head. They were much like the beams throughout the house, but unstained and not as wide.

I put my hand on Judith's arm, taking in the fusty smell and the slanting shadows cast by the arc of light. I was aware how quiet it was, there was absolutely no sound at all. You could almost hear the silence.

"So what does it feel like down here?" I asked curious to hear about Judith's first impressions which were no doubt very different from my own. "Does it feel strange to you or any different from the house? Do you feel any particular vibes?"

"It seems a bit cold of course and really quiet, you realise just how much noise is generated in everyday life," replied Judith. "There's a sort of musty smell, not really damp but more dusty. There's something else. Something I can't place, can you smell it?"

"Yes, there is something," I say breathing in. "I don't know what it is either."

"It does feel different from the house, feels like a different time. Almost feels like we've gone back, back to when the cellar was last used. When would that have been?"

"Now there's a question. I really don't know. Maybe we'll get a better idea when we look round. I don't think it's been closed up for as long as we imagined. That handrail doesn't look that old to me."

Taking Judith's arm I moved over to examine the alcoves. They were about sixty centimetres in length and about thirty in height. Being away from the light they were somewhat cast in shadow but as far as I could see there was nothing on either of the ledges. Grasping the torch I shone the light into first one and then the other. Putting my hand in I felt gingerly towards the back. What on earth would they have been used for I wondered and why at this height?

I felt along the rough brick surface. It was whitewashed like the walls, the surface smooth and cold, my hand skimming the surface, nothing. I moved to the second alcove and felt along its length. Empty too.

And then towards the back I found what felt like a large key. I drew it from the alcove and examined it. It was a heavy and ornately carved key.

"I've found something!" I exclaimed and turned to Judith. Both of us were wearing warm clothing and I could see Judith pulling her jacket more closely round her and tightening her scarf. "There's a couple of small alcoves set in the wall just here, quite high up. Can't think what they're for. Anyway there's a key in one of them. See what you think of it."

I put the key into her hands and she felt it over carefully. "Must be some door by the size of it," she remarked. "I wonder where it is."

I reached up and placed the key back in the alcove unsure what to do with it. Looking down I scuffed my feet in the rough earth in the corner. "I wonder if there's something buried down here." I said. "The flagstones just end about thirty centimetres from the wall. There must be a reason, they're so neatly laid everywhere else."

"Strange. Maybe they ran out of flagstones."

"Seems a bit odd all the same. We really need something like a probe or a fork that we can poke around with. I'll go up and get something in a minute."

As I turned round I realised there was a small wooden door set to the right of the staircase. "There's a door over in the wall by the stairs," I exclaimed. "It must lead through to the cellar under the sitting room. It's arched like the doorway at the other end but a fair bit smaller."

Taking Judith's arm I led her over to it. "Hm, it looks far too small for a key of that size." Although it was dusty and covered in cobwebs I could see it was a fine-looking carved oak door about my height. There was a round metal ring set on the left-hand side. Tentatively I put out my hand and tried to turn the ring. I could hear the latch click but the door was evidently locked.

I could see a keyhole just beneath the ring but there was no key. I tried it again, twisting it with both hands as hard as I could but couldn't budge it.

"Nothing doing?" Judith asked. "Well at least we know this isn't the door for that heavy key." She ran her fingers over the carved surface. "Feels beautiful," she said, "but why have such an ornate door in a cellar? Was it because this particular cellar was an important place at one time?"

"Hm, maybe. I'd really like to see what's on the other side. Why is it locked?" I said impatiently running my fingers round the doorframe and searching with the torch to see if there was a key hanging from a hook or placed in some cranny, but I couldn't see any sign of one.

"We'll have to think about this. I'm sure Raymond could help. He's probably ace at picking locks." Standing back I swept the wall from top to bottom with the torch. "Nope, nothing. We're not going to get in there today. Anyway let's go through that doorway into the cellar at the other end. Surely there'll be something in there."

I took Judith's arm and led her back across the room and through the archway. Somewhat cautiously I flashed the torch and was surprised to see how well the beam illuminated the room. The second cellar was similar in size to the first and I could see that it too was quite empty. I sighed, nothing. The walls were whitewashed brick like the first cellar but with no alcoves. However I could see there was another door set at the far end.

"So what have you found?" asked Judith rubbing her hands together.

"Oh it's just the same as the first one. There's nothing here as far as I can see," I said dejectedly. "Raymond did say he would lend me a couple of portable halogen lights next week. That'll make it easier to see down here. How about we grab a cup of coffee and then bring down something so we can dig into that rough patch back there?"

"That'll be good," replied Judith. "I could do with a dose of caffeine."

Back upstairs we were settling in by the Aga with mugs of coffee when James arrived. I explained about the patch of rough earth we'd found and how we wanted to dig down to see if there was anything buried there. "I suppose a trowel or garden fork might do it, or maybe the poker as it's quite long. Perhaps we'll take them all down."

I collected a couple of trowels and a garden fork from the garage together with the poker from the sitting room and we returned to the cellar. "Quite something," said James looking round him. "This would have taken a heck of a lot of digging, especially if you're right and there are three or four cellars. Just think of the earth and rubble they'd have had to take away."

"You're right," I replied. "I hadn't thought about that. What would they have done with all the rubble I wonder? Maybe that's why the back garden is tiered, perhaps they just dumped it all out there."

James grasped the poker and kneeling down began to prod the rough patch of earth. "This soil is very hard," he said, "we're going to need something a lot more substantial. Can you pass me the fork please."

I passed him the garden fork and he stood up and started to loosen the topsoil, wiggling the fork with his foot to ease the soil. Taking a pointed trowel I poked the firmly packed soil, loosening it so that James could work his fork deeper. I realised with a smile what a sight we must look, crouching there in a dusty old cellar with mud-spattered faces and hands. James looked at me and smiled wryly back.

"So have you found anything?" queried Judith leaning towards us. "Maybe that's something to do with the smell we noticed earlier, that piece of ground. There's certainly an earthy smell down here"

"Nothing so far," replied James working away. Suddenly he jerked the fork and prodded again. "There's something here," he exclaimed. "It may be a stone or it could be something else. Can you pass me a trowel please so I can dig down a bit?"

I worked alongside him tossing the soil to one side and between us we scooped away the earth. Digging urgently we piled the soil away from the hole as our trowels hit something solid.

"It's a box, a wooden box," I said, turning to Judith.

"It's not that big," said James, "only about fifteen or twenty centimetres I should think. Why on earth bury a box down here?"

James dug away at the sides to release the box and then prised it out of the ground. It was covered in dried mud, the wood was cracked and curling outwards in places, the small hinges at the back rusty.

"So what's this!" he exclaimed looking at me expectantly.

CHAPTER 11

A baby, a one-day-old baby. How dreadful, thought Robert. How dreadful to be the one to bury her, to lay her to rest in the carefully chosen corner of the graveyard, to leave her there by herself, forever alone. He reflected on the simple but poignant inscription on her gravestone:

In memory of baby Zara Tegan
Died 31 November 2009
Aged 1 day
Ever loved by Alice and Connor Tegan

The funeral had been disturbing, more difficult than usual. The distraught parents completely overcome, their only daughter born after years of waiting. And now what did they have but just one day of memories of their beautiful baby. Hard at times such as this to understand why these things can happen. What is God's will or meaning in all this he thought?

Now Robert was standing alone inside the church, rapt in thought and gazing at the sole remaining stained glass window at the nave end. In the darkening afternoon it was gloomy and distinctly cold but

Robert was entirely unaware of this as he contemplated the vibrant colours of the glass. Dated 1854 this solitary window was dedicated by Mr and Mrs John Tattam in Victorian times when they left money to provide winter coal for the poor.

Robert Delforth, vicar of Whittlesham for seven years, was interrupted in his thoughts by Jane Marsden, one of the wardens, bustling energetically into the church. She was wearing a thick red woollen coat with a knitted hat to match with large earpieces pulled down firmly on her head. "You'll be catching yer death of cold, you will," she said. "That there coat couldn't keep out the cold, it hasn't got any substance to it."

"Thank you for reminding me. I should really wear a scarf but I never seem to remember," he replied somewhat chastened.

"Anyways I'll make you a cup of tea in a jiffy, that'll warm you up," she said busily straightening the hassocks on the hooks along the pews. She flurried towards the other end of the church occupying herself with the pews and then moved over to the door where she began straightening the prayer and hymn books and the church magazines, carefully arranging them in an orderly fashion.

Returning to his thoughts Robert looked up at the six clerestory windows in the high-pitched wooden roof above the nave as the lowering sky darkened. The word nave is Saxon he thought and yet this place has been here since ancient times when it would probably have looked more like an agricultural building of some kind. Nothing like it does today.

"Here's yer tea then," said Jane handing him a large mug. "I've given you extra sugar to warm you up. Put yer hands round this. It'll do you good."

"That's very kind, thank you," he replied abstractedly. "And how is Peter today? Is he on the mend now?"

"Well, he's still under the doctor. But yer know what it is with men. They just don't know how to look after themselves. He's been going outside in all this cold when he really shouldn't," she said disapprovingly. "Good job he's retired now or he would have insisted on going back to work."

"Pass on my good wishes won't you," said Robert smiling to

himself as she disappeared energetically into the porch to arrange the flowers.

As he turned his head back and faced the altar he was aware of the three stone seats set in the recess in the corner of the nave. These were originally for officiating dignitaries when the priest sat on the highest seat, the deacon and sub deacon on the lower seats. An important Church with a prestigious past.

Not so now. It was him alone who preached to his parishioners and yet he had a goodly turn out on Sundays. His predecessor had discovered that guitar playing and a more modern approach was a recipe for growing and retaining the congregation and Robert had deliberately built on and developed these ideas knowing full well that many Anglican congregations were now sadly in decline. In contrast he thought with the vibrant Catholic resurgence taking place with swelling congregations of newly arrived African and European migrants. And so it was that part of the hymn singing and prayers were accompanied each week by a member of the congregation who regularly brought his guitar with him.

He moved still lost in thought to the far end of the church and standing beneath the belfry became aware of the insistent banging emanating from the bell tower, the heavy and never-ending toll of the wind on the roof tiles. The thudding and the juddering, the constant battering. A knock-knock effect that sounded as if someone was trying to get in.

When he had first arrived at the church he had several times gone to the porch and opened the door thinking someone was trying to enter. Each time there was no-one there and he had now obliged himself to cease responding to the strange knocking.

At times when the swirling winds battered in from a northerly direction the roof leaked relentlessly and it felt as if the roof would be blown away in its entirety. More expense, more fund-raising he sighed to himself. At least when the rains did come in he was able to prevent too much damage by the strategic placing of several large buckets.

As he listened the wind subsided and he could hear instead the welcome and familiar sound of the old clock ticking stolidly above him in the tower. The original Saxon church had had a circular tower but this was replaced and rebuilt in the early 1500s whereafter six bells had been installed incrementally over the next hundred years. He glanced up at the neatly furled bell ropes, red, green and white striped, hanging in abeyance until Sunday, the discordant bright green first aid pouch attached to one of the ropes. He knew only too well of the dangers of rope burn.

And then there was the dreadful incident of a local bell ringer, one William Barnes, being hung by his very own bell rope at the turn of the last century. Hung as oblivious his fellow ringers sounded their bells and it was only as they looked up that they saw his body being swept unmercifully up and away, high above them in the tower. The thick rope crushing and snapping his neck, the lifeless body hanging like a limp rag doll.

The distraught vicar immediately decreed that no bell should ever be rung again from the church tower in memorial of that fateful death. It was believed that they had been jinxed and the tower was placed out of bounds. From that time no-one ventured up the stairs to the belfry, the bells waiting in silence for three quarters of a century.

And then in 1974 the incumbent vicar took courage and determinedly raised money to recommision the bells, committed to once again make them and the belfry stairs safe. He had to cajole the locals to take up bell ringing and arranged bell ringing lessons from neighbouring ringers as inevitably all bell ringing skills had died out. Since then bell ringing had been an important part of village life with bell practice being religiously maintained every Tuesday night and bell ringers of all ages taking part.

As he clasped his thin black coat round his shoulders he heard a movement at the door and a grey-haired gentleman entered the church. "Good day to you," said Robert not recognising him.

"Good afternoon," the man replied moving towards Robert. He looked about him. He was short and well dressed but painfully thin, wearing a blue suit and navy overcoat with a bright yellow scarf tied round his neck.

"I'm just visiting the graves of my parents who were buried here some ten years ago. They lived in the village next to the old fire station. I'm just paying my respects, taking the opportunity to get close to them as I live in Banbury now. I don't get here very often," he said pausing. "This is such a lovely church to visit, so very peaceful and I was just passing through," he added.

Robert nodded and held out his hand to the man. "I'm so glad you could visit," he said shaking hands. "All visitors are most welcome."

The man took his place at one of the pews and knelt for some time solemnly bowing his head, his yellow scarf incongruously bright in the darkening church.

"I'm not long for this life you know," he said almost inaudibly, looking up. "I shan't be seeing Christmas this year."

"My blessings on you," said Robert softly. "Is there anything I can do?"

"Well there is one thing," said the man straightening himself up and stepping into the aisle towards Robert. "You can tell me one thing. Can I be buried here with my parents? Does it matter that I don't live here?"

"Of course you can," replied Robert gently. "You have your ties with the village. It's absolutely fine. Just leave your instructions and it will be done."

"Thank you," said the man looking down at his feet. "You don't know how much that means to me. You see," he paused, "I don't have anyone else. I have no roots. I need to know I'll be in company when I go if you know what I mean."

"I surely do," said Robert. "We all need company."

The man slid himself again into a pew resting his knees on a hassock, closing his eyes seemingly in prayer or deep in thought. After a while he rose and nodding to the vicar he moved silently to the door and was gone, adjusting his scarf involuntarily as he went.

Robert carefully extinguished the lights and took a large key from his pocket. Turning it in the lock he repeated the same prayer he said every night as he closed the church:

"Almighty and everlasting God, I pray thee forever keep this House and your parishioners safe. Help me to do my work in your name and to remain your ever-faithful servant.
Keep from us all things that may hurt us and help us cheerfully to accomplish

what thou wouldst have us do.
Amen."

Suddenly aware that he was by now stiff with cold he made his way the short distance across the graveyard to the old vicarage. The house loomed thick with shadows, large and unforgiving. There were no lights burning, no-one to welcome him. "We do all need company, even me" he thought to himself as he put the key in the lock.

He lived alone, rattling around in the large red brick Victorian building which was far more suited to a vicar with a rumbustuous family. He'd always lived alone and knew that at the age of forty-seven he would most probably always live a solitary life. Once whilst at Exeter Theological College he'd hoped to make his girlfriend Olivia his wife but she had been consistent in her view that she could never marry a theologian and give her life to the church, despite all the things they seemed to have in common.

They shared an interest in film and theatre, the arts and music, they trekked on the moors and shared blustery picnics and flasks of coffee in the wilds. They took sanctuary in off-the-beaten track pubs with roaring fires and good simple ales. They visited cities together and she indulged him in his abiding interest in visiting cathedrals despite being a non-believer. They drank mulled wine together in his rooms and shared blasphemously exotic cocktails in hers.

However his beloved vivacious and red headed soul mate, a trainee science teacher, could not reconcile her future with his. And so she had moved on, moved on and married a solicitor. A law undergraduate from Exeter. Much easier to live with he thought than someone like me.

He pictured her bubbly and energetic vitality and tried to imagine what life would have been like if she had married him. Probably a washout he thought. I could never have kept up with her. What would she be doing with herself here in a rambling old vicarage with someone like me? No good would have come of it he mused.

Sometimes, just sometimes, he wondered what her life was like now. Whether she had had children, whether she was still married? Whether indeed she was still alive? And then he closed his mind to those thoughts and brought himself back to his spiritual beliefs and his work in the parish with the never-ending duties and commitments.

He rekindled the dying fire in the over-sized sitting room, first laying some twigs and small pieces of wood and then adding a few logs and some coal. Then he brought a plate of rough-cut crusty bread with cheese and pickles and set them before the fire. Returning to the kitchen he poured some beer into a tankard and sat by the fireside to eat.

Thinking back to the baby he had buried that day and then the visitor in the church he deliberated about the proximity of death. It is so close, yet so unknown he thought. We can never know what is going to happen. It's my work to be close to those who are dying or bereaved and yet it's sad, so very sad. It will happen to us all and who will mourn for me he asked himself broodingly.

No-one is the answer. My parishioners will be sorry I am sure and they will miss me I hope. They will bury me stoically and the Bishop will say his piece. But what ultimately is the meaning of my life? Surely I must leave more of a mark when I go. Helping others is my work but what of my own life?

He drank thirstily from his mug of beer reflecting about the day's events, his weary body revived by the warmth of the fire, the crackle and glow now brightening the dimly lit room.

The vision when it came was wondrous. He was suddenly in the presence of an amazing coming together of forms, of wraiths and spirits swirling above the newly consecrated part of the graveyard.

Although it was dark he could see several vicars in flowing black cassocks writhing in dance alongside male and female forms, all dressed in clothing as they had been in life. It was as if a party, a celebration, a delight for all. The dresses were red and gold, the faces happy and smiling. And as he looked up he could see the forms raising their glasses as if in cheer, seemingly euphoric about their destiny. Not at all sombre as remembered in death.

As he watched they moved together in dance, a slow and rhythmic uncomplicated dance, one with another twisting and turning, all appearing twice or three times their size in life. Their faces, some known to him some not, lit by an intense light from above, their mouths moving fervently deep in conversation.

And he could hear the music, the strangely moving resonance of long forgotten Elizabethan strains as the harmony of flutes, citole, harp and percussion played in his head. He could taste the essence of the flowing wine and smell the intoxicating aroma.

And he felt pure happiness and absolute serenity as he lay concealed within the shadows beneath them, watching, sharing, transfixed by their presence around him, satiated in turn by their celebration. A joy to behold. The moment imprinted in time.

Life after death he murmured.

CHAPTER 12

"Sounds like witchcraft to me," said Tom. Lying on the floor in the sitting room in front of a glowing fire replete after a takeaway Thai meal James and Tom were poring over a single piece of parchment found in the wooden box.

"What makes you say that?" asked Judith.

Tom read again from the piece of paper:

> OUR DAUGHTER DOTH NOT REST
> SHE LIETH NEAR THIS PLACE
> HER BODIE WETTE, HER BODIE DRIE
> SHE NEEDS TO BE AT ONE
> Signed Thomas and Mary Crabbe

"Just think about it," he said. "The first two lines are fairly plain, we can understand what they mean. Say I'm right and the daughter was suspected or accused of being a witch, then she couldn't be buried on consecrated ground. So what would her parents do if she died? They'd have to find somewhere else to bury her. What better place than a cellar, even more probably their own cellar?"

"But it's the third line that's less clear," Tom went on. "Presumably it means 'her body wet, her body dry'. If so why is it sometimes wet and sometimes dry? And where is the body anyway?" he looked puzzled. "That must mean something. It's like a riddle, as if they're deliberately trying to make it into a conundrum. Something we've got to puzzle out. Is this all there was in the box?" he added looking round for it.

"Yes the box practically fell apart in my hands," replied James. "This piece of paper was wrapped inside an old piece of velvet. There were also the remains of something that could have been a piece of jewellery but it's so crumbled away that you can't really tell what it was."

"Did you look deeper in the hole?" queried Tom.

"Well not much deeper. We poked about just beneath where the box lay. We didn't dig down a lot. Maybe we should take another look. Dig deeper."

"Well that's all very well and fine," said Tom, his long slender fingers holding up the parchment. "But I think this is the clue. This message."

"So what makes you connect it with witchcraft?" I asked.

"There's just something about this riddle. Makes me think there must be a reason for her unrest," said Tom slowly. He picked up the piece of paper again and read it out loud.

"Okay let's just put the message on hold and think about witchcraft for a minute," he suggested. "Right from way back witchcraft was associated with heresy or rejection of the teachings of the Christian church. That's what led to witches being burned at the stake or hung and this went on until the early 1700s. It was only then that laws were brought in which referred to those 'pretending' to be a witch, setting out punishments for those accused who were now considered to be vagrants or con artists trying to trick others. From 1735 onwards they were subject to much more lenient penalties in the form of fines or imprisonment as attitudes changed considerably."

"So they really only burnt and hanged witches in the 1500s and 1600s?" Judith interjected. "I thought it was still going on long after that."

"There were no official burnings at the stake or hangings or drownings after the 1730s, not in this country anyway," said Tom. "However not all attitudes were changing. It is said that lots of people got mixed up on the periphery of witchcraft, maybe they knew or associated with someone suspected of being involved. There was a whole lot of hearsay and general taboos around witchcraft which no-one really understood. You can imagine what local gossip was like."

"Yes in those times news was only brought to the villages by passers by, many of whom might be pedlars or itinerants and who's to say what they knew. They were just passing on what they had heard elsewhere. Gossip and anecdotes becoming myths and rumours and then generating more myths and rumours," said James.

"Some people related witchcraft to pagan rituals or Wicca," said Tom. "Others saw it as the establishment trying to put down women who were early practitioners of herbal medicine and birth control. Midwives had a lot of knowledge at the time and also had access to things connected with witchcraft, for example umbilical cords and foetal placenta. Also don't forget that village tensions were easily exacerbated in close knit villages and communities and casting someone in the guise of a witch could be a way of getting even or just getting them into trouble generally."

"You seem to know a great deal about these things," I remarked with a smile. "Are you sure you're not a witch?"

"I'm no witch," said Tom, laughing, "although lots of so called 'witches' were men as well as women. As a media researcher I get asked to delve into all kinds of things. My first job on my local paper The *Stowmarket Advertiser* involved tales of suspected witchcraft and skulduggery. Nothing ever came to anything but I did find it a very interesting area and it's not the kind of thing you forget."

"Okay," I said. "Let's suppose you're right. The paper seems to have been written by a Thomas and Mary Crabbe. We should be able to find out more about them through the Parish records, see if they lived in the village and whether they are buried here. Also if they have a daughter and where she's buried."

"They might have had more than one daughter," put in Judith.

"That's true," said James. "And their daughter or daughters might have been buried in the churchyard. I suppose we need to go and look see."

This is going to take some time, I thought as I scrolled through endless microfilm on an archaic and cumbersome but surprisingly effective microfilm reader. Seated in the research area in the library I found myself in the midst of numerous other individuals all hard at work, heads bent jotting and scribbling down information gleaned from maps, registers, microfilm and various other sources.

"Do you always get this many people in here?" I asked the duty librarian whose name badge said Hilary Crabtree.

"Oh yes, sometimes the place can be quite full, especially from late morning onwards. Delving into family history is an absolute passion for many, particularly retired people. They spend weeks, even months, poring over old documents. They get quite obsessed. I suppose all the interest has been generated by the many programmes on radio and TV."

"I hope it won't take me that long," I said. Earlier she had deftly shown me how to navigate the Parish Records of burials in Whittlesham dating back to around 1700. It was surprisingly interesting to get a feel for the names of people who had died in the village. The burials were neatly recorded and numbered by the presiding vicar and it was quite poignant to note the number of vicars who were buried by their successor.

"Fortunately the burials recorded at this time were legible and are quite easy to decipher," commented Hilary peering over my shoulder. "Not like earlier burials dating back to the 1500s where the writing is almost impossible to read."

I flicked through the names, scanning for a Thomas and Mary Crabbe who were buried around the same time and after some searching I found a Thomas Crabbe and a Mary Crabbe who died in 1865 and 1867 respectively. Both born in Whittlesham and buried there. Bingo I thought. That must be them.

I went over to the cabinet that Hilary had shown me earlier where the Register of Marriages were kept and took out the microfiche tape. Slotting it into the microfilm reader next to my station I found the record of marriages in Whittlesham after 1800 and discovered that a Thomas Crabbe, born in 1797, and a Mary neé Fox, born in 1798, were married in August 1819.

Returning to the other tape I fast-forwarded it a bit and then scrutinised the burials in the name of Crabbe listed after August 1819. I scribbled everything down on my pad.

> Thomas, John and William all died in infancy in 1820, 1822 and 1824 of fever, weakness and dysentery respectively
> Emmeline b.1824 died in 1884
> Richard b.1825 died in 1876
> Louisa b.1827

No record of Louisa's date of burial but her birth was recorded as 14 October 1827 so it seemed likely that she was the youngest child of Thomas and Mary, their marriage being recorded in August 1819. Quite the norm it seemed for children to die in infancy. It must have been very hard on Thomas and Mary to lose three young children in quick succession.

I decided to turn next to the local paper to see if I could find out anything relating to Louisa in the local news. "Thank goodness for microfilm," I said to Hilary as she helped me to load the spool spanning the 1800s.

However I found this search much more difficult than I had anticipated. *The Northampton Echo* subtitled *Farmer's Journal* and *Advertising Chronicle* was indeed aimed very much at farmers and the gentry and had a forbidding format and extremely small print.

There were no front page headlines concerning local issues. In each issue Notices, Auctions and Sales appeared on page one, followed by Foreign Intelligence and The Markets, then The Farmers Journal and London and Windsor News and eventually Local Intelligence. This must be where I'll find anything if there is anything to find I thought, somewhere after page four.

Meticulous skim-reading from 1820 onwards took a while and brought nothing. I stopped for a quick coffee and sandwich in the rest room and then returning to my position I had a sudden find.

In the Local Intelligence section dated Saturday 19 August 1843 was a single paragraph. LOCAL GIRL DEAD read the first line. It seemed that Louisa Crabbe had been found drowned, face down in

Wookey Hole Spring in Whittlesham on 15 August 1843. She was sixteen years old.

"Did you find what you were looking for?" asked Hilary as she moved around tidying up the outspread maps, piles of books and discarded spools left by my fellow researchers.

"Yes, I think so," I replied. "It says that a local girl was found dead in my village and that the local constabulary are linking it with some strange events that happened in nearby Puxleyridge some months before. I'm trying to find out what happened to her."

"I can see you've got an idea of how the paper is laid out now," Hilary observed. "At least that makes it easier to find what you're after. It's rather like searching for a needle in a haystack in those old papers. The print is so small and the pages are just crammed with quite obscure information. I can't imagine who would actually have read it even then. And of course not everyone could read anyway."

Scanning backwards from 1st August 1843 I discovered that 'strange happenings' had been reported in April and May 1843 in the hamlet of Puxleyridge just by Handford near Whittlesham although there wasn't a lot of detail, just vague hints of suspected rituals and dark goings on.

"Look at this," I said to Hilary as I continued my search. "It seems the local vicar refused to bury Louisa Crabbe. Reported on 26 August it says 'Arthur Coventry condemned the girl as forfeiting her rights to a Christian burial by consorting with those of an evil nature who practice sorcery and witchcraft'. I didn't know that they could do that."

"Oh yes. They could and they did. I've heard it still went on in places like Devon even in the 1950s, vicars refusing to bury girls who were 'sinners', another word for being pregnant, and suicides," Hilary replied.

"Well this is all food for thought," I said carefully rewinding the spool and slotting it back into the filing cabinet.

Back home I sat in the kitchen lingering over a cup of coffee and imagined the Crabbe family living here in the house. Was that what I had seen those months ago I pondered.

Images came tumbling back into my mind. The rough whitewashed walls, the bunches of dried herbs and yellowing hops draped above the lintel, the smell of freshly baked bread and the pungent aroma of stew from the open range. In my mind's eye I could picture Mary busying herself with the meal and Thomas in his work clothes, beer in hand.

And then the images switched and Louisa's face haunted me as I saw her lying face down in the sloping gully as the spring water bubbled over the rocks and gushed over her body, her long blonde hair swept unremittingly along by the torrent, her dress dishevelled and muddied, the blood red poppies along the bank of the stream bobbing their heads in the wind.

CHAPTER 13

Judith and I return to the cellars. Raymond dropped by earlier and loaned me three small but powerful halogen lights which he doesn't need for the time being. Switching the loft light on I tuck one of the lamps under my arm and carefully descend the steps while Judith bumps down the stairs behind me.

It's rather like moving into another world. The secret world beneath my feet. A timeless void that has been shut out of the world as we know it for years, where the internet does not exist, where there is no news, no mobiles, no television. A timewarp back in the last century. Once again the silence wraps itself round us.

Placing the lamp on the floor near the arched doorway at the far end of the first cellar I depress the switch. Instantly a bright light bursts through into the second cellar, the draping cobwebs silhouetted against the walls like angry cartoon characters gesticulating, the peeling whitewash casting an eerie luminosity across the room, the bare stone flags covered in layers of dust.

I return to the bottom of the stairs and guide Judith across the room and through the arched doorway. "So what do you think? Is Louisa buried somewhere down here?" asks Judith.

"Well she could be. If they weren't able to have her buried in the churchyard her parents must have buried her somewhere. We've all heard of bodies in the cellar and stuff. But the flooring is all stone slabs so if she is buried here she must be under the stone."

"If that's the case," Judith says, "we're not going to find her. It would be a huge job, digging up the flags. How would one know where to start?"

"Yeah. You're right. It wouldn't be easy. Anyway you're the perceptive one. Do you have any kind of feeling or premonition that there might be a body buried down here?"

"Not really. There's almost a nothing atmosphere here if you know what I mean. No inkling of another presence or anything. Just you and me, in a place where no-one has been for a heck of a long time."

"Well that's good I suppose. Not that I believe in ghosts really."

"Don't you?" asks Judith. "I do. I haven't seen one but I do feel they must exist."

"I don't know. I suppose if they existed I think I would have seen one. Anyway I still can't believe that these cellars are just empty. Someone sure has cleared up after themselves. I wonder why?"

"Who knows?"

"One thing. I hope there aren't any rats or bats down here," I say cautiously looking round the corners of the room to see if there were any droppings.

"I'll try not to think about what furry fiends or otherwise we might meet down here," says Judith shuddering. "I really do not like rats so keep an eye out for any signs and let me know."

"Rats are a possibility I'm afraid. Don't worry I'll keep my eyes peeled for any sign of them."

"Thanks, I'm relying on you!"

I look round the cellar. It is completely empty but I can see a door at the opposite end. "There's a door on the far wall. I suppose it must lead to the third cellar, under the kitchen. Let's see if this door opens. There must be something down here."

Taking Judith by the arm I lead her across the room. This is an ordinary door, a plain oak door with an arched top and rusty iron hinges. Nothing like the ornately carved door by the stairs. Grasping the solid metal ring with both hands I manage to turn it quite easily.

"It's not locked! I thought it might be, like the other one." The door creaks as I push it open. "We really need another halogen lamp but we can make do with the torch for now. Stay here for a moment and I'll go and fetch it."

Returning with the torch which I had left lying at the bottom of the stairs I take Judith's arm and walk expectantly through the doorway into the farthermost cellar.

I can see immediately that this room is different. Shining the torch methodically from corner to corner my gaze takes in piles of dusty old wooden boxes stacked up along one side and a long old-fashioned trestle table set against the wall on the other, the surface cluttered with old-fashioned utensils, more swathes of shadowy cobwebs dancing in the torchlight.

"There are lots of boxes," I exclaim, "and also a table with bits and pieces on top. At least there's something in here. Oh yes, over at the far end I can see the wooden staircase rising to the kitchen and I can see where it's been blocked off," I explain as I approach the bottom of the stairs. "This must lead to the rose bed by the kitchen. So Harry Furlong was right about that all along."

"There are some strange smells in here which I can't place," says Judith sniffing the air. "Something apart from all the dust and cobwebs."

"I can't smell anything much. It smells just the same as the other cellars to me. Fusty and dusty. I know you've got a better nose then me. Well, where to start?" I ask, moving towards the pile of boxes. On closer scrutiny I can see that they are crudely fashioned boxes nailed together from old pieces of wood with ill-fitting lids. Taking a couple of tissues from my pocket I sweep away the dust from one of the upper boxes and gingerly lift the lid with one hand, shining the torch into the box with the other.

"Yuk, scrunchy remains of what could be some kind of grain or animal feed," I say drawing back from the box. "Not very appetising. Maybe that's what you can smell." Putting it to one side I tentatively open the one beneath. "Hm, piles of dirty old cracked and broken crockery with rather garish motifs, nothing much in this one either."

I work methodically and open each box in turn. They all seem to be alike, made of rough wood and about the same size, dead spiders prostrate in the corner of several of them. As I open them I find bits and pieces of cotton and sewing materials in one, what looks like beer and wine brewing items in another and some old tea towels and aprons in another.

And then near the bottom of the first pile I find a box which seems to be of significance. Opening the lid I shine the torch inside. The box is filled with letters and photos and a couple of old notebooks.

"Yeah," I say, turning towards Judith, "a find at last. There are some bundles of old letters here, tied up with ribbon, and some black and white photos. And there are also some old books right at the bottom. Just opening one of them it looks like a diary. It's filled with spidery writing in black ink and dated 1941 at the front. Let me read you some of the entries.

> '3 September 1941. Today Rose and I took a walk to Puxleyridge and gained a big yield of wild herbs and elderberries as well as elderberry bark to keep flies away, flies being very bad this year. As usual elder is good for our medicine chest and tomorrow we will make wine and dry some bark for winter purging treatments and to keep constipation and arthritis at bay. We will also dry berries to make tea, they should be good by Christmas. The fresh berries should make about four gallons of wine so will need to pick more as that will not suffice.

> '4 September 1941. Unexpected visitors so Rose and I did not manage to effect all that we had planned. Land girls in the village came by looking for rooms to stay. We had some difficulty in explaining our spare room was not available as villagers had told them we have an empty room. More evacuees arrived in the village, the school numbers are getting bigger and classes are held twice daily, children attending either in the morning or the afternoon. As the village gets busier our calm, natural spaces feel invaded. We hope it will not be for too long but who knows with the war what will happen?'

"I don't know if this is going to be a gripping read but it will tell us something about the people at the time who may well have lived in the house." Closing the diary I lay the box on the side. "There's one more in the pile. Let's see what's in it." I shine the torch on the remaining box in the pile. "This one's different. It looks like it's made of mahogany or something. Lovely wood, lovely colour. But oh, it's locked. Maybe James can open it or Raymond," I say laying the box on top of the one containing the letters and notebooks. "Let's take these upstairs and have a proper look at everything."

"What about the other boxes, are there many more?" asks Judith.

"There are at least six in the other pile I should say. Have you got time now or shall we leave them till another time? I know you're very busy at the moment."

"Okay, maybe leave them. I've got several transcriptions to do by tomorrow. All my publishers want things turned round instantly at the moment. Anyway it's very cold down here. I wonder what it's like in the summer months, whether it ever gets a bit warmer?"

※

James is cooking a Vietnamese meal, shredded chicken with coriander, aromas of tangy lime and chilli wafting across the kitchen. Expertly tossing the finely sliced chicken and green beans in a wok, he throws in a large handful of chopped coriander. The rice cooker turns itself off with a resolute click and he fluffs up the rice with the spatula.

"The pak choy is ready too. I've just stir fried it for a minute or two with a dash of light and dark soy sauce. Just how you like it," he says. "Time to serve."

We take our steaming bowls through to the crackling fire in the sitting room on trays and sit eating, the chilli and lime fragrance scenting the air. "Tasty isn't it," I say. "I don't think you've made this one before. So quick to make."

"Yes and the beans are nice and crunchy aren't they? What would we do without the Eastern rim influences on our food I wonder? Anyway what have you done with the box of letters and photos you found yesterday and the other one you couldn't open?" asks James eating steadily.

"I've left them in the study, maybe we should have a look when we've finished our meal. Not that we'll be able to open the Mahogany box. I'm afraid it looks like a strong lock. You've really excelled yourself with the meal by the way, it's great. Just the right amount of chilli and the lime gives it a very subtle flavour."

As soon as we finish eating I get the boxes from the study and place the rough wood box on the floor between us. James takes the bundle of photos and starts laying them out on the carpet.

"Look there are several photographs of these two ladies, sisters maybe," I observe. "They're very alike. I found the name Eliza Cann at the back of the diary and she mentions someone called Rose in that diary entry I told you about. I wonder if Rose is her sister."

Head and shoulder shots of the two women stare back at us. Smiling faces with dark curly hair swept back and pinned with a comb or grip. The elder, about fifty years old, is wearing a light coloured blouse with a cardigan and the other one, about ten years younger, is similarly dressed but in darker clothes. The shots were probably taken in the garden.

A third photo shows them strolling arm in arm in the village, wearing summer dresses belted at the waist, their hair longer but still curly. Both slim and attractive. There are photos of Morris Men dancing outside what was The Eagle pub in the village and some group photos of villagers and what look like Bank Holiday celebrations. "These are a bit earlier than the diary entries, it looks late 1940s," I say. "There's a car in several of the photos and also the clothes look pre-war. The effect of rationing hasn't taken hold yet by the looks of it. And look here's several more of the garden in winter, heavy snow. See there are the outhouses in the background."

"So it seems quite likely that Eliza and Rose were sisters probably living in the house during the 1940s and possibly before that as well." James shuffles the photos and singles out several more depicting the two women. "No sign of any husbands or children in any of these photos. Maybe they were spinsters."

"What about the other box? Are you any good at opening locks," I ask James expecting him to say no, not his forte.

"Oh yes I can pick locks alright. I was at school with a guy whose dad was a prison officer. He showed me how to pick locks with a hairgrip. You don't have such a thing do you?"

It just so happened that I did have some from way back so I fetch one and hand it to James. He takes it in his right hand and carefully inserts the pointed ends into the lock, gently probing and turning. It takes a few tries but then a distinct click and the lock is open.

I open the lid expectantly. Inside there is a black japanned box with brass hinges beautifully inlaid with polished mother of pearl, birds of paradise and oriental flowers shimmering pink, white and blue in the firelight. "This must be a special box, someone's treasure," I say gently opening it. Lying inside the box there are several sheaves of folded papers and a framed black and white photograph signed Gerald B Gardner with the inscription 'To Eliza and Rose, with fond regards'.

"So who is Gerald Gardner?" I ask. "He looks quite distinguished, like an eminent scientist or something. Learned anyway. He's got rather staring eyes and a strong aquiline nose. Quite a formal photo isn't it?"

"Yes it is and he does have striking features. He looks like a very determined man. What about those papers? Anything interesting there?"

"Well," I reply carefully unfolding the documents. "This one here is the birth certificate of one Harry Cann, born Reading 1st May 1928. Mother Rose Cann, father unknown. Well that's a turn up for the books. We've got an illegitimate son now."

CHAPTER 14

Scrambling through the woods on a bright December morning a few days later James and I are intent on finding out more about Puxleyridge. Louisa seems to have had some connection with the place and we want to get a feel for it. It's a small hamlet about two miles from the village. Not much there, mostly woods and undulating farmland.

The sun slices through the tall trees and casts long shadows across the scattered copses, piles of copper leaves heaped in the crunchy scrubland, a light wind rustling the leggy tendrils of undergrowth. There is no-one there, no sign of life, hardly any birds. The place is peaceful and quiet, only barely heard sounds of distant cars way down in the valley below.

The first clearing we come to is small and the trees fold in on themselves, hugging the grassy hillocks, their spindly branches meeting overhead. "Wouldn't this be a secret place in summer," I say. "All surrounded by leafy trees and no way to see inside the thicket from outside."

"You're right. Just look at how closely the trees are growing together, they must've been planted like that."

We spend some time scrabbling away alongside Barnie in the

wooded area but there is nothing to find except moss covered stones, piles of leaves and twigs and some small grassy knolls.

"What are these trees?" I ask as we meander through the trees. "Are they poplars? They're very tall and their trunks are so slender and look at the number of saplings all around."

"I think so," replies James, "but I'm not that good on trees."

Barnie dives off the rough path and following him we suddenly come upon a lone swing hanging from the bough of one of the taller trees. The long rope is expertly tied high up on the branch overhead and there is a chunky piece of wood wedged into the carefully shaped loop at the bottom. James takes the wood in his hands and sets it swinging. It swings mesmerically to and fro like a pendulum, the heavy weight keeping it going backwards and forwards, backwards and forwards.

"Someone's a good climber," he says, looking up the trunk of the tree and across to the sturdy branch holding the rope. "You wouldn't catch me up there. And you'd have to be good at tying knots."

"I used to have a rope swing rather like that when I was a kid. It was tied to a branch near the ditch at the bottom of the garden. When you sat on the knot at the bottom you could swing across the ditch and jump over to the other side. Most of my friends fell into the ditch when they tried it. It was quite funny."

"Very funny for you." exclaims James.

"Oh they were okay. No harm ever came to any of them," I say laughing at the memory.

Moving further into the wood we can see open fields far distant on the other side. Abruptly we find ourselves standing in the centre of a much larger copse, shafts of sun and shadow criss-crossing the broad grassy shroud in the middle. It is such a regular shape that it looks man-made. And then looking round I become aware of a number of what appear to be rough stone seats, oblong blocks of stone set upright with a smaller stone as a back. "What are these?" I ask, moving to examine one of them. Look there's a name and a date on it."

I count eight stone seats set round the edge of the clearing and I notice that most of them are positioned at the foot of a tree. Also they all have similar inscriptions with a name and a date. We walk slowly round and examine each one in turn, finding as well a number of small slabs of stone set in the earth each with a name and a date.

"Look here," James calls. "There's some kind of inscription or poem on this stone in the middle. It looks like Latin. I'm afraid my Latin is far too poor to be able to read it. How about you?"

"Oh no," I reply. "Latin wasn't for me. I was thrown out and made to study Greek Mythology instead. Much more interesting. I wish I'd brought my camera with me. Anyway let's copy it down and see if we can get it translated."

"That's a good idea. I'll find somebody at the University to translate it for us."

"Have you got any paper with you? I think I've got a pen in my bag."

James produces a small pad from his pocket and notes down the words, firstly from the stone tablet in the middle and then moving round the glade noting the names and dates on the stone edifices. "This must have been some kind of tree worshipping sect and their meeting place. It's uncanny but the dates are all between 1840 and 1852. Just around the time when Louisa died."

Standing back we scrutinise the grassy area carefully looking to see if there's anything else of significance. Over at the far edge of the clearing we stumble upon the remains of a large bonfire, almost hidden by the trunk of a fallen tree. It looks as if it has been placed to serve as a seat at some kind of celebration and I notice that there is a box stuffed beneath one end.

"Someone's been enjoying themselves," exclaims James looking at the empty crate of Moet & Chandon.

"So Tom," I said, "What do you make of this inscription and those odd stone seats? You're always a mine of information."

Tom, seated at the kitchen table that evening, pored over the inscription. "It seems to be something about trees, peace and serenity," he said. "I wonder whether it's a Quaker burial ground? There are lots of them across England and Wales dating from around 1650 to the late 1800s. Most of them were originally on the same site as a Quaker meeting house although many of the meeting houses have now been demolished or fallen into disrepair."

"We didn't see any signs of a building in the wood. No ruins or anything anywhere near," I commented.

"Quakers believe that all ground is 'God's ground' and therefore that their dead could be buried anywhere, in fact they actively avoided consecrated ground. Burial grounds were usually very attractive and planted with shrubs and trees, often in secluded rural locations," Tom continued. "What do you think?"

"I really don't know," I replied. "Could be. Would there be a record of it if it was a Quaker burial ground?"

"I should think so. We could try googling it and see what comes up. Are you logged on?" he said getting up.

We moved to the study and carried out a search, finding a number of sites describing Quaker burial sites and even who was buried in them, in locations across the country but nothing at Puxleyridge.

"Maybe it isn't listed on the internet because it's such a small burial ground?" I suggested. "Anyway what we do know is that someone has been up there recently, having a bonfire and some kind of celebration. Must be recent as the box isn't in bad shape. But that doesn't help in relation to Louisa. Maybe it's nothing significant."

"Hey look what it says here," said Tom reading from the webpage:

> 'Quakers could bury their dead at any angle they chose and were not constrained by the Christian belief that bodies should lie in an east-west alignment with the head at the west end, known as the 'axis burial'.'

"Ah. That's probably why the Puxleyridge site appears to radiate out in a circle. It actually makes it a more inviting environment. But back to the Moet & Chandon. Modern day witches wouldn't drink that would they? I thought they drank wine with their cake."

"As far as I know they might drink champagne as well as wine. However if the place really is a Quaker burial ground one wouldn't expect witches to meet there, not white witches anyway. I think you'll have to take me up there and show me the place. We can take some photos. I'd like to get a feel for the place."

"How can we find out more about Louisa and what was going on in Puxleyridge? I'd really like to know if she was a witch or wasn't a witch and also where she's buried."

"Well her parents didn't seem to think she was a witch. If they did they wouldn't be trying to have her body laid to rest. That seems to me what is meant by their words:

> 'Our daughter doth not rest
> She lieth near this place
> Her bodie wette, her bodie drie
> She needs to be at one.'

Most witch lines ran in families in any case so if Louisa was a witch her mother and probably her grandmother would probably also have been witches and they wouldn't have been bothered about burial in the same way."

Putting the name 'Puxleyridge' in the search engine Tom clicked the mouse and came up with a history and description. "Hey, look there," I said pointing at the bottom of the page:

> 'The manor of Puxleyridge, a considerable hamlet in this parish, was in the baronial family of Moels dating from the year 1460. The name Puxleyridge derives from old English word and means *'ridge with a heathen temple'*.
>
> 'Heathens recognise numerous non-human entities, such as major gods, local gods, ancestral spirits and various sorts of wights (elves, brownies and hill-folk). The various pagan place-name elements appear to date from the pre-viking period.'

"Well it seems there are certainly early Pagan connections with Puxleyridge but what that means for the stones is not at all clear," said Tom. "Let's have a look at the Golden Bough on Wikipedia which is all about secret sects and religious groups and practices. You know we're being drawn in all kinds of different directions here."

Tom and I return to the wood with James the following weekend. It's another bright and sunny day as we make our way to the clearing. Tom moves swiftly round, looking at the stones and taking photographs. "It's certainly is an unusual place," he said standing back and taking in the whole setting. "I've never seen anything quite like it."

"Amazing to just stumble upon it," I say. "We probably wouldn't have found it if we'd been looking for it."

"See here. I've got the translation made by a colleague in Oxford," James says taking a piece of paper from his pocket. "This is what the inscription says:

'The saplings may they grow large having been placed
    with care in this place of my companions.
Harmonious and divine to friendship, may they give
           shade to whoever be present.
Be mindful of the sacred grove and I will not be
                 offended.'

"So sacred grove is what they called it," put in Tom, "that doesn't surprise me. It has that kind of feeling about it. Calm, quiet and serene. Maybe it isn't connected with the Quakers, maybe it's something different. Anyway why don't you show me the remains of the bonfire? That's present day stuff, whoever it is they've only just been here."

Moving over to the fallen tree we can see that the Moet & Chandon box is gone. The ashes look more recent and it seems there has been another fire. Tom crunches through the piles of leaves around the bonfire and kicks through the remains with his trainer scattering the unburnt twigs and ashes and sending a shower of dust into the air. He sifts the ashes with his foot and waits for the dust to settle.

"Not much here," he says. "The fire is really well burnt down. They must have been here for some time though. You can see this was a huge bonfire. You'd have thought people would have seen it from the village, given that there are no leaves on the trees."

"What's that?" James asks pointing to the edge of the ashes.

Tom bends down and pokes around in the ashes with a stick. As he does so the hilt of a sheath knife emerges. Grasping it carefully in his hands he exclaims, "Hey, this knife is made of silver. It's a bit tarnished by the fire but as it's right at the edge it hasn't been affected by the strong heat in the centre of the fire."

"Let's have a look," says James taking the knife from Tom. "It's beautiful, see here how it's engraved with some kind of signs. There's a star on the hilt and look at this strange lettering on the blade. Someone's going to be very upset about losing this. Maybe we should leave it here."

"Yes," I say nodding. "We can't keep it. Why don't you take a photo Tom and we can leave it here on the log. Whoever lost it is going to be looking for it. Let's just have a look at your photos before we leave."

Tom scrolls through the photos. In most of them the sun is bright and welcoming and the stones are starkly etched in the crisp sunlight, the copper leaves and swathes of grass captured in their winter beauty. But as he flicks through them a couple of them reflect back to us a different dark and menacing place, a sinister twilight wood with hints of shadowy movement in the undergrowth. The trees are stark and inhospitable, their branches waving like angry arms repelling us giving us a glimpse of the night-time mood of the clearing and setting the scene for the fire revellers to return.

CHAPTER 15

"The dead can be dangerous," I read out loud as I flicked through the pages of one of Eliza's black notebooks found in the cellar. Copiously written annotations flow across the pages in her now familiar spidery black handwriting, interspersed with simple line drawings and diagrams. Jotted down thoughts and ideas, a flow of consciousness, inviting one in to her inner reflections:

> *'The dead can be dangerous though many people, spiritualists and channelers, want to talk to them. Best to leave well alone and to talk kindly of them. It is said that the headstones in graveyards are placed so as to prevent the dead from climbing out of their graves. This must be respected. The dead must be left at peace.'*

Sitting at the dining room table beside Judith, I had decided to trawl through the books and bundles of letters and photos, fascinated by their contents and the breadth of her ideas and experiences.

"I often wondered about headstones," said Judith. "They seem to be so cumbersome. I like that idea of weighing down the dead. I've also heard it said that funeral processions are meant to return from the cemetery by a different route from the way they came in order to make it harder for ghosts to follow the bereaved back home."

"And I've have heard a saying that the furniture in the room where a person dies should be rearranged so that the ghost won't recognise their place of death. Fascinating isn't it, ghost stories and the supernatural. You never know whether to believe in any of it."

"Well you know that even today in some Christian burials the body is purified or asperged before being taken into the church in case demons come in with it, so some magic still remains part of the Christian belief," Judith added. "It's not just in Pagan religions."

"I didn't know that," I said turning the pages of the notebook and scanning through the jottings. "Now this entry looks interesting. I really want to know more about their rituals and what they were interested in:

'Magic is the art of getting results. Rites are the processes whereby we achieve it. Witchcraft undertakes by force of will to bend the supernatural to meet our own ends. It is as old as mankind, the inheritance of an age-old religion which must be passed down the line. There must be a belief in the sacred knowledge being passed from one to another, without cessation.'

"That ties in with what Tom was saying, about witch lines running in families. If they lived in the house and were part of a witch line, say their line went back as far as Louisa and beyond." I said. "And what's happened to the witch line now? Is that why the cellars were closed up?"

"Makes sense," said Judith. "Someone must've bought the house maybe in the 1960s or '70s and not liked what they found down there. So they sealed the trapdoor in the study and just let sleeping dogs lie as they say. You didn't get a feeling of anything untoward or unusual when you bought the place did you?"

"Not at all," I replied. "As soon as I came into the house I just felt as if I belonged. I only looked at three houses. When I saw Middle House which as the third one I knew I had to buy it. I was so glad when the Jenkins accepted my offer, it was actually a bit lower than they were asking."

"Lucky for you, they must've wanted to push the sale through. Anyway do read me some more," said Judith.

"How about this," I said alighting on a page with beautifully etched shapes and diagrams, " 'How to make amulets and talismans from nature'. That might come in handy:

> 'Look for and collect stones with a natural hole in them. These offer protection and power to the wearer or carrier. Depending on the colour of the stone, such amulets will protect or cure. They can be worn on a piece of leather round the neck or carried in a pocket. Also collect parts of animals found in the wood, cleaned up and polished they can be worn as charms for protection, i.e. fur, feathers, claws, bones, teeth, rabbits' feet.'

It seems Eliza was quite an artist, there are some drawings here which are really simple but eye-catching," I said. "I only wish they had raised outlines so that you could feel them. She writes that there are three kinds of amulet: protective amulets, those used for the treatment of illnesses and those containing medical substances and she goes on to say:

> 'In white magic the most powerful amulet is the pentagram, the five-pointed star with one tip pointing upwards, the pentragram conveying a sacred blessing. Another potent sign used on amulets is the eye which symbolises the spirit within and thus gives good protection to the wearer against evil.' "

"I've got an amulet," said Judith, "it was given to me by a friend when I was at Uni. It's a silver bangle with raised fishes and shells symbolising the sign of the fisherman. Apparently it's meant to give one inner strength. I never thought of it as being connected with witchcraft, just thought it was a good luck charm. I'll show it to you. Maybe I should wear it more often."

"What's the difference between an amulet and a charm?" I replied.

"Not really sure."

"From what Eliza says amulets are used for protection and cure and as I understand it charms are also worn to ward off bad spirits and bad luck. So maybe they're one and the same thing. At least it seems Eliza and Rose were involved with white magic. We haven't heard anything about black magic so far."

As I put the journal down on the table several slips of paper fell from the back pages. "There are some recipes here," I exclaimed. "Let's see if they're of any interest.

```
'Four Thieves Vinegar
Take a great many cloves of garlic and red wine
vinegar, big handfuls of rosemary, mint, rue,
lavender, sage and wormwood if you can find some.
Add camphor gum and boil for a few minutes. Then
cool the vinegar down and place it in a screw top
bottle, next filter it and throws away the herbs.
This drink gives great benefit to the stomach and
keeps the user young and supple.'
```

Not sure what camphor gum is," I said, "or wormwood. I suppose they would have grown these things or else found them in the hedgerows. Here's another one:

```
'Panacea
Make this panacea with red wine, using elderberry
wine is good. Add bunches of honeysuckle flowers,
groundsel, lily of the valley and handfuls of mint
plus heather if available. Place in a large jar
and allow to ferment for some months, giving a
shake once weekly. Then strain through muslin and
use as a cure-all or medicine taking one
tablespoon as needed.'
```

"Strange to use honeysuckle," said Judith, "you would have thought that was poisonous and lily of the valley as well for that matter. I wonder what Eliza and Rose died of," she added, laughing. "Maybe you should have a look for their graves. It would be interesting to know what year they died and whether they're buried together."

"Yes. That's a good idea. I'd like to find out more about them. Let's have a look at some of these letters," I said picking up one of the bundles and untying the ribbon. "They're all very neatly folded. They seem to be correspondence between Eliza and someone called Gerald Gardner, written after the war. I wonder who he was?"

26 November 1946

My dear Eliza,

It gives me great pleasure to correspond with you, although it is some time since we met. We share many interests and ideas and it is good to speak of them.

I know it is easier for you to gain new members of the group in your village. You know the villagers and you know their family past. You know who can be trusted and who cannot. With regard to Bricket Wood, it is always a problem to expand members. That is why we work with the naturist club. Those who join can be assessed and approached if they seem sympathetic.

We are developing the study group and now run motor coaches through the beautiful countryside of Elstree past Bricket Wood to Witch Hut in London and museum lunch there. The study group is encouraged to join the Folklore Society (they have cheap rates for students refreshments only!!). They have the use of the University College Library. But likely Students should be told to join the nudist club at the museum (at special rates!). Then on Saturdays and Sundays they can go down to the museum with us. We can have the things out and study them, and try them, and try the old Witch dances, etc. The ones who take to it will be initiated and no one can say anything because they are all members of a Nudist Club.

If it could be managed we could I think get a good and strong cult going. We could probably have a meeting place in London. The Folklore Society can always borrow a Committee room from the London University and I think the Folklore Study Group could also get it, if the secret was kept. But it must be kept.

Yours ever, Gerald Gardner.

20 December 1946

Dear Gerald,

It is good to hear from you too. It seems you have developed a good system for identifying new members. You are right. It is easier to seek new members in the village but we strive to keep the number to about ten. More than ten is problematic, less then ten is too few.

You asked me in your last letter about the first and last house in a village belonging to a witch. Why that dates back from persecution going back to the 1600s. Those practising the craft in the open if discovered could safely run to the first or last house knowing it to be the dwelling of a witch or cult member, known as a safe haven for those who need it. Does this still pertain you will ask. In some villages, yes. In Whittlesham it remains so; but not everywhere. You cannot now rely on it unless you have knowledge of the village. In any case it is not really needed now, it is just a custom which still holds.

Yours Eliza.

4 February 1947

Dear Gerald,

I know that you have been to America and that you were unwell. I trust that you are now recovered and at least feeling able to meet with your members. They will have sorely missed you and your inspiration.

One thing to add to my last letter. We are fortunate as there are passages in the village so that members can enter the house unseen, and also enter other places unseen. These passages date back a long time. This allows us to have indoor and outdoor meetings and to move more freely. There are those in the village who would scorn and decry us, blame us for ill that occurs. What we do is for the good and only for the good as you know.

Yours Eliza.

6 March 1947

My dearest Eliza,

I am so glad to hear from you. I have sadly neglected our correspondence. How can you forgive me? Yes I have been unwell. My travels were difficult because of my health but I managed to meet new friends and contacts. It is essential to meet people and to spread the word, find out about other groups.

I was initiated to my first coven in Christchurch in 1939 through the Rosicrucean Fellowship. Through this I learned a great deal and it was because I wanted to link to other groups in London that I established the Bricket Wood coven in 1945. As you know my extensive studies have taken me into witchcraft as practiced in the past and it is from there that I have been able to reform the ancient religion with the intention of presenting it to the public. I have worked with Aleister Crowley and looked at ancient witchcraft in Africa and other continents. My quest is based on a search for peace and a sense of wonder at what I find. I also imbibe a sense of companionship and good fellowship wherever I go. My desire is to introduce Wicca to the world.

With best wishes Gerald Gardner.

CHAPTER 16

The High Street in Oxford is heaving. It's a Saturday morning in January and James and I are buttoned up in warm coats and scarves. Taking the Park and Ride makes it an easy trip and we start off by spending time in a coffee shop by the bus station drinking Americanos and watching the world go by, enjoying the bustling atmosphere.

The café is busy with a constant flow of tourists buying 'coffee to go' before shooting through, either in the direction of the busy bus depot or drawn by the world-renowned dreaming spires, elegant shops and tourist attractions. As usual there are tourists from all over the world and we listen to the fleeting conversations in a myriad of languages.

Moving on down the High Street we are in search of a different part of Oxford. Somewhere at the edge of this bustle, a place where the shops are more out of the ordinary. A place where we might find out more about the occult.

"Not sure exactly where we're going but I think it will be somewhere down this way," I say. "I used to park down at the far end of the High Street and I can remember a very distinct difference, both in the people and in the kind of shops. Quite unlike this part of Oxford."

The High Street is broad and the colourful blue and yellow buses make their way up and down disgorging eager sightseers. We pass the elegant shop fronts with their perfectly orchestrated mannequins and bright designer clothing, moving out into the road every now and again to pass tourists standing agape at the architecture. There is food, food everywhere. More cafés, restaurants and takeaways than can be possibly needed, all vying to entice customers in at the mid-morning lull.

We pass the golden coloured tower of Magdalen College and the crowds immediately begin to thin, making walking on the pavement easier. Approaching the bridge we glimpse through the stone balustrade the familiar long wooden punts casually moored at one side of the river, looking bereft without oars or cushions.

"Too early in the season," comments James. "They look quite sorry for themselves down there don't they? You can just tell there're waiting for all the action to begin. The boaters and the picnicking, the laughter and the frolics. They must be oh so bored in winter!"

As we reach the far side of the bridge we see a bicycle chained to the tall metal railings. It's a bicycle of sorts really as the wheels have been removed. It lies there with its bright turquoise and royal blue paint, an empty spike all that is left of the saddle.

We pass the monument and crossing the roundabout at the end of the High Street step into the Cowley Road instantly finding ourselves in another world. There are shops with a difference here, some derelict, some tawdry and rundown but others are colourful, full of life and energy.

"This is amazing," says James. "We're only two minutes from the High Street and all the affluence and tourismos that go with it and then we're here. It's like another stepping into another place."

"Unbelievable," I reply looking at the bright red café on the corner, it's name indistinguishable. "What about the café over there? Looks like the …ik …ock. Should we ask there if they can point us in the direction of a shop selling stuff to do with the occult?"

"Oh no, I don't think so. Let's just wander on and see what we can find for ourselves."

"It's strange, shops connected with witchcraft don't seem to be on the internet. There are plenty of on-line and mail order sites across the country but the actual shops themselves don't seem to advertise on the net."

"Maybe that's because they're likely to suffer from attacks from certain members of the public," puts in James.

"You could be right. People can hide their location on the internet if they want to I suppose. Maybe that's why. Anyway let's just carry on down here and keep our eyes open."

This once residential street has small brick-built buildings in direct contrast with the huge shop fronts in the High Street. The windows of the remaining houses are narrow and uncurtained and there is an air of neglect but the passing shoppers are gaily dressed and animated and there is a community atmosphere.

"Bignalls of Oxford, Robemakers," I say reading the gold letters boldly imprinted on a maroon background above a small doorway across the road. "What kind of robes do they make? Maybe we should pay them a visit later."

Above another shop the sign reads 'Delhi Emporium – colourful clothing, fabrics, giftware and more'. The items in the shop window are a wondrous collection of miscellany. A large yellow chicken with red coxcomb and red legs sporting dainty yellow shoes; a shocking pink wig; a stuffed black raven; a black ironwork candelabra; a photograph of Marilyn Monroe; beads and bangles in every riotous colour; a severe looking male mannequin in a red and yellow turban with matching scarf; and a silver and gold shawl made of shimmering coins. "What an array," says James gazing at the crammed window. "So difficult to choose what to buy. Should I go for the mighty yellow chicken or what about the wig?"

"I should think the raven might come in handy," I reply. "Aren't they associated with the supernatural? Looks like it's meant for you. If I was going to buy something I think I'd go for the shawl. At least everyone would know I was coming with those jingling coins."

We mosey on down the street passing rows of boarded up shops where every last inch is papered over and papered over again with posters and leaflets advertising everything under the sun. Glancing at them we are bombarded with out-of-date information telling us about meetings, concerts, readings, societies, open air worship and clubs of every shape and form. "Never a dull moment here," I say looking at James.

Swept along by the medley of shops and cosmopolitan delicatessens we find ourselves beside an enormous display of graffiti which covers the entire end of a three-storey wall. It towers high above us depicting strangely tall and lithesome animations in blue, orange and yellow watched over by a sorcerer breathing out a snake from above, a blazing fire-breathing monster in the corner and a lurid sun with three eyes gazing down from beneath the chimney flanked by an enormous leering moon. The whole painting is intermingled with curious signs and symbols.

Over a small door set in the wall is the sign 'Oxford Opal Moon'. "This is what we're looking for, just the type of shop," I say tugging at James' arm. We push the door open hesitantly and find ourselves transported into a bright and cheerful modern interior hung from top to bottom with objects of every description belying the rather downtrodden appearance of the street. Jangling chimes herald our entrance as we step inside, the fragrance of burning incense wafting a hint of sweet herbs and spice as we stand on the threshold.

"Wow! What a collection," I exclaim. "It's like an Aladdin's cave." And indeed the shop is crammed in every direction. One corner houses the larger items, stacks of cauldrons of all sizes heaped together, some filled with wands and staffs, others filled with besom brooms and a number of strange looking wooden objects.

Straddling the counter and cascading from display stands there are candles and incense sticks, oil burners and sea shells, floating candles and shiny stones surrounded by heaps of crystals of every kind. Coloured boxes of tea spill across a shelf and dried sunflowers and marigolds bedecked with sheaves of wheat and bright red plastic peppers adorn the wall behind the till.

I move over to another corner where an elaborately carved bookstand is piled with handcrafted books of soft fabric, wood and leather. Each one is different and ornately engraved on the front. Picking one up I trace the coiled green dragon and red Celtic knot work on the soft leather, beautifully crafted with slate effect and faux jewels. The book is marked 'Spell Book' on the front but inside the pages are blank.

A tall thin girl in her twenties with flowing dark hair and an aquiline nose moves towards me, "Do you need any help? These are Books of Shadows if you're unfamiliar with them. For personal writings, practices and spells for those initiated into the Craft."

"They're beautiful," I reply picking up a leather book engraved with gold leaf and bound with a golden cord. "And each one is absolutely personalised. This one says 'Earth, Fire, Wind and Rain'"

"Yes," the girl says nodding. "To bring about the flow of psychic energy you must harmonise the four earth elements. Earth, air, fire and water. That Book of Shadows is intended to invoke the elements."

"So everyone has a book of their own like these, where they write down their thoughts and ideas?"

"That's right. Magical journals are used to record personal experiences and insights while doing Circle work. Initiates usually write things down whilst in the Circle so they can ask for clarification later if needed. They also record their dreams which become heightened and especially vivid after a magical working."

"And what about these knives, what are they for?" I ask, stepping over to a glass covered display counter with a large array of short and long bladed knives laid out in star formation on a soft lavender cloth.

"They're athames or double-edged knives. They're used by the sisterhood when they want to cast a Circle. All witches have one. Athames are used for rituals and ceremonies at the altar and symbolise air and male energy," said the girl opening the glass case. "Would you like to have a look at them?"

"That's what we found at Puxleyridge," I whisper to James, picking up a silver knife with an ornate carved wooden handle. "It was an athame. Lucky we left it where it was."

"Athames are forged using the four elements earth, air, fire and water. These are combined with spirit which comes from the inspiration of the maker. If they've not been exposed to the elements in manufacture the buyer must immerse them in the elements before use," explains the girl. "This handle is crafted from oak which has particularly strong energy. Others are made entirely of silver or other metal."

"There's a real beauty in all of these objects," I say turning to James. "Beauty and a spiritual quality. Definitely a presence here."

"Do you have a particular interest in the occult?" asks the girl. "We like to get to know our customers."

"We've become interested in Wicca and Paganism and we're just trying to find out more about what's involved. There's so much to learn isn't there and so much contemporary interest in the subject once you start delving into it. I was amazed at the amount of websites."

"Oh yes," the girl replies. "Since Gardner wrote the Book of Shadows and unleashed modern ideas about witchcraft there has been a complete revival of ancient traditions. He and his contempories bought Wicca and Paganism into the twentieth century. It's connected with the eco and green movements and there are groups and societies everywhere, especially in Oxford where there are deep-seated traditional witchcraft roots. Oh, excuse me I have another customer."

Moving over to assist a pair of blonde teenagers, she opens a cabinet and lays out a range of soft felt and sateen bags. Tipping out the contents of the first bag she displays some sparkling crystal stones beautifully etched with angular symbols. "Did you want wood or crystal?" she asks them.

"I prefer crystal," says one of the girls.

"And I think I'll have wood," says the other. "Have to keep these out of my mum's sight. She doesn't want me to have anything to do with this kind of thing."

"You can keep them at my place," the first girl says. "My dad doesn't give a monkeys about what I keep in my room. In any case with all my artwork all over the place nobody can find anything in there, except me that is," she continued grinning. "That's why I got into tarot and runes, for my art. Now I'm trying to find out more. It's really very interesting. I'm glad you're interested too."

"Let's buy this book here called 'The Learned Arts of Witches and Wizards – history and traditions of white magic," I say to James. "I think it will help us to understand Rose and Eliza a bit more and maybe also give us some clues about Louisa."

"Good idea," replies James. "And what about one of these mirrors? Scrying mirrors it says, they look like crystal balls. How about this one, it's got some beautiful markings on the case. It's probably made of yew. I'll buy it for you if you like."

Taking the mirror in my hands I gaze into the flawless crystal. As I watch it fills with a slight mist, becoming denser and denser and I can just make out what looks like a recumbent figure stretched out in a stream. Louisa. It must be Louisa. Shaking my head I turn away and then back to find the figure gone, the crystal clear.

"Take my card before you go," the shop assistant is saying as I turn towards her. She packs up the books and the mirror carefully in a blue carrier bag with an opal moon on it, thrusting a leaflet into my hand. 'The Opal Moon Occult Society' it reads across the top. "You may be interested in this."

CHAPTER 17

"We've definitely found something. It could be Louisa's grave," said James over a scrambled egg breakfast. "You know at the far end of the churchyard there's a wall and over the other side there's a thick copse. Well Matt and I were running over that way this morning for a change. You know what he's like, he's always looking for a new route. The trees were etched in white by the heavy frost and we ran over to look at them. They were really eye-catching."

"That copse always looks so impenetrable," I said buttering a piece of toast.

"Well, yes it does. But seeing it defined so clearly by the frost we thought we'd try and get a close up of the trees. So we pushed our way into the thicket and then we realised it was less dense woodland than we'd thought. The ground dipped down slightly to the left and as we moved downhill we came to a rising spring. The water was almost iced over and we stopped to look at it. Quite surreal, the frost with a slight hint of mist and the water frozen at the edges," James continued taking a sip of coffee.

"I didn't know there was a spring there although I know there are a couple over the other side near the castle mound."

"Anyway as we moved past the spring we could see the stone wall at the end of the churchyard. Then Matt tripped on a loose boulder. He went down and caught the side of his hand on a slab of rough stone. It was covered in moss. Not sure we'd have noticed it if he hadn't slipped."

"Did he hurt himself?"

"No, apart from a slightly bruised knee. We did have a look at the stone but the moss was thick and stiff with ice and we couldn't get a grip on it to pull it away."

"So what makes you think it's a gravestone, let alone Louisa's?"

"Well it just has a feel about it somehow," replied James between mouthfuls of scrambled egg and toast. "It must've been put there deliberately and there has to have been a reason. Also it kind of looks like a headstone which has been placed flat on the ground."

"Sounds like an interesting find. Let's go and have a look at it when we've washed up," I said collecting up the mugs and plates and piling them on a tray. "The poor girl must be buried somewhere."

⁂

Even mid-morning it's a crunchy and crisp day except where shafts of wintery sun have penetrated the fields and the frost has melted away, leaving stark white-frosted edges round the fields. Our footsteps crunch on the well-trodden footpath as we step across some deep dog prints frozen in the mud. The slanting sun catches the yellow stone of the manor house at Handford across the valley, its imposing presence standing out above the gently interlocking folds of the countryside.

And then we come to the copse. The sun has melted the frost and the trees are starkly silhouetted against the bright blue sky "We went this way earlier," says James, pushing the thick shrubby branches to one side. "It's not very inviting to begin with."

We force our way through the undergrowth, water droplets from the bushes and trees dripping onto our hands and faces. The soft murmur of water bubbling over to our left as the ground dips down towards the church wall. "Look, it's over here," calls James pointing to one side of the spring. The oblong stone is almost obscured by the lush moss whose bumpy texture gives it the appearance of a green underworld of its own.

Taking a couple of knives from his pocket James passes one to me, then bends down and systematically begins to scrape away the moss revealing a worn and pitted surface. I squat down and work alongside him. The densely packed clusters of moss fall away in clumps and I sweep them to one side with my hand.

The jarring calls of the crows as they circle the newly ploughed fields and the urgent calls of the smaller woodland birds accompany us as we work. "The birds are very noisy today," I say to James. "Must be because of all the frozen grubs softening and enticing the birds to a sumptious feast."

Bending down to examine the exposed slab I can just discern a roughly cut inscription in the centre of the stone:

Louisa
Dear daughter, Forever beloved
Forever cherished
1843
TC and MC

"So this is it! This is where she's buried. Well done James. You've found her."

"It certainly tells us something," says James. "Either she was a witch and that's why she was buried here or the vicar held particular views and refused to let her be buried on church land, whether she was a witch or not."

"It doesn't seem right for poor Louisa to be buried here. I wonder, can you have remains moved?" I say slowly, trying to think through all of the ramifications. "How would you go about moving a body?" I add. "Would it have been in a coffin or not? Would the coffin have disintegrated and in any case what kind of state would her bones be in by now after more than 150 years?"

"So many unanswered questions," says James, "but at least we've answered one."

The vicar poured out steaming mugs of coffee as we sat in overstuffed armchairs in the somewhat chilly vicarage. "I don't have too many guests here in the vicarage," Robert Delforth was saying as he placed the mugs carefully on the small round coffee table in front of us. "Do call me Robert by the way. I don't like formality. Even to her own children the Church has in special circumstances refused burial in the churchyard," he continued. "Suicides were unquestionably excluded in the past, along with criminals and unbaptized children. Also lunatics who were said to be possessed by the devil as well as those suspected of being a witch. Although by the date we are talking of in the 1840s the Witchcraft Act had been in force for some time. Witchcraft was no longer the target of rebel rousers as it had been in the past. From what you tell me it seems that the vicar at the time had particularly strong views about witches."

"He certainly did according to the local paper. He was adamant that nothing could make him change his mind. We really appreciate your interest in this by the way," I said. "I know it all happened a long time ago but we've got a particular interest in Louisa. As I said, she actually lived in the house. It makes us feel that we have some kind of responsibility for her."

Robert sipped his tea thoughtfully and sat back in his chair. The room was cluttered with books everywhere and the large desk in one corner was covered with piles of paper, all heavily scrawled with the same neat handwriting, the wilting pot plants lining the windowsills evidence that the vicar had other things on his mind.

"I need to think this through," he said eventually. "The only person who can consecrate ground is the Bishop. Our Bishop, the Right Reverend Richard Davis, was here a few years ago to consecrate the new piece of land which the church managed to purchase in order to extend the graveyard. There was a big ceremony and he said prayers as he blessed the ground."

"I wouldn't think he'd be too happy about being asked to consecrate a bit of ground outside the church boundary," I said. "There must be set rules and regulations."

"You're right," replied Robert. "I'll give this some thought. And now why don't you tell me how you came to move into the village. It's always interesting to hear what brings people to these parts."

A few days later, as the afternoon deepened, Robert worked his way into the copse accompanied by the verger Bill Blacklock. The vicar was carrying a black leather prayer book and a small wooden crucifix.

"You knows where you're going do you?" asked the verger.

"Yes, two of our parishioners have told me the exact location," said Robert as they pushed their way through the scrubland. They could hear the gurgling stream down in the direction of the wall, the looming church tower etched against the sky as the day began to darken.

Robert moved deferentially and the verger followed. He was aware that he was taking a risk, that maybe he should have consulted with the Bishop. But he knew that the Bishop was a stickler for the rules and that should he have ruled against blessing the child he would not have been able to take any action to bring her once again into the fold. This was the only solution, to carry out a blessing quietly and without a fuss. No-one would be any the wiser.

He stood by the rough hewn slab of stone and holding the prayer book in his left hand and the crucifix in his right hand he intoned:

> "Oh Lord hear our prayer and
> Send us help from thy holy place
> Grant we beseech thee, merciful Lord,
> To thy faithful people pardon and peace;
> That they might be cleansed from all their sins
> And serve thee with a quiet mind.
>
> In blessed memory of Louisa Crabbe
> May peace be upon you
> May you rest and feel the love
> And everlasting companionship
> Of your parents, Thomas and Mary,
> Buried nearby in the churchyard
> May you at last lay in rest
> And be at one
> For ever and ever
> Through Jesus Christ our Lord, Amen"

The two men bowed their heads and stood in silence for several moments. "So that's done then," said the verger.

"Yes, I hope so," said Robert.

Silently they returned the way they had come.

※

Robert Delforth sleeps. His eyelids flutter. The room is cold and pale shadows swirl outside in the breaking dawn. The bedroom is square, the furniture plain. Four more empty bedrooms slumber in the vicarage as Robert turns in his sleep, the simple white duvet pulled round him like a shroud.

His dreams are laced with turbulent grey forms, massing and writhing above the church. They are angry, they twist and they turn. The dark wraiths lengthen as they move upwards and then descend, their taut faces gaunt and strained, deathly pale brows lined with deep furrows. They whisper noisily and incomprehensibly to each other and wave their arms, forming and reforming, now blurred, now each one a double image of themselves, frenzied and raging. Their hands raised, fingers outstretched, waving, shaking and pointing at him in the church as he kneels before the altar. And raising his head he can see that they are all around him, twisting and turning at the windows high above the nave, the lengthening grey forms sharpened by the inexorably lightening sky as shadows fall across the church.

He is mesmerised, he cannot move. He feels their anger; he feels their rage. And then he is falling, falling, falling, floating through a morass, gasping and struggling for breath.

In the pale dawn he wakes to find himself half sitting, half lying in the bed, the duvet tossed to the floor. And as he wakes he hears himself saying under his breath, "The dead are offended."

CHAPTER 18

Judith, sitting in one of the deep leather chairs in the dining room, reached out and gently took the glass in her hands. She held it firstly close to her chest and then at arms length and then brought it back to just in front of her. "It's heavy," she said quietly. "I wonder whether it will have any effect on me, whether I will be able to see things with it?"

She sat holding the crystal, silent and absorbed. I could see her forehead wrinkling as she tried to absorb energy from the mirror. Outside the sound of a siren broke the silence as an ambulance raced through the village shattering the quiet but Judith seemed oblivious, her eyes closed and head down.

I could see her fingers tightly clenching the ball on her lap and could feel her concentration. I sat waiting drawn by the crystal, my head bowed as I flowed into a stream of consciousness, my thoughts whirling.

James was there before me as he wove in and out of my mind's eye, his tall form lithe and solid and at the same time ephemeral, now here, now only half seen and then gone. As I watched Tom merged into the images and I envisioned him and Judith locked in an embrace, his hands entwined behind her back, her small hands reaching up to caress the nape of his neck. Moving silently apart they became engaged in deep discourse of which I could hear nothing.

And then he too was gone, replaced now by hazy images of the house. The house in previous times, deep in shadow, more ramshackle and unpainted. The thatch in parlous state like unkempt hair, dipping down towards the pavement making the house appear a shadow of its current size. A horse-drawn wagon wending its way, the back end open revealing loaves of bread and crates of pastries.

With a shock I felt myself start and shaking my head the images faded as I was drawn back to the present. What was I seeing? What did it mean?

I looked up and saw Judith, sitting there with the crystal, still transfixed. As I did so she started to speak hesitantly, uncertainly. "I can see a mist. It's uncanny. There's a mist there in front of my eyes, in my head. It seems to be getting denser," she paused.

"There's something there but I can't tell what it is. It's coming," she said breathlessly.

She leaned back rapt and I could see her hands moving involuntarily on the ball as she tensed. Her face became taut, her mouth tense, as she strove to focus on the revelation beneath the haze.

"No," she said finally, breathing out, her shoulders drooping as she relaxed. "I just can't make sense of what's there beneath the shadows. Maybe that's a message in itself," her frustration and disappointment showed clearly in her face as she raised her head.

She passed the crystal to me disconsolately and I replaced it carefully in its round wooden case, feeling the underlying roughness of the hand-carved wood.

"I just had a thought," Judith said thoughtfully. "Should I be using your crystal ball or should it be personal to you?"

"I really don't know," I replied suddenly anxious that any messages conveyed by the crystal ball might be skewed by two minds coming from different directions.

"What was that other word you used?" she asked. "The one to do with crystal ball gazing."

"Oh, you mean scrying," I said. "I think I prefer crystal ball gazing."

"I know what you mean," Judith replied, "but scrying sounds a bit more interesting somehow."

Later as the languid deepening darkness cloaks the house I feel a calm and tranquillity again flowing through me. Sitting by candlelight at the table in the study I gently take the crystal in my hands and hold it firmly, gazing into the depths. I can see a tiny web of faults blending and weaving through the glass, part of its very essence, the cloudy glow within the ball issuing from my hands.

Clasping it firmly I concentrate completely on the glass sphere, cleansing my mind of all other thoughts, focussing inwards and only on the glass. My body feels pure and relaxed and I can sense my head clearing of all consciousness, mesmerized by the glowing ball in the dim candlelight.

Images flooding into my mind are of the dense woodland thicket at dusk, the boughs of the spindly trees twining and intertwining, and there is Louisa's grave, with her parents standing close by. Thomas and Mary Crabbe. He dressed in an open necked white shirt with dark trousers and a working jacket and she in a navy smock. And dimly in the background some young girls with joined hands dancing as they clasp the hems of their light summer dresses, laughing as they merrily toss back heads with flowing blonde tresses, their faces rapturous and intense. As I watch the glade darkens and the shadows deepen, pale rays of moonlight penetrating the copse.

I speak the words out loud describing what I can see again and again and as the images merge and intermingle the vision becomes blurred and I am left with a haunting last glimpse of two stark figures standing sentinel by Louisa's grave in the shadowy woodland grove. Of Louisa there is no sign.

Next day we are again sitting in the dining room and I'm reading from Eliza's journal:

> 'One of the main aims of magic practice is to link into the energy of the circle, the space between this world and the next. Between the

worlds is the dominion of the gods, a space where one captures and directs one's power and energy.

We of the sisterhood acknowledge the relationship between spirit and matter and draw our energy from the fusion of the two within this sacred place.'

"So that's why circles are important to witches," I said turning to face Judith. "They're extremely powerful symbols and that's why most magic working is conducted in a circle, circles apparently being traditionally nine feet in diameter."

"I wonder where Eliza's circle was," put in Judith. "Nine feet is quite a size, nearly three metres."

"It does say further down that circles can be smaller for witches working on their own but from what we know about Rose and Eliza they worked with about eight others. It would be interesting to know how many men were in the group or whether they were all women. Gerald Gardner was obviously linked to a lot of male witches, both in this country and abroad." I continued reading:

'The most important feature in our sacred place is the altar which represents the goddess, the earth mother, and must be set up facing north in this hemisphere. Here we place our most important symbols to help us touch the magic of the earth, namely earth, air, fire and water.'

"So the sacred place is the circle?" put in Judith quizzically.
"Sounds like it," I replied:

'Our tools include a pentacle, an athame, a wand and a chalice and these we keep both secret and safe. North corresponds with the element of earth, opposite the altar is the fire quarter, to the right is air and to the left is water. Thus we complete our circle.'

"Witchcraft was often practised outside so it's possible that their circle was in the woods somewhere or it could even have been on the castle mound," said Judith.

"You could be right," I said thoughtfully. "The far side of the mound is quite well sheltered from view behind all those trees and shrubs. And of course there would have been fewer houses in the village then."

I poured us both a black coffee from the cafétiere, passing a mug to Judith saying, "I don't suppose we'll ever find out where it was unless of course it's mentioned somewhere in her notes."

"It could perhaps have been in the cellar," said Judith pensively. "That way none of the uninitiated would know of its existence and no-one could just stumble upon it."

"That's true," I said turning the pages of the journal. "However there's no sign of anything like that so far. We may never know. Anyway, here's another interesting entry:

> 'Our Book of Magic is kept safe in its usual place. One must keep these notes and spells in secret, lest they should pass to the unknowing hands or worse to those who would put us down.
>
> 'It is the case that the effect of spells will depend on what one puts into them, the emotion and direct thought and energy drawn from the circle, the self being the origin of power. Knowledge in the sisterhood is instinctive and derives from our closeness to natural forces and intuitive nature.'

I wonder where they kept their Book of Magic?" I said looking up. "That would be some find or would they have destroyed it or passed it on when they knew they were nearing their end?"

"Who knows," replied Judith. "It's not in the cellar anyway, at least not as far as we know. We'll have to keep an eye out for it. It could be hidden somewhere, like under the floor boards."

"You've got a vivid imagination," I said laughing.

"Anyway I'd really like to find out more about Gerald Gardner and the various rituals and practices to be found in other parts of the world," said Judith.

"Yes and of course he then went on to develop Wicca and what we now know as modern witchcraft. He must have been very influential and our Eliza and Rose actually knew him, even living in a small village like Whittlesham. Amazing really," I commented.

"Can you perhaps find anything which gives us a greater insight into what was going on in any of his letters?" asked Judith. "I suppose we can try the internet as well."

Rifling through the pile of letters in the box I picked out several which look significant. "It says here that Gardner found similar rites and witchcraft practices in this country and also in places like the Far East, Africa, the United States and Australia. He was a civil servant overseas and also an amateur anthropologist and travelled widely."

"So perhaps it was his anthropological studies that got him involved and interested in the folklore and religious rites across the world?" Judith queried.

"Maybe that was part of it but he is writing here to Eliza and says that he has been interested in magic and kindred subjects all his life and that he has an extensive collection of magical instruments and charms. I'll read it to you:

8 June 1947

'My dearest Eliza,

.... These studies led me to spiritualist and other societies and I met some people who claimed to have known me in a past life. Here I must say that, although I do believe in reincarnation, as most people do who have lived in the East, I do not remember any past lives albeit I have had curious experiences. I only wish I did.

Anyhow, I soon found myself in the circle and took the usual oaths of secrecy which bound me not to reveal any secrets of the cult. I realised that I had stumbled upon something interesting; but I was half-initiated before the word, *Wicca* which they used, hit me like a thunderbolt, and I knew where I was, and that the Old Religion still existed …'"

"He was certainly well-travelled," said Judith. "He must have had a fair bit of money of his own as I don't suppose the civil service paid very high salaries."

"Maybe," I said. "Strange to think that he was corresponding with people who lived in this very house. I wonder if he ever came here? Anyway his letter continues:

'... I have this past year been fortunate to be in a position to put my findings in writing. I am working on a manuscript which is intended to preserve and share with the world the secrets of the Wicca religion as descended from ancient rituals and practices.

Other books on The Craft have been mainly propaganda written by the various churches to discourage and frighten people from having any connections with what was to them a hated rival – for witchcraft is indeed a religion. Later there were books setting out to prove that this Craft had never existed.

As an anthropologist it is my job to investigate these things and it is my duty, my contribution to the world, to make these works known. As you know I am not so young now and must endeavour to work hard to make sure that my life's work is finished ...'"

"Have you thought about getting hold of a copy of his book?" queried Judith. "Do you know what the title is?"

"I think it's something like *High Magic's Aid*. I saw it when I was on the internet. Not sure I want to buy a copy and I don't suppose the library would have something like that in stock. Why don't we try googling later and see if we can come up with extracts of the book?" I replied. "Here, let me read you another of Eliza's letters. She wrote this in the July:

4 July 1947

'Dear Gerald,

It is always so good to share your correspondence and ideas with Rose. We are keeping well and the village is now back to normal and quieter since the ending of war. We are able to meet and carry out our business without fear of interference. The evacuees were quite numerous and indeed village numbers nearly doubled for a while.

Your writing is a very important task and I think you have been identified in your worldly position to be the conveyor of such wisdom to the world. Maybe there will be a time when all does not have to be concealed from others. Maybe others will become interested in our works and see the good we can do, and join with us also.

It is good also to hear more of the sisterhood in other parts of the world and to know from first hand of their existence, rather than through stories and rumour.......'

Of course things in the village must have been difficult for Eliza and Rose during the early 1940s, quite apart from the effects of the war. All these incomers traipsing round the village, difficult to keep things secret," I commented.

"Sure," said Judith. "There was a huge influx of both evacuees and land girls. And of course the land girls would be working the farms and be out and about everywhere. Easy for them to stumble upon things that were going on."

"Well there doesn't seem to be any sign that Eliza's group was discovered. I'm sure she would have mentioned something like that in her letters to Gardner."

"That's true. They must've been very careful or just very lucky," replied Judith.

Rummaging again in the box I picked up a faded newspaper press cutting from *The Northampton Echo*. It was dated 15 October 1940 and entitled: *War News – Where are all our evacuees?*

"Figures show that there are the highest levels of evacuees in the country accommodated in parts of Buckinghamshire with acute overcrowding in schools and trouble for local households when the children often arrive in scurrilous and verminous condition. Complaints regarding the behaviour of evacuees are varied and numerous.

So far no bombs have fallen in the county despite its proximity to

London. This is disturbing evidence of our enemy's precise knowledge of where the greatest population lies and where the rural boundaries begin.

Following the fall of France in the summer preparations are now in hand for a second evacuation, Bucks being allocated a further 7,700 evacuees. More feeding and rest shelters are planned."

"Interesting stuff," said Judith. "That shows the extent of the problem they would have had with so many evacuees around the village."

"Anyway the coven wasn't discovered by the sound of it. You know I would really like to have been a party to what went on here in the house. It sounds extraordinary."

CHAPTER 19

"What an amazing view," said Tom taking Judith's arm and guiding her carefully along the gently rising path. "I should imagine you can see the whole county of Wiltshire from here."

"It feels incredibly open and fresh," said Judith taking a deep breath. "I'm so glad you brought me with you today. Much better than working!"

He drew Judith along the path until they reached the curved ridge of earthworks surrounding the stone circle at Avebury. Tom was in his element, sent there by *Archaeology Today* magazine to write an article about barrows and stones and draw attention to the recently refurbished Keiller Gallery. He felt inspired by the tranquil atmosphere and was enjoying the opportunity to share his work with Judith.

The springy turf was dotted with buttercups and daisies and holding hands they simultaneously threw themselves down on the grass. Judith was wearing a pale pink and turquoise skirt and looked very young and attractive and Tom felt a sense of inner happiness.

"There's a feeling of karma here," said Judith with a sigh. "It's really potent. I can just feel it, sense it pervading my whole body. I could lie here forever." She stretched out full length on the grass enjoying the soft breeze and the feel of spring sunshine on her bare arms.

Tom lying alongside said, "I can feel it too, that feeling of 'otherness'. The presence of the past and yet of the here and now at the same time. It's certainly an incredibly compelling and vibrant place."

"Isn't it just."

"Anyway," said Tom, "part of my brief is to write about the influence of the ley lines and the reason why the circles are sited here. Which is all quite complex. Also to explain a recent discovery that the henge is in fact astronomically aligned to the midwinter sun." He paused, "This was once a huge and thriving community of a hundred or more people. Not primitive as we like to think of our ancestors. Just imagine how immense their intellectual and practical skills must have been, to envision the monument in the first place and then to incrementally create the largest stone circle in the world. Unbelievable."

"I can almost see the people in my mind," said Judith, "moving round the enclosed pastures tending their animals. What would they be thinking I wonder?"

"They'd be focussing on where their next meal was coming from, I should think!" said Tom with a grin. "You know me, I'm always hungry."

"Seriously and moving swiftly on from your stomach, I suppose the summer and winter solstices were of tremendous importance to them. Their whole lives would have been centred around them." She stretched again and rolled onto her back.

"Yes and one of the main thrusts of my article will be to explain why it has only relatively recently been discovered that the rising midwinter sun is in direct alignment with the southern causeway. That's because the earthworks are now nearer to the stones than they would've been originally. They were moved a couple of hundred years ago for some reason. Nobody realised that before, it wasn't part of their calculations. Once they realised that the earthworks had been moved they were able to establish proof of Avebury's association with the winter solstice. Before that it was a supposition or a maybe."

"Incredible. I wonder what other things we don't yet know about the stones? There's so much to uncover," said Judith idly pulling at the springy turf. "I suppose its all chalkland round here." she continued.

"The grass is very wiry. If I remember rightly early settlements of this kind were traditionally located on chalky downland."

"Oh yes, you can see the chalky fields, beyond the earthworks. And also that path over there looks like a white snake wending its way up the ridge. All to do with drainage."

"They certainly knew a thing or two, those ancestors of ours. Think about the terrible flooding problems people are encountering today because of where new housing estates are located," said Judith indignantly. "You hear about it all the time in the news."

"You're right, what do our town planners today know in comparison?" said Tom laughing. "They think they know about these things but do they? That's what I'd like to know."

"So, how far do you think you can see?" asked Judith.

"I really don't know. I'm not very good at distances," said Tom standing up, "but I should think this span of open countryside is around fifty miles or so in each direction."

"What does it look like, the countryside?"

"Hm. It's fairly flat with rolling undulating downs. Hardly any sign of town or village from here. Population must be very low. Quite a lot of trees and hedgerows round the fields in the distance. One could be in the very middle of nowhere surrounded by all this mystery. Some call it the earth's whispering energies."

"I know. I can feel it," said Judith. "I can almost hear it. The atmosphere is just loaded. You can sense a combination of natural and supernatural forces somehow. It's all around."

"Great for getting me in the mood for writing," nodded Tom lying down again beside Judith. "It's incredible. Just think about it. This place was originally begun around 4500 years ago in an absolutely precisely chosen location in order to channel the earth's natural energies."

"That's what the archaeologists say," said Judith. "But who can be sure of the exact purpose and truth?"

"True, who can say for certain? Its origin is so far distant and it must've been built by generations over time. Communities with complete dedication and commitment to carry on developing the site over literally thousands of years," said Tom.

"Anyway, don't let us get so carried away that you forget your reason for being here. You need to get going on your photographs and your research," said Judith forcing herself back to reality.

"Yes, I've got an appointment with someone called Harry Drinkall at the Keiller Gallery in about forty minutes. Do you want to come with me or do you want to visit the Gallery on your own? I know you're keen to find out more about Avebury and the mystery surrounding the circles. I'm sure that Fee will be fascinated by all this when you see her."

"Too right she will. She was very interested when I told her where we were going although I don't think she's actually been here herself," said Judith pausing.

"Actually I think it would be best if we divide and rule," she continued. "I know we've got all day but you've got a lot to get done and I'll only slow you down. I'll go to the Gallery and have a look round."

"You might be interested in something I found out when I was reading up on this," said Tom. "Apparently researchers have found that the outer standing stones emit a kind of energy or 'band transmissions' as they call it. The taller stones have five bands and the smaller stones three, which both absorb and transmit an aerial form of what is known as 'ley-energy'."

"Interesting stuff. Amazing what they can find out through modern technology," said Judith. "Do they know how the energy is produced?"

"Not really," replied Tom. "All they do know is that these particular standing stones somehow absorb the electromagnetic force which is emitted at Avebury."

"Wow. I wonder what their recording instruments look like. Technology always interests me. I'd really like to find out more about them. Maybe there'll be some information about them in the Gallery," said Judith sitting up. "Anyway, much as I don't want to maybe we should move on. You need to get to your appointment with Harry and you've got a bit of time to take some photos beforehand."

"Yes," said Tom reluctantly getting up and brushing the grass from his trousers. He slung his Nikon round his neck and put out a hand to help Judith. "You're right. We should make a move. Here's my hand."

"So what's your angle on these stones and the earth's energies?"

asked Judith as they set off back down the well-trodden path, Tom with his arm round her.

"Well as I understand it the stones absorb energy electromagnetically. This energy is then transmitted through the bands, effectively linking the stones in what you might call a continuous invisible band of energy."

"So what you're saying is that originally there was an unbroken sphere of energy, like a magic circle. That's when all the stones were in place," said Judith. "I'm just trying to visualise what the original circle of stones would've looked like."

"Yes, it would have been just like a magic circle which they created without any modern day technology. Just think about it."

"But what's the purpose of these emissions?" asked Judith.

"Well as far as the researchers can tell the lower bands emitted energy to nearby stones around them at Avebury and the higher bands emitted energy to stones in other circles. For example Stonehenge and elsewhere."

"How incredibly sophisticated," said Judith. "There's so much to find out about Avebury and its past and all we're doing is scratching the surface."

"I know," said Tom wryly, "But if scratching the surface a bit pays the bills then so be it."

"How did whoever it was all those eons ago discover the power of the circle?" said Judith. "And who made the discovery? That's what I'd like to know."

"Well maybe you'll find out something about that at the Gallery, though I'm not sure anyone will ever know the real answer to that question."

Moving back down from the ridge and towards the Keiller Gallery, Tom led Judith carefully across the winding road leading to the village centre as cars and buses sped by.

"Amazing how much traffic there is on such a small road," exclaimed Tom.

"It must be a rat run from Swindon to Marlborough," said Judith. "A shame really. To have all this traffic running right through the middle of what should be an unspoilt place like Avebury."

Opening the wooden gate on the opposite side they passed into a small tree-lined avenue and then through another gate into a large grassy area bounded on the right-hand side by a curving line of large upright stones.

"There's a very interesting group of people here," whispered Tom stopping in his tracks. "They seem to be communing with the stones. Trying to tap into their energy I suppose."

"What's so interesting about them?" whispered back Judith.

"Well at the risk of sounding rather corny they all look a bit hippyish. Bright striped skirts and big looped earrings, long hair, no shoes," replied Tom keeping his voice down. "And the men are wearing loose fitting shirts and baggy trousers. All ages. Probably a few more women than men. There must be about twenty of them and there's another two over on the ridge. One's standing up and moving his arms in slow motion and the other one is lying down, completely motionless."

He led Judith forward keeping well to the left of the stones. He stopped as they neared an olive-skinned man seated cross-legged in the midst of a circle of uniformly dark green blankets, each laid neatly around him with a pair of shoes placed carefully in the centre. The man was slowly and rhythmically drumming, his fingers moving deftly across the shallow wooden drum on his lap. Tom could see the tautly stretched skin on the instrument as he listened to the insistent but simple tempo.

"The stone worshippers are each doing their own thing," Tom said quietly. "Some are standing up and leaning against their stone. Others are sitting with their backs to the stone and there's one girl lying with her feet up against the stone throwing grass at her legs. Must be a reason."

He stopped and looked about him. "Oh and there's another one over there. Actually lying flat out across the top of the stone in a most precarious position. She looks as if she'll fall off at any minute."

"Sounds a bit odd. Didn't you say something about the force of the bands and the energy they transmit also affecting people?" asked Judith.

"Yes," Tom replied. "It seems that if you stand on tip toe and place the palms of your hands against the stone leaning at an angle of forty-five degrees, the force will push you either to the left or to the right."

"How weird," said Judith.

"Apparently the force varies according to the lunar phase,"

continued Tom. "If I remember rightly it's at its strongest six days after both the new and the full moon. These stones must be on the north side which is associated with the moon, maybe it's all to do with that."

"Maybe that's what they're doing, trying to take in energy from the stones," said Judith, her head on one side listening to the persistent sound of drumbeat. "Perhaps I should have a go later when they're gone. I wonder what the moon phase is today?"

※

"So you see circles are rooted in ancient pagan beliefs," said Judith now comfortably ensconced in my living room, having returned from Avebury with Tom and enjoying a glass of wine.

Sitting on the floor I was stroking Barnie and keen to learn about Avebury. "Did you find out why circles were so important to them in the first place?" I asked taking a sip of wine.

"Well I had a very interesting tour of the Gallery with a really good guide," replied Judith. She bent down and retrieved her handbag from the floor. Opening it she felt around and passed me some leaflets.

"Here I got these for you. You might find them interesting. Anyway the guy told me that our distant ancestors saw the circle as a symbol of infinity," she explained. "To them the earth was sacred and mother of all things. Their lives were dominated by the rhythmic cycle of the seasons. It seems that the henge was of circular construction to keep evil spirits at bay as well as marauders and wild animals of course."

"I've never visited Avebury. Always meant to go," I said looking at one of the leaflets. "It looks amazing, perhaps James and I should pay a visit. The size of the stones is incredible. Do tell me more."

"Well there are two smaller circles within the larger outer ring. The Northern inner circle of twenty seven stones and the Southern inner circle with twenty nine stones," said Judith carefully. "I'm just trying to remember all my facts."

"Do you know the purpose of the inner circles?" I asked.

"It seems that the Northern circle was connected with moon rituals and the Southern circle with the sun. Only recently they discovered that the stones in the south are oriented to the midwinter sun. Apparently the rising sun shines directly through the southern portal. It was one of the most important turning points of their year."

"It all sounds very complex," I said.

"It is or rather it was. There's not so much of it all left now. Apparently most of the stones were destroyed or moved in the 1300s because people were frightened of the pagan rituals which were associated with the place. It wasn't until the 1930s that a man called Keiller carried out a reconstruction of the outer and inner circles and made it what it is today."

"So going back to circles in witchcraft," I said thoughtfully, "the magic circle is a key part of their rituals as we know. And when you think of it amulets are often circular. The purpose of both of them is to provide protection. It's all rooted in pagan tradition."

"And just as at Avebury the magic circle is used to concentrate energy, by forming a sacred space with magical protection," said Judith finishing her wine.

"Say Judith you're most welcome to have another glass of wine but I know you're tired. You've had a long day. Why don't I come round to see you and Tom tomorrow evening and you can both tell me more."

"That's probably not a bad idea. I'll get Tom to show you the photos. He says they're great. Especially the ones he took of the stone worshippers."

"Oh yes. I'd really like to see them. They sound bizarre. By the sound of it none of them fell off their stones," I said laughing.

"No fortunately they all left in one piece."

"Did you manage to find out anything about them?" I asked.

"Yes we did get talking to them. They were really interesting. The drummer is South American and the others were generally an international bunch. Malaysian, Chinese, Mexican, Portuguese, French, Spanish. They were from all over."

"So what's with the drumming?" I asked.

"Well it seems that the sound of the drum is used to raise their level of consciousness which increases the rate at which they can absorb energy. Apparently it kind of synchronises the mind and the body."

"So that's how they managed to stay put in all their precarious positions I suppose," I said. "Amazing."

CHAPTER 20

It's a rainy Saturday morning in March. Sitting in my study marking assignments I'm glad not to be out in the torrential downpour. Barnie's walk will have to wait I thought, at least until the rain is lighter. Suddenly Tom emerges noisily from the trapdoor under the stairs breaking across my thoughts. "There's something we need to show you," he gasps. "Come and see. We've found a bricked-up doorway in the cellar, the far cellar under the kitchen. You can see where the bricks are irregular."

"It's obviously an in-filled bit of the wall," says James clambering out after Tom. "You can tell the bricks have been added later. You can see that the edges run in straight lines, just about the width of a door. The surface is rough and uneven and it's obvious the bricks are different even under the whitewash."

Dropping my pen and papers onto the table I follow the others hurriedly down the wooden staircase and through to the furthest cellar. Tom has placed one of the lamps to one side and James shines the torch to highlight the wall. It's easy to see the bricked-up area, the bricks are plainly of a different type and feel slightly bumpy to the touch.

"Look, you can see a bridging brick every five or six layers," says Tom, "to marry up with the bricks in the rest of the wall."

"How strange," I say examining the wall and running my fingers over the rough lines along the brick edges. "You were the one who said these cellars might have some more secrets. You know what, this doorway is very similar to the two doors on the front of the house which were bricked up at some point. You can see the bridging bricks just the same."

"So what next?" asks Tom excitedly. "Are we going to open up this wall and see what's behind it?"

"I don't know," I say gazing at the wall.

I stand back suddenly thoughtful. What might we find behind it? Images crowd my head as I picture an adjoining cellar, its walls rougher, dank, dark and dripping, the floor rutted and uneven, the menacing shadowy corners and low ceiling. There must be some reason for bricking it up, some sinister secret maybe. Was it anything to do with Eliza and Rose and their secrets of the other world?

"I'm not sure," I say hesitantly. "We could be opening up a can of worms or worse. We just don't know what we might find through there."

"Well you didn't know what you'd find in the other cellars and that didn't worry you," put in Tom swiftly. "What's there to lose by taking a look?"

"I'm not usually bothered by these things but I'm beginning to think maybe we've investigated all of this enough. We've made some great finds and we're still unravelling things. I think perhaps we should leave it at that for now. Also it would cause a whole lot of mess, opening up the wall."

"You really are a bit uneasy about this aren't you?" says James putting his arm round my shoulders. "We don't have to do anything at all about it if you don't want to. No-one is going to make you, least of all us."

I can feel a tingling at the back of my neck as I stand looking at the blocked doorway and my shoulder muscles tighten. Where is all this going to end I thought. I'd been excited about buying the house mesmerised by its charm and charisma and then gripped by the secrets of the cellars and I was increasingly becoming obsessed with its past. Now it seemed that the house was putting out ever-widening tentacles and I could feel that I was in danger of being swept along without having any say in the matter. I tried to articulate this.

"It just seems too much, a bridge too far." Taking a deep breath I went on, "We've had a great time unravelling things from the past and we've learned a whole lot, all of us. But we've got to stop somewhere before it takes us over. We're in danger of becoming fixated on the past. I've just got a feeling that there's something untoward on the other side of that wall. I can't really explain."

I can see James studying my face seriously and I know that he understands, as if he too accepts that things should probably be left the way they are. Tom however is fidgeting, restless and edgy his slender fingers unconsciously tracing and retracing the uneven edges of the doorway. "Are you saying you're nervous?" he says looking surprised. "You're usually the decisive one, intrepid, the explorer. You're the one who wants to find out more about the house."

I move away from the wall deliberating. Are my worries irrational? Is it just my over-active imagination? Or is there something really underlying my unease. I wish that Judith was here with her instinctive knowing and her logical way of thinking.

"I know I usually take things in my stride and that I'm generally curious but this somehow makes me wary. I just don't feel I want to move on it, not now. I think we need to take our time and give it a whole lot more thought before we do anything," I say finally, uncertainly.

Tom steps back from the wall looking despondent. "Okay. Have a think about it. Maybe in a couple of weeks we could do something, call Raymond in and get him to at least take a few bricks out at the top and see what's there. Just think what we might find. Could be something valuable or of archaeological interest, who knows?"

"Well let's just say, not at the moment," I reply thankful that he is accepting my caution.

"Of course. Whatever you think best," Tom says. "I don't want you to be worried about things. But we've pushed on this far. If we leave it completely you'll always be wondering what's on the other side. You need to bear that in mind."

"I know. I will."

Easter holidays and the children and youngsters in the village are noticeable during the day for once, drawing attention to the fact that they are usually invisible, heads down in their classrooms and hidden from sight.

As I open the gate and Barnie follows me through I catch a fleeting glimpse of two young girls aged about twelve darting across the road. One with blond hair and a ponytail is wearing a white top and pink trousers and the other is strikingly dark-haired and dressed in a black tee shirt with bright orange cut-offs. They fly across the road and disappear into the drive next door.

I wait, expecting them to re-emerge. Maybe they're hiding or maybe they're doing a leaflet drop. They certainly don't live there and my neighbour is out, evident by the lack of her black BMW.

Standing by the gate I wait for them to reappear. Nothing. There's no sound, no young girls giggling and chattering as they sneak onto some one else's property.

I glance round and then move towards the drive. No-one. Perhaps they went into the drive beyond but no I would have heard them open the gate. I look over the low fence dividing the two houses. No sign of anyone. And I didn't hear the sound of a door so they can't have gone inside. I look around me. Where can they be?

Cautiously I turn the heavy black ring on my neighbour's side gate expecting to find resistance as it is normally kept locked. To my surprise the door opens and I can see the long stretch of grass and overrun flower borders sloping away at the bottom of the steps.

There is no-one there and not a sound. All is silent about me.

The sitting room was pungent with the comforting warmth of burning logs as the evening drew on. Buried deep in my book about Gardner and oblivious to my surroundings I read, my attention rapt:

> "Cardell claimed to be a Witch, but from a different tradition to

Gardner's. He managed to get a woman called Olive Green into Gardner's Coven, and told her to copy out the Book of Shadows so that Cardell could publish it and destroy Gardner.

He also contacted a London paper and told them when and where the Coven meetings were held and of course the paper got quite a scoop. Cardell led people in the Coven to believe that it was Doreen Valiente who had informed on them."

Curling my toes involuntarily on the chaise longue I stretched my legs and yawned, thinking it would be time for bed soon. I glanced up casually from my book, taking in the sprawling length of James stretched out on the soft leather sofa he favoured after dinner. Absorbed in his book he was gently stroking the outstretched Barnie by his side.

My gaze was drawn to the smouldering fire and as I looked I saw in the centre of the burning coals a skull-like shape with deep-set eyes, flickering and watching me, the high forehead and square-set jaw sputtering and glowering in the embers.

Starting up, I hear myself saying urgently, "Look at that, the skull in the fireplace," as I point at the smouldering coals in the grate. "That's weird, what does it mean? It's watching us, can't you see. Look at those sunken eyes and the high forehead."

James looks up distractedly. "What did you say?" he murmurs.

I indicate the glimmering shape formed by the fusion of burning logs and coal in the fireplace. The grinning skull looks back at me as it glimmers and crackles in the yellow-orange firelight, an unexpected silhouette lit from behind by the flickering flames.

James stares at the fireplace. "Your imagination is too vivid for your own good," he says as he returns to his book.

I watch for some time, fixated by the still smouldering skull, waiting for the burning coals to die down and take the charred remains of the leering skull with it. As I gaze intently the coals beneath shift and the crumbling object is shaken reluctantly into the embers and in an instant is gone.

CHAPTER 21

"Dead at thirty three. Just like that," said James taken aback. "Oh Fee, how unbearably sad."

"Yes it was sad. It was a complete and utter shock when he died. We'd only been married a year."

"I don't know how you managed, how you coped and turned your life around."

"Well it took time," I said slowly. "I was numbed and in shock for months and months and then I just gradually came to, as if I was waking up from some deep nothingness or oblivion," I paused remembering the pain and the hurt, the deep depression. "The blackness seemed to lift and I felt somehow I was able to move on and see things again," I continued.

"You must have been very brave."

"No, not really. Lot's of people have to pick up the threads of their life like that."

"I'm glad you've told me more about it. I know it's hard to talk."

"It is hard but it's good. Mark was an amazing person and somehow I need to tell you about the way he was, what he gave me."

Curled up in the welcoming hotel room with its soft pastel walls and spotless white duvet relaxing after the drive James and I were snatching a short break in Cornwall. Boscastle had been my suggestion. It was somewhere Mark and I had been going to visit before his sudden death during a squash match.

"Did he have any signs of anything wrong beforehand?" asked James hesitantly.

"Not really. Not that I was aware of although he had felt a trifle breathless on occasion. We put it down to the fact that he was always rushing about, always on the go. What with work and sport and everything else."

"But there was nothing that could have been done, no cure for it?" James queried.

"There are a range of drugs that could've been prescribed if he'd known. I don't think there's a cure. The doctor told me it occurs in about six people per 100,000 every year and that many of them die, especially those who are young like Mark and are unaware that they have a problem."

James sat silently for a moment and then he slowly got up and moved over to the open window. He beckoned to me to follow. "Just look at the view. You were right when you told me it's an absolutely charming and enchanting place."

Through the window I could see the road over the river, the stone wall a golden yellow in the sun and farther down a second newer looking road crossing the river with a trickle of tourists ambling leisurely across. Slate cottages with grassy banks nestled along the far edge of the water and I could hear the burbling of the fast moving river as it flowed down to the sea.

I remembered that friends had told Mark and I some years ago before we were married that Boscastle was a magical place, unspoilt and alluring. A place to relax they had said, to walk and feel the soft winds blowing on the cliffs, hear the sputtering throb of the fishing boats and the ever-present chink of lobster pots. It had sounded so idyllic and it was a place I knew I had to visit.

I'd found a picturesque hotel centrally positioned by the head of the estuary and now we had the long May Bank Holiday weekend ahead of us. Time to remove ourselves from the house and its summons from the past, time to immerse ourselves in each other, to live for the now.

Arriving at the hotel we had been immediately struck by the fast flowing river coursing its way right through the middle of the garden accessed by a simple arched bridge. On the far side rising terraces of large round wooden tables and chairs beckoned, their bright orange and cream umbrellas inviting us to take our cups of coffee over and offering shelter from the unexpectedly warm spring sunshine. Above, the deeply incised wooded valley with its emerging tresses of pale green foliage provided a mantle of protection to the village, sheltering the hotel and houses along its sloping banks

Later we crossed the road and set off along the path opposite the hotel skirting the scattered whitewashed cottages along the estuary with the smell of salt and the sound of gurgling water as the river trickled softly downwards to meet the gently lapping tide. Swathes of primrose clumps and dotted celandines cloaked the grassy hillsides to our left and Barnie now unleashed was snuffling and nudging along the dripping slate cliffs.

"What a strange rock formation," I exclaimed to James. "Layer upon layer of higgledy-piggledy folds of slate."

"Yes and look how the water trickles out almost all the way along this part of the rock face," he replied pointing.

"How odd."

"The water must rise in springs high above on the cliffs and then just sheet its way down interspersed between the layers of slate. I've never seen anything of the kind before," said James staring at the dripping rock.

"Barnie seems to like it anyway," I said chuckling at the wet dog, his fur flattened by the incessantly dripping water. Putting out my hand I caught some of the cool droplets of water in my palm where they lay like pearls.

Turning James pointed to the long line of gulls strutting like sentinels along the shore line where river met sea.

"You get a really good view of them from here," he said.

"They're magnificent birds aren't they," I replied.

"Majestic, haughty and probably quite vicious. Vicious if you're a fish that is," James added laughing.

As we stood and watched the incoming tide picked up speed and gushed inland up the estuary moving rapidly towards the village, a stark reminder of how fast the water could move without warning. Images shown on television of the terrible flash floods surging down the main road a few years ago came to mind. Swirls and torrents of fast-moving water sweeping away buildings as if they were toys, causing villagers and tourists alike to clamber onto rooftops or cling to trees as the rushing water swept relentlessly on its path to the sea. Hardly any sign of that tragedy now. Only a few small bright orange diggers still busily digging out and reinforcing the sides of the now widened river bed with carefully placed stacks of slates backed with cement higher up near the main street.

"They've certainly rebuilt very painstakingly and sensitively," I observed looking over towards the Youth Hostel, a long stone and slate building on the other side of the estuary its yellow brown walls blending seamlessly with the surrounding buildings.

Our gaze was drawn to a girl driving an old brown land rover pulling a trailer with a neat speedboat down the sloping track towards the riverbed and the incoming tide. Clambering from the cab she expertly unfastened the boat from the trailer and with the help of her unusually tall partner who jumped out of the passenger seat manoeuvred it into the shallow water, the waves lapping at her calves. The man climbed into the driving seat of the land rover and drove back up the riverbed heading for a place to park. The girl, her bright pink skirt dipping into the rising water, stood motionless, her light tee shirt flapping in the wind as she stood hands grasping the prow of the boat waiting for him to join her.

We meandered on along the bank of the estuary as it imperceptibly widened to embrace two stone jetties, one near and the other slightly further down protruding from the opposite side of the river, placed I imagined so as to maximise the protection of the village. Beyond we could see a craggy headland interlocking with the cliffs, the jagged rock formation protruding in places like giant crocodile heads.

Wending our way we passed massive stacks of lobster pots with their brightly coloured red, green and yellow flags neatly propped up alongside colourful marker buoys. Reaching the harbour wall at the end we found several steep steps set in the side of the cliff. Encouraging

Barnie to scale the rough cut slate steps we found ourselves before an enchanting view. The shimmering turquoise green of the sea edged with delicate white-crested waves gently lapping against the rocky promontory, a gaping cave set low down beside the tide line.

"Just look at that island," exclaimed James pointing to a rocky outcrop out to sea. "You can see that the birds have taken it over. It looks as if no human could ever have scaled it, it's so sheer."

"Lucky birds," I replied. "Fancy having a safe haven like that without fear of ransacking egg-collectors preying on them."

Exhilarated we squatted on the shaley slabs of slate overlooking the calm waters and breathed in lungfuls of fresh salty air. I felt quite tranquil after my outpourings to James, glad that I had been able to share more about my past with him, the traumas and the nightmares. I still felt numb when I talked about it.

Climbing up the narrow twisting path we looked down on the rugged slate cliffs tumbling towards the mill pond sea and felt the euphoria of being in the open air with a gently fluttering breeze and the warm sun soft on our faces.

As we passed a couple with a Springer spaniel who were seated on a stone bench the girl stopped us and asked what breed Barnie was.

"Oh he's a Labrador mix," I replied.

"Lovely coat, seems very friendly," the girl said. "Are you walking far?"

"Don't really know, we're just going for a wander and to get a view of the sea from higher up."

"So what do you think of Boscastle? Are you enjoying your visit?"

"Well we've only just arrived but so far we've found it a lovely place. So much to see and very natural," said James.

"Yes," said the girl, "it is quite unspoilt. Lots to see and do. By the way, have you been to the Witchcraft Museum yet?" she added in a friendly manner. "All the visitors seem to go there."

"Witchcraft Museum. What Witchcraft Museum?" I asked quickly. Turning to James I muttered darkly, "I thought we'd left all that behind us."

"Haven't you heard of it? The museum is world-renowned. It's really quite something," the girl replied. "We've only just moved here and it's been a very interesting place to visit. It seems that Boscastle has strong links with witchcraft, both past and present."

"Yes there are all kinds of amazing and scary things in there, some of them a bit far-fetched," her companion added.

"Far-fetched, what kind of far-fetched?" put in James.

"Well there's what's meant to be a petrified witch's hand. It's all black with disintegrating fingers, quite revolting really. And there's other stuff like that."

"Sounds weird," said James.

"Apparently the museum suffered a lot of damage in the 2004 flood but it's been rebuilt and restored now so it's pretty much as it was," the man said. "I'd recommend a visit if you have time."

Thanking them, James and I moved on along the path. "I can't believe it. Why would we choose to come here probably the only place in Cornwall with a Witchcraft Museum when we're trying to escape from that very same thing?" I said gloomily.

"Goodness knows," said James, "but it must just be a coincidence. Shall we try and forget about it for now? After all you can't beat this scenery and the weather is just perfect."

"Okay," I said. "I'll do my best to put it out of my mind. "Who wouldn't enjoy being here," I added looking around me.

We climbed the now steeply rising path which ascended high above the bay to explore an isolated whitewashed building at the top. "I wonder what this was," I said as we examined it from all sides.

"No saying. It's an odd sort of building" replied James peering through the grimy windows. "Come to think of it, maybe it's the place I read about in one of the brochures," he continued. "I think it was originally lit up as a beacon telling sailors out at sea of the 'ladies of the night' to be found on the shore, telling them that this was a good place to land."

"Amazing. I knew that lighthouses had their purpose but luring sailors for pleasures of the flesh is altogether different. I'll bet these coastal areas could tell many a story. If only we knew the half of it."

I took a few steps forward nearer the cliff edge and sat down on the springy turf which was dotted in all directions with clumps of pale pink thrift. Gazing down at the shimmering blue green sea I could make out darker patches of shadowy clouds reflected in the water.

"Well," I sat back and looked about, feeling somewhat dismayed, "what do you know. It seems we haven't managed to escape from everything back home. We seem to be right in the middle of it again here in Boscastle when we're meant to be having a relaxing break."

"Yes," said James. "It rather looks that way."

"It's the last thing I was expecting," I said over a crab sandwich in the hotel garden. Sitting on the highest terrace with the warm wind gusting in swirls down the valley and watching the hooded jackdaws swooping down to pounce on small prey in the river we were enjoying a late lunch. Glasses of soft fruity Chardonnay and a half empty bottle in a wine cooler completed the setting.

"I certainly didn't know anything about the Museum but from what the girl on the cliff said it seems to be well known and many of the tourists come to Boscastle because of it," said James.

"Well it didn't come up when I was googling about witchcraft these past months. It's a complete surprise to me and I'm not sure I like it. After all we came here for a complete break."

"Hey you, we don't have to get wound up by all this but maybe we should pay the museum a visit as we're here," suggested James. "Who knows what we'll find?"

Entering the dark passageways of the Museum is like going back in time. Witches on broomsticks, cauldrons and ducking chairs abound. Spells, charms and potions lined up neatly in rows with careful descriptions as to their use and a huge display of healing figures and poppet dolls made of pastry, clay and wax, peppered with pin pricks looking for all the world as if they contained Braille messages. The plaque below reads:

"When the witch has recited a spell as she forms the healing figure, she coats it with egg white, varnish or paint, and leaves it to dry in a

safe place. Nowadays the use of photographs is becoming more popular with pins being stuck into the picture of the intended victim."

There are pots and jars of herbs of every description imaginable. Wormwood, matico, valerian root, hemp nettle, Russian sturgeon, witch hazel, monkshood, willow bark, white hellebore, arnica flowers and henna leaves, the list goes on and on.

We find ourselves standing in front of a large ceramic Hare-woman, brightly glazed in cream, blues, browns and turquoise. James reads the inscription:

> *" 'It is believed that witches can transform themselves into hares, also known as "shape shifting". Stories of hares disappearing after being shot abound in all parts of the country; usually an old woman is found soon after with gun shot wounds.*
>
> *It seems Hare-woman was found under a caravan near Goonhaven in 1996 and has since been on loan to the museum. She has the body of a voluptuous woman and the head of a hare. Although the hare is usually associated with fertility, abundance and good fortune, it is also associated with madness.' "*

"That's interesting," I say thoughtfully. "I've seen hares in the fields when out with Barnie. They're certainly huge and impressive and they look very powerful. Completely different from your average rabbit."

"Can't say I've ever really seen one," says James.

"One hears of the mad March hare boxing its rival and all that. I hadn't quite picked up the association with witches, had you?"

"No," he replies. "The 'mad as a March hare' saying is about all I know of them. Look at that plaque, it's a spell witches used to transform themselves into a hare and back by repeating each verse three times:

> *"I shall go into a hare,*
> *With sorrow aud sych aud meikle care*
> *And I shall go in the Devil's name*
> *Ay while I come home again*

And to return to human form they say:

Hare, hare, god send thee care.
I'm in a hare's likeness just now,
But I shall be in a woman's
Likeness even now."

❦

"So who's a witch then?" I say to James as we eat our evening meal in the cosy hotel restaurant. I'm eyeing up a buxom black-haired girl wearing a tight red jumper sitting at a small table in the corner with an older woman. "Do you think she's a witch? Perhaps they both are."

"What makes you say that for goodness sake?" laughs James quietly.

"It's her face, she just has that look about her. I'm sure she's a witch. Look at her eyes."

"You're incorrigible," replies James squeezing my hand. "Whatever would I do without you to amuse me?"

"Well it makes you think doesn't it. If witchcraft is alive and well in Boscastle, and there's every indication of that in the museum, what about witchcraft being alive and well in Whittlesham. Who do we know that's a witch under our very noses?"

"We'll have a careful look at them all when we get back," he says smiling.

"And what about my digital camera. Those photos I took up by the museum, they didn't come out."

"So your camera's not working. Nothing inexplicable about that. Anyway your other camera seems to be working so not to worry," James says savouring his final mouthful of roasted monkfish. "This food is divine."

CHAPTER 22

Next day we are back in the darkness of the museum, moving once again past the grey-haired old hag cackling at her table surrounded by her familiars and staring into her fishing float crystal ball. Glad to get out of reach of the monotonously intoned charms and spells, we make our way upstairs to check out the other rooms.

Beyond the displays of fetishes used for curses and ill wishing, where darkly knitted poppet dolls with strikingly resonant faces lie starkly stretched out beneath the glass topped cabinets alongside labels exhorting their harming powers, my gaze is irresistibly drawn to a display depicting the Green Man. Pressing a large green button, James and I hear a taped voice from a recording machine located somewhere above our heads clicking into action:

> "You will find The Green Man appears in roots of Paganism and Christianity throughout Europe since Roman times. He is one of the most important male fertility spirits and is found carved in wood or stone. Visitors will have seen these carvings in many churches and abbeys probably without knowing the significance..."

"Would you look at those masks?" a passing American visitor says loudly, bearing down on us as he jabs the button repeatedly, his gaze riveted by the dense foliage of branches and vines sprouting erotically from the face. "And that one there, it's spewing out all kind'sa stuff," he drawls. "Weird or what?"

His companion, a short blonde girl with long hair tied back in a red band pauses and then adds, "Those eyes, they're weirding me out. I've seen the likes of him back around," she intones as she hastens on passed the display obviously on a whistle stop tour of the museum.

"Reminds me of the Green Man pub in Finchley," jokes James. "I seem to remember there are lots of pubs called the Green Man, all over the place. Must have some significance."

"Sure, pubs and ale houses date from way back. There used to be more than twenty in Whittlesham alone. They've always played an important part in villages and towns. Who's to say what went on in them? Maybe they're connected with witchcraft."

And then as we turn from the curiously familiar sculpted masks and pagan woodland imagery we find directly opposite and dramatically seated on a large throne a grim-faced Bahomet, his power radiating across the room engulfing us as we look into his eyes.

He is the Goat of Mendes, half human and half goat, with furled eagle-like wings sporting both male and female organs, his horned head glaring at those who behold him, the glowing sign of the pentagram on his forehead, *"Do what they wilt shall be the law,"* imprinted large on the darkly scored background behind him.

Enthralled despite himself, James reads:

> *"Bahomet has been portrayed as a synonym of Satan or the devil, a member of the hierarchy of Hell. He also represents the Union of Opposites. His humanity is represented by his two breasts with the rod standing as his genitals symbolising eternal life."*

"Spooky. Remember him in *The Wicker Man*," I say shuddering.

"That was a really powerful film," says James. "Scary stuff. Edward Woodward being burnt alive inside the giant wicker man in front of all those crazed pagan worshippers."

"I'll never forget him incessantly chanting his prayers over and over again as the flames engulfed him in the crackling inferno, his hands wildly scrabbling at the straw walls," I say remembering the powerful images of Christopher Lee at his best cast as the fanatical Lord Summerisle.

"All that bestial animal imagery. Very haunting film. Do these things still go on?" James asks.

"It makes you wonder," I say meditatively. "I think I've had enough of all this," I add moving towards the steep staircase leading to the exit.

"I'd just like to have a look at this one last room," says James. "You don't mind do you? We may not get back here again."

"I rather hope not." I reply somewhat sharply moving to the top of the stairs.

I turn and stand watching him as he focuses on the last of the long glass showcases stretching the length of the back room, his dark hair cut short and his freshly shaved stubble a familiar sight. Was I getting too close to him?

I had always been fearful of total involvement with anyone after Mark's death, scared of the fragility of life. Cognisant of how things can completely change in a fraction of a second when a life is snuffed out. And now here I was totally bound up with James. Should I be more careful, hold something back?

"Look, here's the witch's hand, the one that couple on the cliffs told us about," James cut across my uncertain thoughts. "For some reason it's sealed in a box."

Reluctantly I move over to the showcase beside James, "Ugh, see those disintegrating fingers, there're disgusting. It looks as if they're decomposing before our very eyes."

"Apparently it belonged to a whole line of witches all of whom claimed that with the help of the hand they could work all kinds of magic," James says pointing at the caption. "And look there, it seems the last owner had a great deal of trouble with it:

"...the damm thing has a will of its own – it has refused to do what I tell it."

"And so it was passed to the museum. How odd," exclaims James continuing to read:

"Cecil Williamson, the founder of the museum, writes that he has had the powerful hand for twenty-six years and during that time all was peaceful, apart from one major disturbance when the hand was in a storage warehouse which it did not like."

"Well I sure don't like the look of it. I'm off," I say abruptly, re-crossing the room and hastily descending the wooden staircase. I find myself in a dimly lit narrow room leading towards the exit.

The museum is strangely quiet. Yesterday there were numerous visitors scattered around the museum, some moving quickly through like the Americans and others lingering like us, obviously engrossed in the wacky legends and bizarre exhibits. Today there is barely a soul to be seen.

Absorbed in thought I make my way towards the brightly lit shop at the end of the elongated room, contemplating a repeat lunch in the hotel garden. Could I resist another crab sandwich? It was Cornwall at its best. Fresh crab and the crispiest salad imaginable washed down by a bottle of dry white wine. Sheer heaven.

Then stopping in my tracks I find myself before a large oval mirror with elaborately engraved wooden frame brightly painted in reds, greens, yellow and gold. Behind it hangs a deep purple cloth and the black painted wall is dotted with pinpricks of sparkling light refracted from several small crystal balls placed nearby.

Below an inscription describes it as a 'dark mirror' believed to have particularly powerful magical qualities, formerly belonging to Cecil Williamson:

'A black mirror, made to reflect everything about itself that humanity will not confront…'

It's an arresting sight and as I move closer I can feel its power drawing me towards it, sensing the attraction of the unknown. Subconsciously I can hear the sound of muted voices emanating from its depths.

Now is not the time for this I say to myself hurriedly, forcibly moving away from the mirror. Too many things have been happening unbidden. Time to go. The exit is just in front of me. I can see the small leaded window at the front of the museum ahead, the sun illuminating the black witch astride her broomstick, her tall pointed hat reaching to the top of the window. I move to pass the mirror holding my breath and avoiding looking to the left endeavouring to avoid the magnetism of the greeny-black depths of the glass.

Suddenly concerned, I turn to gesture to James but there's no sign of him. Where is he I wonder. Should I go back for him? There's no-one around and it's so quiet I can hear the silence.

Then as I turn back towards the exit unwittingly I catch a glimpse of my own reflection. Trying to avert my eyes I find my gaze is irresistibly drawn to plumb the depths of the glass. I cannot help myself, I am inexorably taken over by the power of the luminous black glass.

I find myself standing transfixed before the mirror. I cannot move, my eyes are held, locked into the beyond. At first I see nothing, then my gaze is gradually brought into focus and a slight mist fills the glass and slowly, slowly, little by little I become aware of an image emerging.

It is a double image, a double image of myself, set to the fore of the brightly coloured oval mirror. The first image is undoubtedly me as I am now, the second image I cannot properly discern. I can't quite make out the features but I know it's me. Is it me in the future or me in the past? Why can't I see my face? I feel I must know. I must know what the meaning of this is, what is the mirror or those beyond trying to tell me?

> 'A black mirror, made to reflect everything about itself that humanity will not confront…'

I shudder as I remember the words. Is this something that those in another world or time feel I cannot face up to? Why can't I see? And once again I feel the pure power surging through me emanating from the mirror. It is taking me over, I have lost control. Who am I, where am I going, where am I being led?

Then I see a line of moving figures reflected in the glass behind me, some are gesticulating, some are standing stock-still, others walking by. They are young, they are old, they are familiar, they are strangers. Where have I seen them? I hear voices whispering, the siren so ordinary tempting me to turn and see who's there. The irresistible demand that I must turn around, I must look, I must get a glimpse of them. Who are they? What do they want of me? But hanging grimly on I manage somehow to defy them. I blink my eyes, hush my ears and concentrate resolutely on controlling my will power, on being in command and I do not turn round. I have heard of the danger of looking directly at those you see in the mirror.

How long I am there I do not know but it feels like an eternity. What is going on, what are these powers beyond my control, what spirits are exercising their will over me?

"Come on," says James suddenly appearing behind me and grasping me gently by the shoulders. "I think you've had enough of that mirror. You've been looking at it for ages."

I come to with a start and feel myself wilt into his arms, "I'm exhausted," I say taking a deep breath. "Let's away from here and into the sunshine, this place gives me the creeps."

"Me too," he says.

As I turn from the mirror I move warily towards the exit conscious that there is no-one in the room apart from James and myself.

CHAPTER 23

Standing on the hotel bridge I'm sipping coffee in the garden following a lazy breakfast. Feeling languid and relaxed after a romantic evening meal and a walk by the estuary after watching the last of the fishing boats return to the harbour and listening to the chink of the lobster pots as they moored, the stars bright in the cloudless night. We managed to get far away from worries about the supernatural and settled in to enjoy the quiet break we had planned.

I can feel the warm sun on my face and am conscious that James and I have really moved on with our relationship. We are in harmony, playing one and the same tune. It's good. James is on his way down the High Street to buy pasties for lunch and then we're off to explore the cliff path further, beyond the square white building along the overhanging cliffs. We're going to head for Tintagel and if we make it all the way there we can always catch a bus back if dogs are allowed.

Suddenly the sound of my mobile pierces the silence abruptly shattering my thoughts. Grabbing the phone from my bag I cross the bridge and sit at one of the tables on the far side, the brightly coloured furled umbrellas blowing gently in the light breeze.

"Hi there. Judith here."

"Hi, how're you doing?" I answer.

"Fine. How's your break?"

"We're having a great time. Boscastle is really beautiful. It's quite a small place with a very natural harbour. The hotel is right in the middle and we can walk everywhere. Lots of pubs and restaurants. Great stuff!"

"Glad it's going well. Tom's been working away for a few days so I haven't seen him. Been catching up on emails and phone calls. You know what it's like when you get a bit of extra time."

"Yes, I really need to do some of that myself. What else have you been up to?"

"Oh this and that. Work is piling up as usual so I've been hard at it. Doing a bit of reading too, nothing special."

"Be good to see you when we get back. You'd really love it down here. It's rather a quaint and old-fashioned place but with lots of charm. And the food, it's just great."

"You know me and food. Maybe Tom and I will make it down there say around June, before all the crowds descend for the summer."

"I'll give you the details of the hotel. It's very welcoming and you can have a good laugh with the staff. They're a right bunch."

"There's one thing I wanted to talk to you about," puts in Judith hesitantly, "I don't want to upset you while you're away."

"What do you mean?"

"Well, I've been doing a bit of scrying, trying to do it properly this time. Develop my third eye as they say."

"Oh yes, how did you get on?"

"Well it was fine to start with."

"What happened?"

"I seemed to manage with the concentration part and get myself focussed okay which I didn't manage before. You remember when I tried your crystal?"

"Yes, it just didn't happen."

"Well this time I could feel myself really relaxing and then there was a sort of swirling mist materialising before my eyes, inside my head. It was weird, but it wasn't frightening."

"And then?"

"Well, that's just it. Things got a bit scary. I'll tell you all about it when you get back but the main thing is I think I got a bit of a warning."

"What kind of warning?" I ask suddenly worried.

"Something about the future, something's going to happen. Not sure to whom."

"So what medium did you use? My crystal's at home isn't it?"

"I was surfing the net the other day and I found a site about scrying. It said that you can use a silver ring or rings so I used that. I've got several silver rings. It really worked very quickly."

"So what happened then?"

"Well I managed to focus absolutely on my inner thoughts and was able to develop my visualisation technique using a mantra to clear my mind. Then I affirmed what I was thinking out loud as the website said."

"Sounds like you were doing it right."

"Yes I just focussed on the images arising in my mind. But then after a time I began to feel cold and I could sense some kind of vibes, bad vibes I think. I can't quite explain."

"And then what?"

"Well I seemed to get the feeling of disaster or chaos, some kind of violence. I felt I was being warned that something ghastly about to happen."

"What kind of disaster?"

"I don't know. Must be in the future or we'd know about it. Things became very dark and more and more chaotic. I think I may have blacked out. I felt really bad when I came to."

"Goodness, how awful. I'm glad you're all right. How do you feel now?"

"Oh I feel fine, just concerned about what it all means."

"I'm sure, very upsetting. When did this happen?"

"On Friday morning, yesterday I suppose. It seems like so long ago."

"It seems eons ago to me too," I say thinking of all that had happened during our short break in Cornwall.

Thinking fast in the midst of our conversation I am becoming increasingly perturbed. Not only am I being affected by these strange happenings but now it seems that Judith is also being touched by it, whatever 'it' is. I resolve not to tell her about the black mirror and the strange photographs which haven't come out. I haven't even told James about the mirror and my experience yet. I'm still trying to make up my mind what to do. How to seek expert advice, how to put a stop to the whole thing.

"Promise me you won't do any more scrying for the time being," I add concerned about the growing menace, the fear of the powerful and the unknown. "It doesn't sound safe, just leave it alone at the moment."

"Too right. I'm not going to dally in that for a long time, if ever," Judith declares determinedly.

"Oh I'm so concerned about you. What a horrible experience. It must have been so scary."

"It was not good I can tell you."

"You'll have to tell me all about it when I get back. We'll be home for Bank Holiday Monday, actually travelling on Sunday to avoid traffic. Try not to worry. We'll think of a way to stop this in its tracks, you'll see."

"Okay, I'll try to put it to the back of my mind for now. By the way, Mum doesn't know anything about it so don't breathe a word when she's around. She'd have a fit if she knew this was going on under her very nose."

"I'm sure she would. She probably wouldn't believe any of it."

"Anyway do carry on having a good time and enjoying yourself. Tom's back today so we'll see you on Monday. I just wanted to say, do be extra careful on the road."

"We will. Not sure I'll say anything to James just yet. I don't want to worry him and it's been great to have a bit of real time together."

"Yeah, it'll do Tom and me good to get away for a break if we can. I'll have a chat with him about it when he gets back. Look after yourself."

"Look after yourself too. Bye for now."

"Bye," says Judith and as I disconnect my mobile I stand motionless wishing I hadn't got her involved with any of this. Bad enough that I was being hounded by something unseen and unknown. It didn't seem right and now she was being scared by events. I resolve to try to put a complete stop to either her or myself dabbling any more. We need expert help I thought.

Just how could this kind of thing happen in the twenty-first century when all I'd been trying to do was explore my own cellars. It didn't make sense. I'd have to think very carefully about what to say to James. Would he think it was all happening in my mind? How much did he know about what was going on?

CHAPTER 24

Robert Delforth stood patiently by the sink waiting for the kettle to boil. Wearing loose-fitting black trousers and a pale blue open-necked shirt he seemed casually familiar and comforting. "I do understand your fears," he said empathetically. "It must be very unsettling."

I was becoming increasingly unnerved and edgy as my fears sent my imagination running riot. My innocent quest in trying to open up the cellars seemed to be unleashing something unexpected, a powerful force in its own right. And something had drawn me to the house and then the cellars in the first place. Something outside of myself, some unexplained magnetism.

As soon as I'd moved into the house there was a lure towards finding out about the cellars. Something made me feel I had to find out about them, find out about the past. Previous occupants hadn't felt this I was sure otherwise they would have opened up the cellars themselves.

"It's certainly disquieting," put in James. "These things seem to be happening to Fee alone, not to me or anyone else. Even when I'm there I'm not affected."

"It's often that way," said Robert. "It's rare that more than one person sees a ghost or spirit at the same time, though they often appear to different people at different times. It's said that some people are immune to ghostly presences due to their date of birth or even their birth order within the family."

"How weird," said James. "How can your date of birth possibly have any connection with this kind of thing?"

"Hard to say," replied Robert. "I've even read somewhere that those born between midnight and dawn on a Friday are the opposite in that they become particularly sensitive to the appearance of spirits."

"Can we take ourselves back to what's been happening," I said somewhat tersely as I became increasingly nervy and anxious. "There's so much going on. I just don't seem to be able to get away from it. Especially in Boscastle, some very unusual things were happening."

"I know," said Robert, "we need to really try to understand what has been going on."

"Even the fact that my shoelaces were constantly becoming undone. I don't know if I mentioned that. It seemed as if something, someone was trying to trip me up, sometimes in dangerous places like the cliff path."

"Well shoelaces coming undone isn't really that unusual," said the vicar gently.

"No not in itself. But when it happens more than three or four times in a couple of days it certainly makes you wonder, especially linked with those images and the magnetic force of the dark mirror. And then there's the photos that didn't come out," I said in a rush. I paused, conscious of the weird nature of what was happening. "I don't want to have to move. So how do you explain those kind of things?" I went on, taking a deep breath and directing my question at Robert, trying not to sound impolite but feeling distraught and tense. "Why are these things happening and why do they only happen to me?"

James put his arm round my shoulder and tried to calm me down. "Fee, you're okay, you're amongst friends. There's nothing threatening you here. Let's try to work things through with the vicar. That's what he's here for," he said reassuringly.

I knew that James was trying to help and was conscious that allowing my nerves to get the better of me wouldn't help the situation. With a sigh, I tried to relax and release the tension in my neck and back. I was determined to find an answer and some way to allay my fears, things couldn't go on like this.

"You're right, James," said Robert pouring out three mugs of black coffee. "Let's go on into the sitting room and talk this through. I'm sure we can make some kind of sense of it."

We were standing in the kitchen at the vicarage. It seemed to be over large and looked unused. The pale cream cupboards lining the walls were rather old-fashioned and the red-tiled floor was bare and cold. I could see racks of dusty herbs over in the corner behind the cooker and a few tins of baked beans with several tins of soup on the side. Even so there was a homely atmosphere tinged with somewhat faded neglect.

The vicar's expression was warm and friendly, hospitably he had invited us into the kitchen so that he could make us coffee. Now he led the way through to his bachelor sitting room where he had given us coffee some months before whilst discussing the blessing of Louisa's grave. Piles of cluttered papers still lined the desk and were now additionally strewn across the large table by the window, effectively leaving no space to eat. It seemed so long ago since we were here before I thought. What a lot had happened in between.

"Well," said Robert thoughtfully as he moved to sit down on a chair to one side of the fireplace. "There seems to be two distinct things happening, one is your contact with witchcraft, seemingly past and present. The other is linked directly with the spirit world. Although there are links between them, they're not actually the same thing."

"Yes, I can see that," said James. "That's quite helpful, making the distinction."

"We may need to deal with each aspect separately," added the vicar. "Anyway, first of all tell me more about the two little girls you saw recently."

I talked through the experience by the gate when the two girls appeared from nowhere and crossed the road, only to disappear in an instant.

"They didn't look as if they were from the past," I told the vicar. "They were in modern clothes, pink trousers and orange cut offs. That pretty much dates them to about now."

"Some people talk about ghosts as having no real matter, describing them as a ghostly presence," said James. "But those girls don't sound like that. They sound as if they were very real, substantial even."

"You're right," agreed Robert, "when people talked about ghosts in the past they were often described as without substance or translucent. But the surprising thing is that ghosts seem to be seen more commonly now than in the past, often as very real people like the young girls you saw."

"But why would I see the ghost girls? Why me and what's their relevance?" I exclaimed looking at James for support. He was seated next to me in one of the vicar's overstuffed and rather uncomfortable armchairs. He took my hand and squeezed it.

Taking a sip of coffee Robert continued his train of thought, "Well, there are at least two separate schools of belief about ghosts. One is that they are spirits seeking solace from the living before departing and finding rest. The other is that ghosts are what are known as 'psychic imprints' or residual energy, left behind by those who died in violent or emotional trauma or circumstances."

He paused, before adding, "Some ghosts haunt individuals whereas others haunt places, which is more often the case."

"So the girls may just have been there and Fee just happened to see them not because they were anything to do with her?" put in James.

"That's right," said Robert. "Nearly all ghost sightings are unexpected and unwanted. Most people are not looking for them. They just occur, which seems to have been the case in this instance."

"Too right," I said trying to come over as a bit less tetchy. "I wasn't looking to see anything. I was just taking Barnie for a walk."

"Nowadays you may not realise it but ghost-belief and giving parishioners support is an important part of a theologian's work," said Robert seriously. "The offering of prayers is often seen as a way to lay ghosts to rest. That may be one thing we need to consider."

"You know what I'm thinking," I said, interrupting the vicar's flow. "There was a death just along from where I saw the girls, about twenty years ago. For some reason Bernard, my neighbour, told me. Apparently a mother and child were knocked down and killed by a car which ran out of control and mounted the pavement. I think the girl was about twelve years old and she was accompanied by her friend Katie, who as far as I know wasn't hurt. They didn't say what happened to her subsequently."

"Well that's one avenue to consider. The sighting may be linked with that incident. Although why there are now two girls involved when only one was killed, strange," said Robert pensively. "Anyway ghost appearances or hauntings are generally not seen as evil. More often they help the living in some way by making sense of things or by showing the way forward."

As Robert spoke, his words suddenly took me back to an uncanny experience from the past as I remembered another haunting. "And now I come to think of it, I can remember another ghostly experience," I said breathlessly. "It was when I lived in a rented house whilst at Uni. I was asleep in bed, it was November time and I was awoken sometime in the early hours by an awful wheezing and rasping noise. There was no-one else in the house, my housemates were all away." I stopped, bringing my distant memories to the fore.

"I just lay there," I continued, reliving the experience. "Not exactly frightened, just waiting, trying to make sense of it. Trying to understand what was going on. It sounded like someone was dying, like their last hoarse rattling gasps of breath. I know it sounds weird but that's what I thought."

"So what happened? What was it?" asked James. Robert too was paying close attention.

"Well, I lay there for some time. I didn't feel threatened or frightened really. Didn't know what to do as my two neighbours were elderly and I didn't think they would be much help. I suppose I eventually got back to sleep. Anyway, later that week I was talking to Sylvia the girl who used to live in the house and she told me that the occupant before her had been an old lady who had killed herself shortly after losing her late husband. She died in my bedroom, an overdose I think."

"Time of day is apparently significant in the study of the supernatural," said Robert. "Some ghosts or apparitions are seen in daylight but the vast majority are seen nocturnally. That presence could have been related to the time and night that she died. Anyway she didn't cause any harm by the sound of it."

"No she didn't. I never heard her again. Even though I lived in the house for several years after that. I must say I'd forgotten about the incident until now. Makes me feel a bit better somehow. That experience was a one-off, maybe the other incident will be the same."

"Well," said Robert. "Thank you for sharing this with me. I feel as if I understand more about the things you've been going through." He stood up.

"What I'm going to suggest for now is that you contact the Right Reverend Bishop Richard Davis," he said, moving to his desk and rifling through untidy piles of papers. "I've got his phone number somewhere here." He swept the papers to one side, revealing a well worn leather address book. "Here it is." He scribbled the number on a scrap of paper. "He'll be able to put you in touch with the Archdeacon or Bishop within the Diocese who looks after the paranormal. These days it's an important aspect of pastoral care. You'd be surprised how many people seek help with this kind of thing."

"Thank you so much for your help and support," said James rising from his chair.

Putting out his hand to me he added, "What about the fourth cellar? Should we open it up to see what's there? It may have a bearing?"

"Of course. I'd not thought of that," said Robert. "I think you do really need to know what's in there. But I think you need to have someone with you. Maybe an expert of some kind. You need to think about that before you do anything."

CHAPTER 25

I was awoken by the urgent ringing of my mobile abruptly recalling me from a chaotic dream. Groping for the phone I shook myself awake conscious that the motionless James beside me could sleep through anything.

"Hello," I said glancing at the alarm clock which showed 5.30 am.

"Oh Fee, it's me. Judith."

"What's happened? You sound terrible."

"It's Tom. He was a victim of a hit and run mugging last night. He's in a London hospital, not badly hurt. I don't think they'll be keeping him in but I have to go and collect him."

"What happened?" I gasped. "I know you said he was working somewhere in London last night."

"It seems he was knocked over by a crazy motor cyclist who grabbed his camera, ripped it from his neck. He was thrown sideways. Nearly into the path of a car coming the other way which fortunately braked and just missed him. I think he's got cuts to his head and maybe bruised ribs. As far as I know there aren't any bones broken."

"Oh Judith. I'm so sorry," I said shocked.

"Really why I called is that I need a lift. Mum can't drive all that way. It's too far and London's a nightmare."

"Of course I'll take you, Judith. Do you want to go right now?"

"Oh yes, if that's okay with you. I'm ready to leave anytime."

"I'll get dressed and be with you in about ten. I'll just need to tell James where I'm going. Which hospital is it?"

"The Royal London Hospital in Whitechapel. I'll google instructions for you. I'll print them off in Braille so I can read them out in the car. Thanks Fee. See you in a minute."

※

"Wow, what a building," I said as we walked into reception. "This hospital is amazing. Trust Tom to get sent to one of the latest and most high tech hospitals in the country. Not just any where for him."

"What's it like?" asked Judith. "It certainly smells pristine and sort of brand new."

"Well it sure is state of the art. Looks more like an ultra modern office block than a hospital. It's massive. High-rise blue glass with windows just everywhere. And this reception area is really tasteful. Soft beige and brown colours with orange seating and cream slatted seats, very spacious and really welcoming."

"Anyway," I added looking at the signs, "I think Casualty is this way. Let's find Tom. I'm sure he can't wait to get away despite the amazing surroundings he's managed to find himself in."

"It sounds as if it's quite busy for this time in the morning, it's only around 7.30 am," said Judith turning her head towards reception where a number of people were gathered.

"Yes it is rather busy for early morning. But the staff seem very efficient at meeting and greeting people and helping with their queries," I said as I led Judith in the direction indicated.

We walked along a brightly lit corridor and found the entrance to Casualty at the far end. Walking through the swing doors I could see Tom sitting in a corner talking to two uniformed police officers, a man and a woman.

"We'll have to wait a minute," I said softly. "He's over there. Looks fine but he's with the police. They're obviously questioning him about the incident. He's got a couple of plasters on his face. Looks like it must be a few minor cuts. Oh and I think his left hand is bandaged. But that apart he seems to be in one piece."

"Oh thank God," breathed Judith. "I feel all funny now we're here. I wasn't too bad on the way."

"You coped really well Judith considering the shock. We both did. Listen I think you need to sit down just here and I'll get you some tea," I said guiding her to one of the settees.

"Thanks, I could do with a cuppa," she said attempting a small smile. "He'll probably see us in a minute anyway. He knows we're coming."

She sat down looking pale and wan. Her face was lined with anxiety and she looked quite frail.

"It was just such a shock. You get a phone call in the middle of the night and there's nothing you can do. I just wanted to be with him and I knew he was so far away. It made me feel helpless and I couldn't even get here to help him on my own."

"Well you did get here and you'll be the best support that he has," I assured her. "Just hang on a minute and I'll get our drinks."

I found my way to the drinks machine and bought back two cups of steaming tea. "Hope it's not too vile," I said. "Hospital tea is not exactly known for its flavour."

"Actually it's not too bad," said Judith beginning to perk up. "By the sound of it Tom seems in reasonable shape so it doesn't look as if too much harm has been done. I think he was very lucky indeed."

"I think so. Could have been a whole lot worse," I said.

"It seems the guy on the motor bike just drove at him. He knew what he was about alright. He must've seen that Tom's camera was an expensive Nikon and he was just going for it. Apparently it was a really mean machine, all black and the rider was in black from head to toe. Quite scary I'm sure. What's going on over there?" she asked.

The two police officers were sitting facing Tom. One was clearly writing notes and the other was asking the questions. Tom himself looked fairly relaxed and composed, just like his usual self. His bandaged hand was not a good sight and I wondered just how badly injured he was. I wasn't going to worry Judith unnecessarily by speculating so I turned back to her.

"Nothing dramatic," I replied. "They're just asking him questions.

One is taking notes. Tom looks fine. You guys are pretty close aren't you," I added. "Do you think it's the real thing?"

"Oh goodness, I don't know," said Judith shrugging slightly. "We really get on, better than I've ever gotten on with anyone. But who knows? You know me. I'm in no rush. Like you I rather suppose."

"Me? I'm certainly in no rush. Look what happened before. I was widowed within a year. I'm not going to push my luck by getting married again. Not for a long time." I breathed in deeply. As always being reminded of my own traumatic experiences was unsettling. One never really gets over these things I thought. How can you? Mark was somewhere, out there, dead at the age of thirty three. Would I ever meet up with him in the afterlife? What would happen if I did and he was thirty three and I was eighty? I pushed my thoughts to one side. It was all too complicated.

I could see the police officers standing up now and taking their leave of Tom. His hair was rumpled and he looked a bit dishevelled, not like his usual immaculate self. But his composure remained and I was thankful. That in itself would reassure Judith.

It must be so hard not to be able to see the person you loved or do something like drive them somewhere when in need. But Judith did so much for herself. She was so brave and self-reliant. I could see what Tom saw in her. She was fiercely determined and independent, witty, clever and attractive. And in contrast there was also a certain softness, almost naivety, about her which made her appear somewhat vulnerable and at the same time something of a maverick. An amiable rebel.

Now I stood up and taking Judith's hand said, "I think we can go over now. Take a deep breath and just feel fine. He's alright you know."

"Let's go," she said.

Tom greeted us both eagerly. "Sorry to bring you here in such a rush like this but I do really appreciate it. Apologies for all the drama. It must've been terrible for you," he said looking at Judith and putting his arm round her. "And you too," he added turning to me. "Thanks for bringing Judith all this way to collect me."

"It's nothing. We're both just glad you're okay. It must've been a horrific experience. Being mugged in a hit and run and pushed into the path of an oncoming car. How did the driver manage to avoid you?"

"With difficulty I think," Tom said wryly. "He was quite a youngster. He swerved violently to the right and hit a couple of wheelie bins. Not too much damage to the car as far as I know but the dustbins were a fine old mess. But what beats me is how the guy on the bike could tell the make of my camera from such a distance."

"Maybe he'd been following you," suggested Judith. "That's what they do I think. They have scouts on the ground who watch out for someone worth robbing and when they see someone they call their mate on a bike, give them a description and bingo. The guy on the motor bike knew where you were and what you had that was worth nicking. I suppose it's lucky he didn't break your neck," she said rather edgily.

"I hadn't thought of that," said Tom. "Perhaps you're right. Bastards. That camera was worth a fair bit but I could've been killed!"

"Those sort of guys wouldn't even have given that a thought," I said abruptly. "Getting say £500.00 for a camera worth £1,500 is all they'd be thinking of. You need to think about that when you get a new one. Just a thought, a friend of mine always puts their expensive camera in a battered case to put them off the scent."

"That might be a good idea," said Judith. "We can't have this happening again. I'd have to make you give up your job!"

"Not sure about that," said Tom but he did look as if he was taking our comments seriously. "Anyway it seems the damage to my ribs is very minor. Just a bit of bruising where the car hit me as the driver managed to take a detour into the wheelies."

"Thank goodness he was on the ball," I said. "Some drivers might not have reacted as quickly."

"No," said Tom. "At any rate the police have taken a description of the motor bike guy for what it's worth. Mind you how can you describe someone who's wearing a black crash helmet and black leathers? The bike looked like a BMW Sport, black and flashy. I gave them the details about that but I hardly think they'll catch anyone. I don't think there were any witnesses apart from myself and the car driver who was busy crashing into the bins. Neither of us got the number plate properly although I think it was an 08 reg."

"Well you look as if you've got a few scratches on your face but what about your hand?" I asked.

Tom put out his left hand. It was neatly swathed with only his fingertips showing, the thumb carefully strapped to his forefinger. "I may have a dislocated thumb. They've strapped it up, to keep the thumb straight. I've got to see my doctor or go to the hospital locally tomorrow. They've emailed the x-ray to my doctor already. That's how they work these days apparently."

"How does it feel?" asked Judith anxiously.

"I can't move my hand a lot as you can imagine," he replied. "It does feel a bit bruised. Don't know if it's any worse than that, can't really feel the thumb much. We'll have to wait and see. Anyway," he paused, "shall we get out of here? I could murder a good breakfast. A one handed job," he added. "There's a Mega Bite Café just near here if I remember right. How about it?"

"You and your stomach," said Judith. "I don't know if I'm going to be very hungry but we'd better fill you up or you'll be a right pain."

CHAPTER 26

The garden is at its best, the silver birch with its delicate leaves, the acer in full burgundy brown and the pampas grasses spilling over the edges of the border. And all about the lower flowerbeds magnificently plump fuchsias in every shade of pink, purple and white.

James and I seated at the table behind the garden house in the early evening are finishing a pork and lentil dish, flavoured with sage, lemon and garlic.

"Delicious," said James clearing his plate. "That is some dish. I love the leeks and peas with it. It's great, you cook French and I cook Pacific Rim. What a team."

"Yes it's a favourite alright. I love Joanne Harris' cookery books. Her recipes actually work. And the illustrations are very evocative. Little cameos of rural France alongside pictures of the dishes themselves, you can't fault her and her desserts are great too."

"You can just sit and look at the pictures," said James. "They tell so many stories."

"Yes the photographer is brilliant at capturing the essence, the very Frenchness of France."

As we sat with our glasses of wine, a small squirrel chased across the grass, his long tail delicately furled, resplendent in the lengthening shadows. He played in the grass searching for seeds and other delicacies then moved to the flower bed and started scratching away looking for earlier hoards of food.

"They're so persistent," said James watching intently. "I know you call every squirrel Sebastian for some reason. Well the other day I saw Sebastian ferreting away with a nut down the bottom of the garden. He seemed to eat part of it and then rebury it. And when he left a crow swept instantly down from the silver birch and dug it up for himself. Amazing."

At that moment Barnie came racing down the garden and flew at the squirrel. The squirrel bounded off gracefully and scaled the fence with one leap. Barnie brought to a sudden halt barked fiercely at the disappearing squirrel. Giving up after some minutes he started scrabbling away in the soft earth, at first in a desultory fashion and then digging more and more urgently

"Must be a mole," I said. "I think he knows when there's one burrowing away underground. I expect you noticed those molehills appearing over the last couple of days. I flattened them earlier. Stuck a few sharp sticks down to deter the moles. Maybe they're trying a new route."

"I'll try and stop the pesky digger if you like," said James getting up and moving across the bank.

He pulled Barnie away from the deepening hole and stooped to brush the loose soil from his face and paws. "What a dirty dog!" he said laughing, brushing the spatters of earth away as Barnie ran off. He turned and began to scrape the soil back into the hole with his foot. Suddenly he stopped and crouched down.

"Hey Fee," James began excitedly. "See what Barnie has uncovered. Some sherds of pottery. I've never seen anything like them. They must be quite old. Do come and have a look." He knelt and pulled several jagged pieces of dark green and orange pottery from the hole.

Moving swiftly I joined James and squatted down beside him "Gosh, I've found pieces of old pottery in the garden before," I said, "but as you say nothing like these."

"Just feel how it's slightly coarse to the touch and see how the orange glaze is mottled with that unusual green colouring. It's glazed both inside and out. This could be pottery from around the fifteenth century you know," said James earnestly. "I'll get a trowel," he continued as he stood up, "and we can see if there are any more fragments. It could be a great find even though the pot is broken. I've seen antiquarian pieces of pottery something like these in the Ashmolean in Oxford."

"What a find," I said. "And all down to the squirrel you could say."

James returned from the garage and kneeling down began to dig gently through the soil with the trowel. "Oh yeah," he said elatedly. "There are some more pieces here. Larger than the first and the same green and orange glaze. I really think we might have something here."

He worked on carefully pulling more pieces from the ground and as he did so I laid the sherds out neatly on the lawn like a jigsaw trying to get a sense of the shape of the pot. "You're right. They're certainly from the same piece. I wonder if there'll be any more pots here? You often get things buried together."

"You know what I think?" said James leaning back on his heels. "I need to give Charles Latty a call. You remember me talking about him? I think I told you he's one of the few black British archaeologists around. He's at my college in Oxford, works in the same department as me. He'd certainly be able to date these fragments for us."

"That's a good idea. We really need to find out more about them."

Fetching an old seed tray from the garage I laid a piece of newspaper at the bottom and then carefully placed the pieces of pottery on it. "Will you take them with you to work tomorrow?" I asked.

"Yes. I think Charles'll be around. Anyway I'll certainly see him sometime in the week," James replied. "I think I'll get something to cover up this hole to stop Barnie having another go. You know what's he's like, never gives up."

"Let's finish our wine before we go in," I said returning to the table. "I know you want to watch that film tonight but it's only about 7.30. Still plenty of time."

James covered the hole with a piece of thick plastic and weighted it down with bricks before coming over to join me. "Good idea," he said sitting down. "By the way, I was going to talk to you about Tom's accident," he continued, "before all the squirrel shenanigans. I know he's back safe and sound and staying a few nights with Judith but what exactly was he doing in that part of east London on Friday night?"

"It seems he was doing an article for a magazine called *Contemporary Writing,* something about the East End Academy Exhibition."

"*Contemporary Writing.* Not a magazine I've heard of," said James pouring out the remains of the wine. "Lovely Rioja isn't it."

"Yes great Rioja. You certainly know your wines. Anyway you know how Tom covers all kinds of things on the arts and history side. Apparently it's a very well known exhibition which takes place every three years. It features both emerging and established painters. He was at a preview."

"I suppose it's inevitable that he gets himself into all kinds of places what with his work. It's all quite risky really."

"Yes it is. Judith doesn't like it at all," I said hesitantly thinking of that nagging worry at the back of my mind. Was Tom's accident the disaster or violence that Judith had been warned about whilst we were in Cornwall? Was there some kind of external force at work which was now involving Tom as well as myself and Judith? I really didn't want anyone else mixed up in this, especially James and the others.

I could feel the temperature dropping as the summer evening drew in and wondered again whether or not I should share my fears with James.

※

From:	Charles Lattey
To:	Fee Hunter
Subject:	Hi Fee

Hi Fee,

James has given me your email address. He showed me the sherds of pottery you found. They look v interesting indeed. Definitely quite old as you both thought. Will carry out some dating techniques and get back to you.

Maybe I can come over next weekend and we can dig the site further? Is that convenient to you?

Charles

From: Fee Hunter
To: Charles Lattey
Subject: Hi Charles

Charles,
Many thanks for taking the time to work on the pottery fragments. Much appreciated. Looking forward to hearing the results.
It would be great if you can come and help us search the area further. How about Saturday morning around 11.00?
Regards Fee
PS There is one other thing. James and I have been exploring the cellars under my house and we've been finding some interesting things. Weird as well as interesting I should say. Anyway there's a fourth cellar we want to open up. Maybe you'd be able to help us with that? I'll do you a nice lunch to make it worth your while!

CHAPTER 27

This time I am nervous as reluctantly I approach the cupboard under the stairs. Charles has arrived and James is showing him round the house. I am tasked with opening up the trapdoor so we can take a look at the last cellar, the one under the sitting room. James will have to pick the lock.

Despite being nervous about the prospect of opening up this last cellar I am nevertheless intrigued. Why is it locked? What if anything are we going to find?

I lift the catch and unlatch the small door beneath the staircase. Slowly I take hold of the iron bolt on the trapdoor and slide it back. Although uneasy and rather on edge about what we might find I am determined to get it over and done with. After talking at length to the vicar I have decided to have the house blessed in order to remove any spirits or lingering forces and this last unopened cellar has to be dealt with before we can move on so there's nothing for it except to go forward and take advantage of Charles' offer of help.

Gingerly I drop the trapdoor flaps down into the void. The cellar is dark and uninviting, the familiar mustiness rising from below. Realising that my hands are cold I rub them together to warm them and then taking a couple of deep breaths I switch on the light at the top of the stairs. Peering down into the now brightly lit cellar the stark brightness of the unshaded bulb makes the cellar look less forbidding.

I think back to my excitement the first time Judith and I explored the cellars. Was it really only last November? It seemed so long ago. We were so full of expectation. Little did we know then just what the ramifications would be. I remembered the key we'd found in one of the alcoves. Would we ever find out which door it fitted? And the discovery of Thomas and Mary Crabbe's riddle that had led to the blessing of Louisa's grave. That was surely one good thing to have come out of all this.

But getting involved with Eliza and Rose's past and their association with Gardner. That had been ill-fated. It's not Eliza or Rose who are causing me harm I say to myself. I'm sure they were good people. Just villagers doing what they could to help both themselves and local folk. I don't imagine they ever did bad magic. I'm sure these weird goings on are linked in some way to their activities of the past but something tells me it's not actually them. No, it must be other forces that have somehow got drawn in.

Now I can hear Charles and James approaching. Just act normally I tell myself and keep your edginess in check.

"So you can pick locks?" Charles is saying to James as they enter the study. "Another sign of a misspent youth by the sound of it."

"It sure is," replies James grinning. "And that's only part of it. I won't even begin to tell you the rest. Anyway Fee you've opened things up. Great."

"What amazing cellars," Charles says leaning over my shoulder and peering through the trapdoor. "And you say there are four separate rooms down there?"

"Yes. We were surprised at the size of them although the ceiling is quite low. You'll have to watch your head."

"Well let's get on with it," says James. "Charles is keen to start working on the dig behind the garage when we're done. He's also got some info on the pottery."

"That's great. Anyway it's all ready for you. Just follow me down the stairs. The steps are quite solid by the way Charles. We've been down several times."

I ease myself through the trapdoor and carefully descend the wooden steps. Charles and James follow and soon we are all three standing by the carved oak door. I remembered speculating with Judith all those months ago as to why it should be so ornately carved and she had said that it might be because it was an important place. Now we were going to find out if she was right.

James grasps the round metal ring with both hands and gives it a turn, probably out of habit because both he and I knew it was locked. Then he takes a bradawl from his pocket together with a couple of screwdrivers. Inserting the pointed end of the bradawl into the lock and using one of the screwdrivers he tries to click the lock open.

"No good," he grunts after a few tries. "Charles do you have any better instruments? I need something pointed, maybe with a small hook on the end. I must admit I've never picked such an old lock. I thought it would be easy."

"I'm sure I've got something. I'll go and have a look," says Charles. Climbing the wooden staircase he disappears through the hatch. Minutes later he returns carrying a few tools. "Try one of these."

James looks carefully at each of them and then selects a long thin instrument with a hook at one end. Inserting the bradawl in the lock again and using the hook he feels his way carefully inside the keyhole trying to locate the locking mechanism. "Ah," suddenly as he deftly manoeuvres the instrument, "got it." With a click the lock opens. "Here we go. We're in!"

Grasping the metal ring he twists it with both hands. This time the door swings open as James expectantly shines the torch through the door.

⁕

I couldn't believe my eyes.

"Look at all this stuff!" said Charles in amazement. "Did you know it was here?"

"No of course not," I said shocked at the sight before us.

"We've never been into this cellar before," added James. "We had no idea what was in here. We did know that previous occupants in the

1940s were practising witchcraft. We found a few photos and recipes and bits and pieces but nothing like this."

Even in the restricted torchlight I could see that the room housed an enormous cache of witchcraft related paraphernalia. There was a large circle marked out centrally on the floor in black paint and each quartile of the sphere was marked in red, N for north, S for south, E for east and W for west. So this is Rose and Eliza's circle I thought. This must be where the coven met. We'd often wondered where it was.

I could see that at the far side there was a raised altar covered in a richly embroidered cloth. Two candles still stood beside a pair of tall carved figures as if awaiting the return of Eliza and Rose. To the front of the altar was a large book. Maybe it's their Book of Shadows I thought apprehensively, wondering what it might contain.

Round the edges of the room neatly placed on uniform wooden shelves were all kinds of objects. My eye took in a number of half burnt candles, what looked like some chunky pieces of slate, a set of large copper pans, some silver-coloured chalices and some bone china cups and saucers. And on the floor under one of the shelves over to the right was a large black cauldron next to a couple of smaller brass cauldrons. Hanging from a hook in the far corner I could see several black cloaks with pointed hoods and white linings. The hoods were embroidered with intricate patterns in silver thread.

"I'll go and get one of the halogen lights," said James looking stunned as he moved away from the open doorway. I could see that Charles was just as surprised as James and myself.

"Never found anything like this then?" I asked him somewhat drained but determined to keep my cool.

"No never," he replied in astonishment as he gazed at the objects amassed before him.

"Although as an archaeologist one does get to know quite a lot about the occult and the paranormal," he added, "what with all the links back to pagan times and all the myths and ritual."

"I know," I said. "I looked into these things on the net when we found the original items."

James returned carrying one of the small round halogen lights. "Let's have a closer look at this hoard. They must've been a lot more active than we thought," he said stooping as he passed through the low arched doorway. I followed him uneasily with Charles close behind me.

James switched on the lamp and placed it in the centre of the black painted circle instantly illuminating the room. Although everything was covered in layers of dust it was obvious that the objects were solid and well made. Where had they obtained all of these things from? And where had they got the money? Rose and Eliza hadn't come across as ladies of means.

Torn by my desire to close up the cellar and get myself well away from this unexpected cache and my conflicting reluctant interest in the find, I picked up one of the silver chalices. The metal felt cold in my hands. It was heavy and slightly flared in shape. The stem was elaborately embossed and the bowl was delicately engraved with unrecognisable rows of signs and symbols.

"Just look at these," I said brushing the dust off with my hand. "They're beautiful. And see, there are more than a dozen of them. I suppose one for each member of the coven."

"Eliza said something about ten being a good number if I remember rightly," said James. He moved over to examine one of the large pieces of slate on the far shelf. "There's some kind of labyrinth carved on this slate. Very intricate. I think I'm right that labyrinths are connected with the underworld?" he said tracing the raised path with his finger.

"You are," said Charles. "The labyrinth is associated with Mother Earth and the entrance to the underworld."

"So what use would a labyrinth have been to Eliza and Rose?" I asked.

"It's what is known as a maze stone. As you know, in witchcraft the circle is an important symbol. It's seen as the space between worlds, somewhere witches are able to develop their powers by channelling the earth's energy," replied Charles moving over to where James was standing. "They would have used that maze stone within the circle to help draw down power by 'finger walking' the path. Much in the same way as you're doing," he continued as he inspected the stone in James' hands.

"Maybe I'd better stop," said James quickly. "I'm not sure I want to get involved in all that."

"Certainly not," I put in sharply

"They talk about the 'riddle of the maze stones'. I believe you can also get a reading from them, a bit like working tarot cards. Not sure how it's done," Charles went on. "Stones like these are found all over. It's the sort of thing that's quite often found on digs."

"You must have to know about so many different things as an archaeologist. It's quite mind-blowing," I observed.

"I suppose one does cover a lot of ground one way and the other," replied Charles. "But if you're interested in things of the past then it's not onerous. I love my work and there's always so much that's new to discover. Like this, for example and like your pottery in the garden."

"Well we're not doing badly," I said with a faint smile. "What with one historian and one archaeologist both conveniently on site."

"Anyway," put in James. "What are we going to do with all this stuff? It's probably quite valuable or at least some of it is."

"I don't know," I said, carefully avoiding the circle in the middle as I skirted the room and walked over to look more closely at the altar. I put out my hand and felt the heavily embroidered cloth. It was cream with bright reds and greens almost like a church altar cloth. I noticed that the statues at the back were standing on some kind of raised podium which was covered with a dark blue and gold cloth. The ornately sculpted bronze figurines had an eastern appearance and elaborate head dresses, a god and goddess each seated on an extravagant throne. What do they represent I wondered. They must have some significance.

I could not bring myself to touch the book but I was sure it was Rose and Eliza's Book of Shadows. Beneath the dust I could see that the cover was made of soft green leather and there was a large gold pentacle embossed in the centre. Underneath was the name Eliza Cann.

"This is amazing!" said Charles. "It's just great to find all this stuff." He took out his camera. "Hm," he said putting it away again, "I think I'd better wait until we can give these pieces a good old dust down. Best to get a good shot of them."

James was quiet and obviously deep in thought as he walked slowly round the room staring at the objects. He picked up a large flat piece of wood and brought it over to us. It was gold-coloured with letters of the alphabet painted in black across the middle. Round the edges were writhing serpents and I could see the words 'good and evil' at the bottom and 'past and future' at the top.

"It's an ouija board," exclaimed Charles. "I haven't seen one in a long while."

"Look there," I said pointing at the bottom of the piece of wood. "It says Sorcerer's Apprentice Weejee Board. That's not how you spell it is it?"

"No," said Charles looking closely at the board. "The proper spelling is O U I J A. I suppose there must be a reason for spelling it like that. Beats me."

"Hey," said James suddenly. "What about donating all this stuff to the Witchcraft Museum in Boscastle. You know Paul McEwan, the chap who owns it, I'm sure he would know what's worth displaying in the museum and that way we could get rid of it quickly."

"Yeah," I said brightening up, "that's not a bad idea. We could get rid of all this stuff in one fell swoop."

"And you'd be preserving Eliza and Rose's collection," said James. "In some ways I think you're duty-bound to keep them together. They'd probably even get a mention on the displays."

"I suppose the thing to do is for me to give Paul a bell and see what he thinks. I'm sure they're always looking for new artefacts," I said walking carefully back round the edge of the circle. I stopped as I reached the doorway.

"What do you think Charles?" I asked.

"Well I haven't been to the museum but I have heard of it," he replied. "I think it sounds like a good idea. Anyway shall we shut this room up and get on with the dig? I'm itching to get going."

"Good idea," said James picking up the halogen lamp and bending his head as we filed through the door. He pulled the door to behind him and twisted the metal ring decisively until it clicked shut.

"I think we'll leave the rest of it untouched," I said soberly. "Maybe Eliza and Rose were involved in more than we'd thought. I'm not sure I want to go there."

CHAPTER 28

Judith was sitting in one of the leather armchairs in the dining room. She cut a diminutive figure, being less than five feet tall. She probably doesn't really know what tall means I thought. There was something on Breakfast TV the other day about a man who was seven foot four. How can you imagine that when you are five feet tall and cannot see?

"Anyway I'm worried about Tom," she was saying. "I really don't like the dangers of his job."

"Well I think it was just bad luck. His being in the wrong place at the wrong time," I said lightly trying to be more ebullient than I actually felt. "Let's face it, lots of journalists and researchers carry valuable cameras and other equipment in all sorts of places. Being mugged is not that commonplace."

"No I know that," said Judith looking tense. "It's just all these strange things that have been happening and then those bizarre finds in the cellar. It's all getting to me."

"I know. It's been getting to me too," I admitted. "But we've got to get on with life. Paul McEwan is coming up from Boscastle next Saturday. He'll be taking the whole caboodle away. So let's hope that will clear things up. Now I've got to get on with organising the blessing of the house and cellars."

"How are you going to go about that?" asked Judith. "I know the Bishop wasn't much help."

"Heck no. He was no help at all. His office point blank refused to allow me to speak to him or anyone else. This woman just said I should look at a site on the web, something called the Acorn Christian Foundation. A fat lot of use. There was nothing of help to me on the website."

"So what next?" asked Judith.

"Well Dan Ellis from the Chapel said I should speak to the Methodist Superintendant, someone called Llewellyn Price. Apparently he's the equivalent of an Anglican Bishop but on a smaller scale. And hopefully much more helpful." I said indignantly.

"I thought there was supposed to be someone within the Diocese of each Bishop who carried out exorcisms?" said Judith looking surprised.

"Well so did I," I replied, "but not this Bishop. Unless his assistant is over-bossy as well as over-protective. Anyway I shan't contact his office again. I've got the Super's telephone number and I'll ring him later."

"Is that what they call him, the Super?" asked Judith.

"Apparently so."

"So Dan Ellis thinks the Super will be able to help?" said Judith looking a bit more reassured.

"I do hope so," I said vehemently. "I really want to get this sorted. As soon as possible."

"Too right," said Judith. "It's been going on long enough!"

"I'll give Llewellyn Price a ring a bit later and try to get him to visit next week. After Paul McEwan has been up from Cornwall to clear the cellars. He seems quite excited about our finds."

"Well I'm glad someone is excited about it," said Judith abruptly. "Sorry I do sound rather grumpy at the moment. You know that's not like me."

"Of course I do. I'm the same. I've been quite short with both James and Tom lately. They probably think we're a pair of old witches!"

"Don't even joke about that, Fee. I really don't want to tempt fate," Judith paused looking worried again. "Anyway, tell me more about the pottery finds in the garden," she continued and I could see that she was anxious to move away from the subject. "You said Charles was very helpful."

"Yes, he's a great guy. Of Jamaican descent, born and bred in the UK. Decided he was going to be an archaeologist because he was wanted to find out more about Black British heritage in this country."

"I don't suppose there are too many black archaeologists?" put in Judith.

"No. I shouldn't think so. Anyway interestingly what he found is that our Black communities go way, way back, as far as AD 208. To when a group of north Africans came here from what is now known as Libya. And there may possibly have been even earlier migrants."

"That's interesting," said Judith. "I seem to remember that history books imply it was the Slave Trade that brought black people to this country."

"Yes and that's what he wanted to disprove," I said. "Which he did. He wanted to prove that the Black British population have a distinct heritage here long before that."

I paused, rummaging through the sheets of paper Charles had left with me. "Anyway getting back to the finds here's what he said," I continued, pulling out the note he had written about dating pottery:

'The sorts of things I would look for are:
— whether the pieces are handmade or wheel thrown?
— is it earthenware or stoneware?
— the type of pot it's from (i.e. jar, jug, bowl, etc)
— the texture of the pottery (is it coarse? smooth? sandy? soapy?)
— is there a glaze — what colour/type is it?
— the shape of the rim
— are there inclusions in the fabric of the pot and if so what are they made of?
— is there any decoration?

The list goes on. It's a combination of experience and looking at all of these factors which enables me to date pottery. Sometimes you simply can't tell, for example if there's not enough of it or if it's badly worn.'

"So that's how they go about it," I said looking up from the sheet.
"I thought you'd find it interesting."

"It certainly is fascinating," replied Judith. "It's great having people in the know to help with one's questions. By the way what's an inclusion?" she added.

"I think Charles said that it's anything foreign encased within the clay. Like small stones or grit for example," I explained. "Anyway because he knows his stuff he was able to date the pieces at around the fifteenth or sixteenth century, almost certainly parts of a smallish jug made at the kilns at Brill which is fairly close."

"Amazing to be able to tell so much from just a few small pieces," exclaimed Judith. "What would the jug have been used for?"

"Wine I should think," I said laughing. "The monks used to love their wine and beer. I don't think this jug would have been big enough for their beer. What he goes on to say is," I said looking down again at Charles' carefully written notes:

'Basically the next thing I would do to confirm an estimated date is to look at and handle pieces of similar pottery that are of known date. If we haven't got anything similar I would go to the Ashmolean. A guesstimate isn't good enough. We have to back up our impression with hard evidence.'

"Sounds intriguing to me," said Judith. "Quite off-the-cuff and yet quite scientific."

"I know what you mean but they've got to start somewhere when they're dating an unknown piece," I commented.

"What else does he say?" asked Judith.

"Well he goes on to talk about the pottery from the Brill kilns:

'Brill-Boarstall ware, (so called because it was made in kilns at Brill and Boarstall) is very common all around the area and beyond. Pots were being made there from the 13th/14th century onwards, right up until the 19th century.

By the 14th century we see patches of very attractive speckled green glaze on the pots, the green being caused by copper oxide in the glazing mixture, over a pale orange fabric. Jugs, bowls, and jars are the most common sorts of pot produced.

Later on, the green glaze is replaced by clear, or brown glazes, but over the same orange fabric, as different oxides were used in the glazing mixture.'

"That's definitely it," I added. "The sherds we found are just like his description. Well that dates the jug at around the fifteenth or sixteenth century."

"As old as that?" said Judith looking surprised.

"Apparently," I answered slowly. "I'm just thinking about all this. Maybe the house was built on what was part of the grounds of the abbey? Maybe it was their kitchen garden or something. The grounds would've been vast and stretched in all directions from the abbey."

"Yeah, I think you might be right," said Judith thoughtfully. "That explains the pieces of broken pottery, it might have been their refuse tip."

"Thanks a bunch! Now you're saying that my house was built on top of a rubbish dump."

"I don't quite mean it like that," said Judith laughing.

"I know, I'm only joking," I said laughing with her. "They would have to have buried their rubbish somewhere."

"And you said Charles found more pieces of pottery?" asked Judith.

"Yes he found quite a lot more. He said they were probably pieces from several jugs of the same type and date. And there were also some plain terracotta pieces which may have come from some bowls of similar age."

"Well that seems to indicate that it must have been some kind of household waste tip," said Judith.

"Yes it does seem likely. Charles also found some bones. Animal bones he thinks. He's not sure yet how far they date back. He's coming back to extend the dig at the weekend."

And then I had a sudden idea. "You know Judith, maybe that's it. May be the house is called Middle House because it's bang in between the castle and the abbey. Maybe it was given that name when it was built in the 1540s or at some later time."

"Could be."

"It's been intriguing me since I first moved in as you know. I just want to know where the name came from, what is its relevance. I wonder if I'm right?"

"Names generally come from somewhere," said Judith practically. "But I'm afraid if you are right I don't think we'll ever really be able to confirm it. The dead can't speak."

❦

After Judith has gone home to get back to work I stand looking out of the dining room window across at the house where once the abbey stood. Could that really be where the house name came from, Middle House, situated exactly between castle and abbey? It's logical enough. I wonder when house names began to be used. Who would have named it Middle House? Maybe Michael Baines can help on that one.

A bit later I'm heading for the fields with Barnie. Waiting to cross the road I turn and look back at the house, an unusual house with its long low frontage overshadowed by a steeply sloping roof. As I turn, I catch sight of a dark haired man, who looks to be in his early forties, dressed in a lightweight black shirt and black trousers just level with my neighbour's house and walking in my direction. He is moving swiftly and with purpose.

Turning away to check the traffic I cross the road, Barnie pulling at my side eager to reach the fields. Instinctively I glance back towards the man, a stranger who I've never seen in the village before. As I watch he reaches my gate and then to my surprise I see him apparently glide seamlessly through the wall of my house. In an instant he is gone.

It's like a scene from Harry Potter. Just like the young Harry when he walks through the wall of Platform 9A at the railway station with Ron Weasley. I can't believe my eyes and yet I saw him. I know that I wasn't imagining things.

So, if he walked through the wall of my house, where is he now? Is he in the sitting room or where has he gone, which room is he in, has he been there before? If so what is he doing watching me and James? Why can't we feel his presence? A maelstrom of unanswerable questions hurtle through my mind as I stand and stare at the far end of the house.

Is he dead, a ghost? What is he, who is he? And remembering what Robert Delforth said is the connection with me or with the house? It's uncannily like what happened with the little girls. They too disappeared completely and I've never seen them again although that doesn't mean that they aren't around of course.

I stand looking at the corner of the house for some moments waiting to see if the man re-emerges. There's no sign of anyone and I'm left standing, wondering what is going on, wondering whether I could in fact have imagined it after all.

But no, I'm positive I did see him. I saw him pass through the wall into the sitting room. He was there. I can describe him in detail with his lightweight black clothes, his dark curly hair, slim, between forty and forty five, maybe five feet eight or nine tall.

So just what does all this mean, am I surrounded by ghosts?

CHAPTER 29

"I managed to find out quite a lot about your family tree on your father's side," Robert Delforth said to me as we sat in the garden. "I remembered that you said your maiden name was Linnell and also that your uncle Eric might be buried in the churchyard. So I did some investigations and surfed the net."

It was early evening and the warm summer day was coming to an end. Robert turned up unannounced, unusually for him as he is always rather formal. I invited him in and we meandered down the garden with a cup of coffee.

"I thought you didn't like PCs let alone the net?" I said with a smile as we sat down at the table on the patio surrounded by tubs of brightly coloured fuchsias tumbling from their pots, a riot of pinks and purples.

"Too right, I don't. They're confounded modern things I could do without," he replied wryly. "However given they're there one might as well make use of them. I also used the library, it's much more user-friendly. Wonderful fuchsias by the way, much more prolific than mine."

"Thanks they do seem to like it here, south facing I suppose."

"Anyway," Robert continued, "what I discovered is that your uncle Eric is indeed buried in the village. His gravestone is unusual, very long and flat. It seems he married someone called Cann, Jennifer Cann in 1944. Died very young at the age of thirty two in 1952."

"Hang on. Did you say Cann, C-A-N-N?" I asked incredulously sitting forward in my chair and looking earnestly at the vicar. My uneasiness returned and I felt a frisson of fear. How could this be? How on earth could I be related, even if only by marriage, to Rose and Eliza?

"Yes, that's right," said Robert.

"That means it's possible I'm related to Eliza and Rose, the two sisters who lived in the house. The two witches I told you about! Their surname was Cann. I can't believe it. How can that be?"

"Hold on," said Robert putting his hand on my arm gently. "It doesn't have to be the same Canns. It may be a common name round here. And anyway would it matter if you were related to them?"

My mind was racing. Why had I felt compelled to buy the house? It had been a forgone conclusion, a done deal as soon as I looked at it. I had to buy it. Was it somehow mysterious events of the past that had brought me here, something to do with family connections of which I knew nothing?

"Have you got all this written down?" I asked rather abruptly trying to act rationally despite feeling quite unnerved.

"Well I have," said Robert alarmed at my reaction. "I'm afraid it's all on some scrappy pieces of paper," he continued reaching into his pocket.

"Just tell me more about what you found out. Please." I tried to be less sharp. "My father was Albert Linnell, born in 1934. He died aged 59 in 1993. Did all that tie up with your findings?"

"Yes," said Robert opening up the folded papers and flattening them on the patio table. "See here, if you go way back to the 1800s a certain Richard Cann had a son, John, and he was the father of Jennifer Cann who married your uncle in 1944," he said as he pointed to the roughly drawn family tree on the first piece of paper. He traced the line through to Jennifer Cann and there was her marriage to Eric Linnell in 1944, pencilled in on the side.

I gazed on in shocked disbelief, clasping my hands together tightly as he pointed again at the paper.

"You can see that Richard Cann had five children. The first died in infancy, then Eliza born in 1889, Rose in 1896, John in 1898 and Ronald in 1891," he went on.

"So let's get this right. Jennifer must have been the niece of Rose and Eliza. Am I right?"

"Yes, that's the way it seems," said Robert.

"It's just too far-fetched," I exclaimed staring sceptically at the torn piece of paper. "No way! I can't believe it. Me related to Rose and Eliza."

"Well, I don't think I've made a mistake," said Robert gently. "I managed to find some of this on the internet and then I checked it out carefully at the library. They're very helpful you know with tracing family trees. They seem to know what they're talking about."

"What about my father's side and my uncle Eric," I asked uncertainly. "Did you write that part down too?"

"Yes," said Robert reaching for the second piece of paper. "Look Gordon Linnell married Patricia …."

"That's right," I cut in. "My grandfather was Gordon and my grandmother was Patricia. Patricia Thorn." I pulled the piece of paper closer towards me and blinked doubtfully at the roughly sketched family tree in Robert's tiny black handwriting.

"It's right," I gasped. "There's Eric and my father and his five other brothers and sisters. It was a large family. And there's me born in 1978, only child. Albert and Priscilla, my parents."

I felt utterly bewildered and bemused. What did all this mean? "I'm going to have to think about all this," I said. "Long and hard. There's been so much happening here since I moved into the village and now all these uncanny connections with the past. It just doesn't seem possible. Where's it all leading?"

I moved over to the patio edge and stared down at the grass apprehensively. Was I really related to those two women? What was it that which had brought me here, to the house? What hold had they got over me? Should I put the house up for sale and get the hell away from it all?

Someone, something was drawing me in, sucking me into some kind of peculiar machination, some kind of conspiracy. I didn't seem to be in charge of my own life anymore, just when I thought I was making new beginnings.

"I think you've just got to take your time and try not to get too upset," said Robert, standing up and moving over to my side. He was trying not to let his concern show but I could see that he was worried. "After all does it matter?" he added.

"I don't know," I said pensively. "It might matter. It might be the reason for all these goings on, then again I suppose it could just be a coincidence. Life is full of coincidences or so they say."

"Coincidences do seem to be part of life's rich fabric," said Robert. "And they don't always bode ill." He paused and put his hand on my shoulder. "Anyway," he added, "you tell me that the Methodist Superintendent is going to carry out a blessing of the house on Friday. That sounds like a good thing. I'm just sorry the Bishop couldn't be of any assistance. I don't know what's going on there, it's absolutely part of his remit."

"It doesn't matter. The Superintendent, someone called Llewellyn Price, sounded really helpful. Immediately said he would come over and carry out a blessing. Said that he was sure it would be of help. He made me feel a whole lot better I can tell you."

"Good, I'm glad to hear that," Robert said. "You must tell me how it goes. Maybe I can call round after he's been?"

"Of course," I said. "You've been a great help in so many ways. Thank you very much. You must have enough on your plate without all this."

"It's my job. It's what I do," said Robert warmly. "I do hope I haven't upset you too much. I was only trying to help."

"Well I suppose I had to know sometime. Maybe it's a good thing after all. At least it helps to explain my connection with the house, the inescapable allure of the place."

"I think you're right," said Robert. "Sometimes these things are meant to be. All part of the grand scheme of things. Anyway I must go. I've got some more visits to make." He moved over to the end of the patio.

"What a lovely garden this is," he said leaning over the balustrade. "I like the way it slopes down in three different levels."

"Yes I love it. It's such an unusual garden. Another one of the reasons I had to buy the house actually," I said momentarily distracted from my worries.

"Such a wonderful view of the fields, rolling down the valley like that," said Robert his gaze following the sweeping landscape. "And this must be the dig you told me about, where you found the pieces of medieval pottery?" he asked turning to the plastic sheet covering the flowerbed at the end of the garage.

"Yes," I said. "Now that was a coincidence. Barnie was chasing a squirrel and when it escaped over the fence he must by chance have found something interesting. That's when he started digging madly. James went over to stop him and uncovered some very unusual pieces of pottery. He took them to Oxford and a colleague of his was able to date them. I can show them to you if you like."

※

Tom leaned across the kitchen table, peering over my shoulder, as I opened up the laptop and booted up. Now that Paul McEwan had taken every last item from the cellar I felt a tremendous sense of relief.

The house seemed brighter and more cheerful. Ever since James and I had opened up the last cellar with Charles there had been an uncustomary darkness about the place. I had felt a sense of foreboding, something I couldn't put my finger on. The shadows somehow seemed longer, the rooms chilly despite the heating. Now I felt as if things had returned to the way they were before. The house was warm and enveloping and seemed to wrap itself around me as the nights drew in.

Typing 'Boscastle Museum of Witchcraft' into the search engine I pressed search and up came a whole list of websites connected with the museum. Strange to think that before April I hadn't even heard of the museum. Now here I was donating an enormous collection to them and Rose and Eliza's names would take their place in history, the very same Rose and Eliza who were apparently related to me. It was unbelievable.

"This is the best website," I said clicking on the sixth web address down. "See you can take a guided tour," I continued pressing the tour button. "Look there's a labyrinth or maze stone like the ones we found." I flicked through the artefacts. "And those are similar to the chalices. And this copper pan is almost identical to one of theirs."

"Amazing," said Tom. "You realise how widespread witchcraft was and probably still is when you see all of this. I'm sorry I only got a quick glimpse of everything before the guy from the museum took the stuff."

"Well you've been away quite a bit recently and I wasn't going to delay things I'm afraid," I said apologetically.

"Oh no, I wouldn't have wanted you to. I know you needed to move quickly on this. I just might have taken a closer look at it all. Could have been an article there," he said with a chuckle.

"Maybe but it's for the best that it's all gone now. I just wanted to get rid of the lot of it and I don't really want to be connected with it anymore, not even in the form of an article. Anyway it's gone to the right place."

"Sure," said Tom. "And Eliza and Rose would have been glad if they'd known what was going to happen to all their prized possessions. Better than splitting all the pieces up and either throwing them away or giving them to people who wouldn't appreciate their intrinsic qualities."

"You're right. Staff at the museum will research and display the most important pieces and the rest will go into the archives and possibly be shown at a later time. I certainly feel it was the right thing to do."

"Anyway Judith and I will be going down to Boscastle for a long weekend later this month or early in October," said Tom. "We may even be able to see some of the things in situ, depends on whether or not they've had time to research and catalogue any of the items."

"I suppose that would be something, to see dedications to Eliza and Rose. I only hope my name won't be mentioned. I don't want anyone getting wind of where all the items came from."

"You did say that to Paul didn't you?" asked Tom. "The fact that you wanted to remain anonymous."

"Oh yes, but maybe I'll email him and just remind him," I said. "Good point. He might just forget in all the excitement of his new-found additions to his collection. He did say that it's not often such a big cache is discovered in one place."

"It makes you wonder you know, if you had such a collection under your very feet whether there could be other hidden collections elsewhere?" said Tom thoughtfully.

"I rather expect there must be. Some of the items on display in the Museum were found or donated only recently. Apparently there's a particular connection with witchcraft and Cornwall," I said remembering some of the write-ups in Boscastle.

"I imagine it was, and probably is, just as prevalent all over the country. The Museum has more than likely highlighted it in Cornwall when actually it's all over the place."

"I'm just glad we've got rid it all," I said thankfully. "I'll email Paul and then we can walk over the road to The Black Horse. James said he'll give us a bell when he gets to the village. He's going to pick Judith up and meet us there. I'm sure you could do with a beer."

"Too right," said Tom as he straightened his tall lean frame. He went and leaned against the kitchen sink.

"And how are you now?" I asked. "After the mugging. I know it's been a few months now but do you feel you're completely over it?"

"Oh I'm alright. Fit as a fiddle," replied Tom. "No real damage done except for my camera. And I'm getting on very well with my new one, another Nikon D3."

"Well just you be careful," I said soberly. "Things could've been a whole lot worse. You could have been killed or very seriously injured."

"I know," said Tom equally seriously. "I won't let them catch me a second time."

CHAPTER 30

Whichever window I looked out of I could see the leaden sky was dark and heavy with low lying rain-filled clouds stretching in all directions. Even though it was mid-morning it seemed like five o'clock in the afternoon. Cars swooshed by every so often, their windscreen wipers battling to keep up with the drenching downpour. The rain was running like a fast-moving river along the road and the gutter in front of the house was already full to the brim. As I peered out of the front I only hoped the drains would contain the gushing rain which seemed to be never ending. Already it had lasted for hours.

Inside the house was dark and dreary. I had just gone round the house and switched on the lights in all the downstairs rooms and turned the central heating on to make the place more welcoming. Now I stood at the window looking out for my visitor. As I watched a small red car pulled up outside and a man dressed in a black raincoat emerged. Taking a black bag from the passenger seat he reached towards the back seat and took hold of a large grey umbrella. He unfurled it and walked hurriedly over to the side gate.

Quickly I rushed to the front door as he came round to the back of the house. Opening the door I ushered him inside, taking his dripping umbrella from him and stowing it carefully in the downstairs toilet.

"Do come through," I said. "I'm Fee Hunter. You must be Llewellyn Price."

"Yes, that's me," said Llewellyn extending his hand. "I don't think we've met before although I'm often in the village. Next door to you at the chapel."

"No, we haven't met," I replied appraising the softly spoken man as we shook hands. He was of medium height with greying curly hair and strikingly blue eyes. As he took off his wet raincoat and passed it to me I could see that he was dressed in well cut soft grey trousers and jacket with a cream shirt and integral dog collar. He was carrying a small black attaché case in one hand. There was something about him that right away made me feel special, that his whole attention was fixed solely on me. I could sense that he was a gentle person and someone I immediately knew I could trust.

"I've never actually met a 'Super' before," I continued with a nervous laugh as I closed the front door. "What do I call you?"

"Oh Llewellyn will do very well," he said genially. "We're really all very informal in the Methodist church."

"What about this terrible rain?" I said gazing out of the back window in the study. "It's like a cloud burst."

"It certainly is," Llewellyn said. "I was beginning to think that my poor little car wouldn't get me here. The roads are like rivers all the way from Buckingham."

"Well you may have to swim home," I joked tentatively, unsure as to whether it was appropriate to crack jokes with someone from the church in his position.

"I do hope not," he rejoined with a smile. "But fortunately I can swim." Feeling reassured I ushered him into the sitting room and offered him tea or coffee.

"No thank you," said Llewellyn. "I've already had several cups of tea at my last port of call. I sometimes find myself awash with it."

Gesturing to him to sit down on the settee I seated myself expectantly on the chaise longue opposite him.

"So tell me," began Llewellyn Price fixing me with his compelling blue eyes. "Tell me just what's been happening to you. Tell me all about it right from the start."

Barnie was lying sprawled out on the floor beside me motionless, cocking his ears every now and again when he heard a word of interest. Stroking him absentmindedly I carefully recounted all the events leading up to the present time, culminating with the male apparition I'd seen vanishing through the front of the house the other day.

"It was unnerving," I said edgily. "He was so real. There he was and then, as I watched, there he wasn't. It just makes me feel as if the house is full of ghosts."

"Oh I doubt that," said Llewellyn softly. "A haunting or an unrested spirit is usually a solitary one. Ghosts hardly ever make collective appearances."

"Well how come I've seen the two little girls, as well as the dark haired man?" I asked quizzically.

"I'm not sure," said Llewellyn, "but that doesn't mean the house is overrun with other world spirits."

"Well it does seem strange. These ghosts or 'other world spirits' as you call them have only appeared to me. James, my partner, hasn't seen anything," I said anxiously.

"From my experience," he paused for a moment, "ghostly appearances do not result in any danger to the person. In my thirty seven years in the church I've been involved in exorcisms in a fair number of places, mainly houses, and no real harm has befallen those who called me in."

"What do you mean, 'no real harm'?" I said picking up on his words.

"By that I mean no harm other than causing the person some anxiety, as in your case. Nothing more," he replied reassuringly. "So that's the second sighting you've seen isn't it?" he added.

"As far as I know," I said. "It does make me wonder if I've seen other things which weren't there."

"I do know what you mean," said Llewellyn understandingly and I was again struck by his eyes. "These things begin to make you doubt your very self."

"You're right. I just don't know what to believe or what to think anymore. And I haven't actually finished telling you the whole story. The other day Robert Delforth, the vicar, discovered that I may in fact be related to the two women I told you about. The ones who practised witchcraft here in this very house in the 1940s. You can't get much more entangled than that!"

"That does seem to be an odd coincidence," said Llewellyn looking somewhat surprised. "But if that is the case it's another reason why they wouldn't want any harm to come to you. Anyway," he continued, "as I explained to you over the phone the traditional way to remove unwelcome spirits is to carry out a blessing or exorcism. I've brought what I need with me," he said indicating the black bag lying next to him on the floor.

"Do you have to use a special cross?" I asked.

"Well it's customary to use quite a large cross, larger than I would normally carry about with me," replied Llewellyn reaching down and picking up his case. "Here. This is the one I use," he went on as he clicked open the clasp and pulled out a soft black velvet bag. Loosening the drawstring he carefully drew out a heavy-looking gold cross about eighteen centimetres in length.

"That's quite something," I breathed. "It's beautiful."

"Yes it is beautiful isn't it?" he replied. "It's a special cross, given to me as a present."

"Must be very heavy."

"It is. It feels special. Would you like to have a look at it?" he asked.

"Oh may I?" I put out my hand. The cross felt cold and heavy and I could see that it was engraved with an intricate design. "What are these," I asked indicating the markings.

"Well this is a Celtic cross. As you probably realise I'm Welsh," he said smiling. "And this cross was given to me by my father when I was quite young. I had already decided I would go into the church. He gave it to me to bring me the love of God and for it to stay with me throughout my life."

"It's lovely," I said handing the cross back to him. "Very special indeed. It has a good feeling about it, conveys a kind of peace and tranquillity somehow. So what will you do next?" I continued keen now to get on with things.

"Well I'd like to take you and your partner into every room in the house and then into the cellars and I'll say a prayer for you in each place. I'll pray that all evil be banished and that you will no longer be bothered by any presence," Llewellyn said.

"Oh dear, I'm afraid that James isn't here. He's away at a conference. I didn't think he needed to be here."

"I don't think that will matter, particularly as James doesn't seem to be affected by these things. In any case he will be included in my prayers."

"Do you use a particular or special kind of prayer?" I queried.

"Well Methodists are generally more informal than the Church of England and so I usually put together a suitable prayer myself which is what I shall do today. By the way you did say that all the artefacts would be removed from the cellar. Has that happened?"

"Oh yes, thankfully. The chap from Boscastle Museum came up at the weekend and took everything away. He was absolutely delighted. And so was I, I felt really good when it had all gone. The room is completely bare now."

"That's good," said Llewellyn. "It's always a good idea to remove anything from the house that might beckon or draw a presence to the place. Well done. You seem to have organised everything very efficiently."

"I do hope so," I said vehemently. "I'd just like to have this all over and done with and get things back to normal. James and I have painted out the black circle down there, so even that is gone now."

"Okay," said Llewellyn standing up. He held the gold cross in his right hand and gestured for me to stand too. "I think we'll start in here."

I stood up and moved over to where he was standing, aware that the rain was still gusting heavily against the windows. "Will either I or you feel anything?" I asked anxiously.

"No, I don't think so," he replied reassuringly. "I bring my infinite belief in God which is an absolute part of me to this place and you will feel the protection of my belief. You won't feel anything, except I'm sure relief after we have finished."

"That's good," I said breathing a sigh. "Shall we begin?"

Holding the cross in his hand Llewellyn slightly bowed his head and began:

"God, creator of all things, infinitely perfect, stand at my side now
As I pray to rid this place of those who are unrested.
May God who is everywhere, and here in this place, here in this
   room,

With your love so immense that nothing can ever separate us
     from you
And claiming the victory of Christ in his death and resurrection,
Help us now."

And at this point, he held up the cross in front of him, focusing all his concentration on it.

"We pray that all evil be banished from this place
And all that is harmful will leave. That the presence of God,
Which is beyond all human understanding,
Will settle in this place and within the hearts and lives of all who
     live here.
In the name of Jesus Christ. Amen."

He stood solemnly in silence for several moments before bowing his head again and then turning to look at me. "Shall we move on to the next room now?" Going through the doorway Llewellyn turned to me and said, "Nothing untoward about that was there?"

"No," I said, "I felt absolutely fine. Very peaceful. I could feel your inner strength being conveyed to me in some way. It felt all powerful, all embracing."

"That is what happens," he said nodding. "Because I have my absolute conviction it serves as a protectorate, to both you and myself. You really don't need to have any fear."

And so he went on to say a similar prayer in each of the downstairs rooms. Then he asked me to show him the way upstairs and carried out the same rite in the bedrooms and the bathroom.

"Now we need to proceed to the cellars," Llewellyn said gravely. "From what you say that would seem to be the most likely place for a presence to be felt."

We descended the stairs and I showed him into the study, opening the small wooden door under the stairs and revealing the wooden trapdoor. Pulling the bolt to the side I dropped the flaps down and switched on the light, flooding the cellar with its luminous glow.

He followed me down the steep staircase grasping the rope handrail behind me.

"Goodness me," he said looking about him in astonishment. "What a place. I don't think I've ever seen cellars quite like these. They must be very old."

"Yes, they are. 1540s or thereabouts. Hard to be precise as you can appreciate."

"And you say that they've been closed up for quite some time?" he asked.

"Yes, could be forty or fifty years or more."

"That could have a bearing," Llewellyn said thoughtfully. "You see your house has been lived in all that time whereas the cellars have been closed up. That could be why spirits from the other world have inhabited this place. They would have had nothing to keep them at bay."

"Oh," I said fearfully. "Does that mean they will be hard to banish?"

"Possibly. I may have to strengthen my prayers," he said quietly. "I just need to give it a bit of thought."

He stood with his hands clasped in front of him, his head bent, gazing at the stone floor lost in thought.

I was becoming concerned again. What if the blessing didn't work? Where would that leave James and I, would we have to move? I really couldn't face the thought of leaving the house and the village. Drawing my scarf and jacket more closely round me, I stood quietly in the cool cellar waiting for Llewellyn to make a move.

I gazed around the familiar white painted walls of the cellar. It remained bare just as it was when we had first opened it. I had no desire to keep anything in the cellars, not now, maybe never. I glanced back at Llewellyn. He was still standing motionless, deep in thought.

After some moments he said, "Yes, I have it now. I can begin if you're ready."

"Oh yes, I'm ready," I said hastily.

Llewellyn moved carefully to the centre of the cellar. Holding the cross in his right hand he began:

"In the name of Jesus Christ, our Lord and God,
   We undertake to repulse the attacks and deceits of all unclean spirits,

All invaders and those who wish the occupants of this house ill.
All evil spirits will be destroyed through the power of the cross,
Christ be with us and help us to rid this place of those who are unrested."

Again he held up the cross in front of him.

"All objects are freed from the possession of evil.
We pray that all evil be banished from this place now and forever.
And all that is harmful will leave.
We pray that the presence of God,
Which is beyond all human understanding,
Will settle in this place and within the hearts and lives of all who live here.
In the name of Jesus Christ. Amen."

He stood still with the cross held in front of him, his eyes closed and his head bowed.

I waited.

CHAPTER 31

The fire crackled and hissed as a lump of coal spat suddenly, sending bright red embers shooting sideways across the hearth.

"Lovely fire," said James lazily as he lay outstretched on the sofa. "One real consolation about the end of summer I suppose. Being able to light a fire."

"Absolutely," I raised my head from my book and glanced at the fire. "It's just great to shut out the world and be holed up in here on our own."

"It sure is," said James. "Anyway it seems you had a bit of an interesting time today," he added sitting up, "with Llewellyn's visit."

"It was definitely an unusual kind of day," I replied. "What with the dreadful weather. It was like all hell had been let loose. And the house was so dull and gloomy. I had to have all the lights on."

"Sounds like Llewellyn had to come through hell and high water to get here," said James laughing.

"Yeah, you could say that. And the rain was still absolutely torrential when he left. He got soaked getting back to his car. I could see from the window."

"So tell me a bit more about it. Did you feel anything unusual whilst he was here? What was the atmosphere like? Did you feel anything, any kind of presence in any of the rooms?"

"Well no, not really," I said. "I don't think I felt anything strange or untoward. I was surprised actually. I think I was expecting to feel the proverbial 'chill in the air' or weird atmosphere that you get in movies about the supernatural but there was none of that."

I paused. "Llewellyn did say that the strength of his belief would protect both him and myself. And that's what seemed to happen. There was no strange atmosphere, no feeling of another presence, nothing. I suppose it was his strong convictions and also his special Celtic cross of course."

"Extraordinary," said James. "I wish I'd been here."

"So do I. It would have been interesting to have had your view on what went on and to know whether you felt anything."

"And he went through the whole house, saying a prayer in each room you said?"

"He did. It took a while even though it didn't seem to at the time. It all went by in a flash although I can remember absolutely every single detail. The way Llewellyn moved, the way he held up the cross in front of him, the strength, the power of his words. Everything. It's imprinted on my mind."

"And Barnie. Did he seem to take notice of it all? I know what that dog's like."

"Well he was there in the sitting room when Llewellyn said the first prayer and he didn't seem to bat an eyelid. Didn't even move. So no, I don't think it affected him at all."

"What next?" enquired James. "Do we have to do anything?"

"Not as far as I know. Llewellyn just said to try and be relaxed and as normal as possible and things should be okay. I said I'd call him in a few days time."

"Well it's a relief isn't it?" said James, "getting rid of all that stuff and finding Llewellyn to help us. There can't be too many people around these days who are exorcists, or at least exorcists on the level."

"No, you're right. I wouldn't have wanted to let a quack loose in the house," I said lightly.

"Anyway, moving on," said James getting up and putting a couple of logs and some more coal on the fire, "Charles and I had lunch yesterday at The Elephant and Child. He was filling me in on some recent finds. He said to say hi."

"I like that pub. Food's good. How was he?" I asked. "We must have him over for a meal soon. He's been really helpful."

The building is large and cavernous and there is a mass of motionless black creatures crowded together at the far end. Blinking to refocus my eyes I can make out hundreds maybe thousands of bats hanging in the crumbling ruins of a huge barn of a place. The once magnificent roof has almost completely caved in. Fallen amber-coloured tiles and thickset rotting beams lie strewn across the floor, but in spite of the ruinous state of the place a slight cover or awning remains above the ingeniously sheltered bat colony.

I stand transfixed. My eyes glued to the black mass of rubber-like shiny bodies. They look unreal. Shifting my feet I wonder if I'm in danger of them swarming towards me but there is no movement from the roost. Remembering that bats sleep in the daytime I take a couple of steps forward trying to see what they look like more clearly, but as I do so I catch a slight ruffling movement on the right hand side of the mass. It might be the wind. It might not.

Stopping in my tracks I turn round and move swiftly back, retracing my steps towards the entrance of the derelict building. The huge doors have long since fallen from their hinges and smashed down on to the rocky ground, splintering into long jagged fragments which stand like fallen sentinels on guard in this now ruined shell of a building.

As I reach the portal I stumble and fall.

Suddenly awake I recall the dramatic images of my dream. A heaving mass of bodies. A bat colony. As I come to I remember. It was in Curacao on honeymoon with Mark. Visiting a dilapidated landhouse on a long disused plantation we came upon this massive maternity roost. A couple of Curacaons we met were showing us the usually unseen side of the island when we spent a completely unexpected couple of days looking at things the average tourist would never see.

Images of the bats and the immense ruin are still imprinted vividly in my mind and I shake my head to distance myself. I turn to take comfort from a sleeping James who is snuggled down, almost hidden beneath the duvet. Reaching out to stroke him I slide out of bed.

I'm sure I will get no sleep now that my mind is so active so I make my way soundlessly downstairs to the kitchen and boil milk for a cup of drinking chocolate. Barnie follows me and plumps himself down by my feet. I sit at the kitchen table idly glancing at yesterday's unopened post and take a few sips of chocolate.

※

Feeling tired the next morning after my night of broken sleep I glanced out of the kitchen window whilst making breakfast, surprised at the lack of traffic. To my concern I noticed that there were several long spidery cracks in the middle of the road emanating from a slight dip. A couple of workmen were busy inspecting the cracks and I could see that they had put up 'Road Closed' signs with red and white temporary barriers about twenty five metres apart. Alarmed I ran out of the house, through the side gate and accosted the men.

"What's going on?" I asked.

"Road subsidence," said one of the men abruptly.

"We've had t'block off the road and divert the traffic," said the other.

"But why?" I asked, shocked. "These things don't just happen. The road was alright yesterday. There's never been any sign of a problem here before."

"Well these things can be caused by all kinds of things," said the second man.

"And we're busy," said the first man impatiently. "We've got other places to go to."

"What sort of things?" I asked looking at his more sympathetic colleague.

"Well you can get cracks like these when there's been a build up of water. Can be caused by what's known as a swallow hole or depression underground. They're sending out the Highways team t'take a look," he replied glancing sideways at his surly companion.

"Is it likely to get worse?" I asked anxiously looking back towards the house.

"Can't say," said the man. "Anyway we're putting up diversionary signs at either end of the village. That'll stop the traffic making it worse at any rate. We've applied for a Traffic Management Order. That'll last for fourteen days in the first instance."

"And what about my house," I said, "and my neighbour's house? Is all this going to affect our houses?"

"Don't rightly know. I suppose it could have an effect."

"What kind of effect?" I asked.

"Well it's possible that it could impact on your foundations."

"It was just so sudden!" I exclaimed feeling distraught. Bernard my neighbour joined me looking at the cracks in disbelief.

"Never seen anything like this," he said apprehensively. "It doesn't look good. We don't even get that much traffic now. Not as much as we used to."

The surly colleague was starting to walk back to his van so I asked the more helpful man what would happen next.

"Well they'll likely carry out a ground radar survey t'see if there's danger of further subsidence," he replied. "And they'll also do some bore hole scans t'see what's going on under the road surface. They'll be taking advice from a structural engineer so you don't need to worry. They're experts."

"How soon will they be here?" I asked dubiously. "I'm mostly worried about our houses. We need to find out about the risk to our foundations."

"Won't be long. Can't say exactly. This morning I should think," he said looking up the road towards his colleague who was standing at the driver's side of the yellow council van glowering impatiently. "I'd best be going," he continued. "We've got a heck of a lot of jobs today after all that rain."

"Well thanks for explaining things," I said uneasily. "We do appreciate it."

"Yes at least we know a little bit about what to expect," said Bernard. "I've never seen anything like this. Road subsidence in a road like this overnight just like that."

"No," I said. "Neither have I."

CHAPTER 32

"Hi Fee, this is Llewellyn here. Llewellyn Price. I'm just ringing to find out how you are?"

"Oh Llewellyn, hello," I said. "You took me by surprise. Thank you for ringing."

"I just wondered how things have been since I was there?"

"Well I don't really know how to answer that," I said uneasily. "The house has been fine. I haven't felt any presence or seen anything unusual." I paused. "But there has been a major calamity."

"What kind of calamity?" asked Llewellyn worriedly.

"You're not going to believe this but the road has subsided right in front of the house. It was the day following your visit, the day after we had all that rain. The Highways Department blocked off the road and sent in a team to try and ascertain what caused it."

"My goodness," said Llewellyn shocked. "How awful. How unexpected. No wonder you're upset. What did they find?"

"Well they sent the Highways engineers out. They did come quickly, before midday on the day it happened. There was quite a team of them. They carried out some kind of search using radar and other technical-looking equipment and then they started drilling holes in the road. They were all milling round in their hard hats and bright yellow coats. I must say it looked rather like a small mining operation."

"At least they acted swiftly. Did they tell you what caused the problem?"

"They told me it was probably what's known as a swallow hole. That's a hole which forms suddenly underground caused by the infiltration of excessive water. In this case they think the sub-base underground is limestone which is porous anyway. Apparently swallow holes are often found where there's limestone subsoil. They said the heavy rain a few days ago, the day that you visited me, could be a likely cause."

"It was certainly torrential," put in Llewellyn.

"Yes, it was. It seems that large amounts of moving water flowing through the surface fissures can dissolve limestone and form large potholes or caverns. Hence the subsidence and hence the speed of it all."

"Poor Fee. It's all been happening to you lately. Would it help if I came over to see you?" asked Llewellyn gently. "There's not much I can do but sometimes a friendly face does provide some comfort."

"Oh would you?" I said gratefully. "I've taken a couple of days off work until the road issue is sorted or we know at least the extent of the damage."

"I'll come this afternoon, around two o'clock if that's alright?"

"That'll be great," I said feeling a sense of relief.

⁂

"Just look at these cracks," I said to Llewellyn as we stood in the road outside the house. "Unbelievable isn't it?"

One of the men who seemed like the boss had allowed us to accompany him behind the high metal fencing which now kept the public away from the scene after giving us safety helmets and a hi-viz jacket each.

"Don't go near the fissure," he had said. "I'm only letting you in here because I know you're concerned about your house. Just you be careful."

A couple of men from the Highways team were busy by the side of us, adjusting a large hydraulic pump. Suddenly the pump leapt into action and I quickly took a few steps backwards.

"It certainly is incredible," said Llewellyn looking taken aback. "The cracks are really quite extensive and they seem to be coming from there." He pointed over at the hollow in the road which measured about thirty centimetres across.

"I just don't know what's going on. How can this just happen? Just like that, over night. It's an absolute nightmare," I said worriedly.

"I'm sure it feels like that," said Llewellyn. "But things may not be as bad as they seem. Don't forget your house has stood here for hundreds of years. It must be built as solidly as a rock otherwise it would have fallen down long ago."

"I suppose that is a point. But you'd be worried yourself if your house was right by this hole."

"I would," said Llewellyn. "I certainly would and I really do understand your concern. You've just got to hold it in your head that the worst may not happen. The road might not collapse any more than it has now, especially as the Highways men are onto things. They've been working on it for several days by the sound of it. They must have got things more or less under control by now."

"Well yes. They have been working hard. They've been pumping water out of the hole for a couple of days now. So maybe you're right, perhaps there is less chance of further subsidence. It's just that it's all happening so close to the house and there seems to be nothing I can do. I just have to stand about and watch."

"I know. That always makes things harder if there's nothing you can do," said Llewellyn. "What happens at night by the way, does all the work stop?"

"Oh yes. They leave it all lit up with those special lights you can see round the edge of the fencing and there's a security guard too. We shouldn't really be in here ourselves. Perhaps we ought to leave."

"You're right," said Llewellyn taking my arm. "Let's go inside. It's quite chilly out here."

"We're off now," I said to the man who had let us through the fence. "Thanks for letting us have a look. In some ways it does make me feel a bit better. Seeing exactly what you're doing. Your men are working really hard."

"They sure are. They know how you're feeling I expect," said the man. "No-one would want to be in your position. They're working as quickly as they can."

We made our way round to the back of the house and I took Llewellyn into the kitchen and made us a cup of coffee. "You take it black without sugar like me, don't you?" I asked.

"Yes please. I could do with a coffee to warm me up. It's not very warm out there," he said holding his hands over the Aga. "I do envy you your stove. I was brought up with one in Wales. There're a great comfort aren't they? Thanks," he said as I handed him a mug of steaming coffee. "Do you want to talk to me about the road or would you prefer us to stick with small talk?" he said with just the hint of a smile.

"Well much as I'd like to forget about it, it does actually help to talk about it. I rang the insurance company again this morning. They were really very helpful."

"So what's the position? I'm sure you must be covered for land subsidence. I would have thought that it's a general feature in all home insurance policies these days," said Llewellyn sitting down at the kitchen table and pulling out a chair for me.

"Yes I've got the policy here," I said picking up a thick document from the table. "I'll read you what it says:

'Buildings and Contents are covered for loss or damage caused by:
Subsidence or heave of the site or landslip
Including underground service pipes and cables, sewers, drains and
    septic tanks
The cost of making the building safe including architects/solicitors
    fees and consulting engineers as agreed in writing beforehand
Costs relating to any escape of water
Costs to restore any garden damage.'

So all that sounds good."

"It certainly appears to be very comprehensive. That must put your mind at rest somewhat," said Llewellyn as he took a sip of coffee. "And what about policy excess?"

"Oh I hadn't thought of that. I'll have a look," I said flicking through the policy and reading the small print. "It's always someplace you don't expect to find it, the finer details. Ah here it is. It says that generally there's a policy excess of £50.00, but in the case of subsidence, landslip or heave the excess is £1,000. Well, I suppose that's not too bad."

"No. It could be a lot worse. However it may not come to anything. As we said the damage to the road doesn't seem to be worsening." Llewellyn took my hand as he spoke. "You know, you're coping very well with all this. You're a real stalwart. You're doing just great."

"Thanks," I said. "I've had a lot of help. From you, from James and my friends and also Bernard my neighbour. I just wish we could put an end to it all and get back to normal. I'm beginning to forget what normal is," I added with a laugh.

"You've just got to hang on in there as I think they say. I'm not very good with the modern lingo you know," Llewellyn added somewhat self-deprecatingly.

"Yes that is the saying. And you're right, the cracks don't seem to be getting any worse," I said standing up and moving over the front window. "The Highways guys are still beavering away out there. They seem to be working on the unaffected areas round the edge. Maybe they're trying to stop the spread."

CHAPTER 33

There was a light knock at the front door. As usual Barnie alerted me to the fact and raced ahead of me to the door. I could see one of the men from the Highways team in his hi-viz yellow jacket through the window as I approached the porch.

I opened the front door. "Hi. My name's Mike, Mike Thompson. I'm the Highways team supervisor," said the man. "May I come in?"

"Of course." I stood back and ushered him in.

"I'll just take off my boots and leave them here. They're a bit wet," he said as he carefully unlaced his heavy duty boots. "And I'd best take off my jacket if you don't mind."

"Fine," I said taking his jacket from him and hanging it on the hook behind the front door.

"Do come through," I said opening the sitting room door and indicating the sofa.

"There's been an interesting development," said Mike Thompson sitting down. "When our chaps did the ground radar survey and bore hole scans they realised that there's more than just the swallow hole we told you about which is causing the problem. There seems to be some kind of void under the road. Just a long shot but I wondered if you might know what it could be."

"Well," I said carefully, remembering what James had discovered, "my partner James did read something in the library in Oxford about a subterranean passage which is said to run from the castle behind the house to what was an old abbey over there," I said pointing across the road.

"Ah. I see. It's quite possible," said Mike nodding. "It's well documented that a whole system of tunnels was constructed across the country at various times to allow the lord or baron and his family to escape when a castle or mansion house was under siege. And monks had a similar need to be able to escape or keep their movements secret. So it's quite feasible there is a passage."

"I know. James said the same thing but he also said tunnels of that nature are usually in larger places than this."

"Oh you can find tunnels in all sorts of places," said Mike. "You'd be surprised."

"Well it does seem strange that I might be living within feet of one. So what next?"

"My team will do some more checks and if they have any reason to think that there is an old tunnel like you say they'll call in the county archaeologists."

"Why the county archaeologists?"

"Well anything that has to be disturbed that might be of archaeological interest has to be investigated by the experts. My men might inadvertently do some damage to what might be a historic find."

"I suppose that makes sense. Anyway it's lucky in the circumstances that James read about the tunnel. At least you can check it out."

"That's right," said Mike. "A lucky coincidence you could say."

"So can I be of any further help?"

"I don't think so. Local people with local knowledge are always a help in this kind of situation. Also I wanted to keep you in the picture," said Mike. "You need to know what's going on out there and maybe you could let your neighbours know."

"Oh right. Will do. It's very good of you to keep us informed. It has been a bit of a strain. It was all so unexpected as you can imagine."

"I'm sure," said Mike sympathetically. "It's the last thing one expects to happen just in front of your house."

"It sure is," I said. "I can still hardly believe it. By the way, would you like a cup of tea or coffee? I should have asked before."

"Oh no thanks," said Mike. "I must be going in a minute anyway."

"Do let me know if there is anything else I can do to help you in any way."

"We'll let you know," said Mike standing up. "First I'll get my men to do some further investigations. And I'll alert Sam Wright in Archaeology that we may need some help from him just so he's at the ready. We don't want this to become protracted and drawn out. We need to get the road fixed as soon as possible, for your sake and for the sake of the general public."

"Yes," I said. "I'm sure we all want that."

⁂

I picked up the phone. "Hi Fee, it's me Tom."

"Hi Tom. How are you doing?" I said taking the telephone through to the study and sitting down on the small sofa by the fireplace.

"I'm fine thanks. Just calling to see how things are going. Judith told me about the apparent tunnel find under the road."

"Yes, it's all quite bizarre the way things are happening at the moment," I said thinking of the tumultuous events recently.

"You've had a lot to cope with," said Tom gently. "You know we're all behind you. You must let me know if I can be of any help."

"Oh I know that you're with me. I don't think I could have got through this far without you guys. I'll certainly let you know if there's anything you can do."

"Just one thing," said Tom hesitantly. "You know a while back I was banging on about that bricked up wall in the cellar under your kitchen. I just wondered whether you ought to tell the Highways man about it? Could be significant."

"Oh," I said. "I hadn't thought of that. In fact it had completely slipped my mind. I suppose I've been trying not to think too much about the cellars too much as you can imagine."

"It's just that it could be helpful to them. Might be another way for them to access the tunnel under the road, if there is one. Let's face it," he said pausing, "there must've been a reason for having a door or bricked up cupboard in that cellar in the first place."

"Goodness I hadn't thought of that," I exclaimed. "I wonder what's behind that wall. You've made me all wound up again."

"I'm sorry. I didn't mean to do that. I was only trying to help."

"I know you're trying to do the right thing. I do appreciate it Tom. I'd better give Mike Thompson a ring and run this by him."

"I think it might be a good idea. It could speed things up as well. I'm sure you want all this over and done with as soon as possible."

"I certainly do. It's a bit like living in the middle of a disaster zone at the moment. There seems to be dozens of men swarming around out there most of the time. Well, four or five anyway. And they've got so much equipment what with excavators and pumps and the high metal fencing and there are even security guards at night."

"Incredible. What a thing to be going through, right in front of your eyes as it were. Anyway Judith and I'll be seeing you later. How about all of us going over to The Black Horse for a meal tonight? It'd be good for you and James to get out and at least none of us would have to drive."

"Great. See you later. About seven thirty?"

"Yes, fine. See you then. And good luck with your Mr Thompson. You can fill us in on any developments when we see you."

"Bye," I said looking out of the window thoughtfully, trying to see if the Highways boss was around.

❦

"So you discovered this back in May," said Mike Thompson as he looked carefully at the uneven surface. He ran his fingers over the rough brick edges. "It's certainly a bricked up doorway, your friend's right about that."

"Do you think it will help if you guys open it up?" I asked.

"I'm sure it will," said Mike. "It's got to lead somewhere. I'll get my team onto it right away. What we'll do is take some bricks out along here," he said tracing the top line of uneven bricks. "If we take out a couple of layers we'll be able to see exactly what's there and then we'll know if it's worth taking out the whole doorway."

"This is all a bit weird," I said. "I was the one who stopped my friend Tom pursuing the idea of opening up the wall. I just had a funny feeling about what we might find. It made me feel quite uneasy. Anyway you've got to do it. So fine, please ask your guys to get on with it."

CHAPTER 34

Nervously I make my way down the cellar stairs to find the place brightly lit by several of the portable lamps. Two men from the Highways team have been working at speed to open up the brickwork in the cellar under the kitchen and have called me down to take a look. Mike Thompson ushers me excitedly through the cellars to the far end.

As I enter the cellar I'm acutely aware of how significant this moment is. There have been so many finds and happenings already. Whatever is going to happen next I wonder? I wish it were all over and done with and that James and I could just get on with life. I love the house to bits but I just want to live here undisturbed, for James and I to get back to how things were before. We're planning a holiday before Christmas and I really want to be thinking about that. But at the moment all I can think of is rain, road subsidence and underground passages.

Until earlier when I showed Mike Thompson down I haven't been in the cellars for a while and I am reminded again of Rose and Eliza, their belongings still lying discarded in the piles of dusty old wooden boxes stacked against the wall. The trestle table has been cleared of the various bits and pieces of kitchen paraphernalia by the Highways men who have propped it up in the far corner by the bottom of the wooden staircase. It all brings back a flood of memories about Eliza's life and the various notes and letters she had stored there, her spirited correspondence with Gerald Gardner and all that I had learnt about Wicca and the occult. All that seems like a long time ago I reflect as I stand motionless in the doorway.

Jerking myself back to reality I follow Mike to the far side of the cellar. Two of his men have skilfully removed the bricks and shored up the wall with a couple of steel support poles. I can see that they're held in place with thick pieces of wood running through the brickwork to meet two further poles on the other side. The uneven bricks jutting from each side of the hole every four or five layers have been cut away roughly and behind the wall there is a heavy-looking oak door studded with rusty nails.

"As you can see we've uncovered a door," one of the men says, a tall thin man with gingery blonde hair, "a bit unexpectedly."

"I suppose we'll have to pick the lock," adds his mate bending down to peer through the key hole. "It shouldn't be difficult. Or should we wait for Ben Wright from Archaeology? He should be here any time now. You know what he's like."

"Perhaps we'd best wait," Mike Thompson puts in. "We don't want to get in trouble with the resident 'expert'. And if we do open the door now we won't be able to hold ourselves back from taking a look."

"Maybe," the ginger-haired man says looking disappointed. "Why is it he gets to have all the fun? We know just as much as he does about these things."

"Well maybe you should become an archaeologist Jim if you like their work so much," Mike says sardonically.

"I'm just thinking," I say slowly, "when my friend and I first explored the cellars, back at the end of last year I think it was, we found an old key. A big old key. It just might fit this keyhole." As I speak I walk swiftly back to the first cellar at the bottom of the wooden staircase under the study. Mike follows. Indicating one of the alcoves set into the wall I reach up saying, "I'm sure I put the key back in here."

Feeling with my hand across the smooth surface of the alcove I grasp the key with my fingers remembering back to the time when Judith and I first explored the cellars. Recalling how we dug in the loose soil right there beneath my feet and discovered the wooden box with the cryptic message about Louisa that Tom had unravelled, then the drama of discovering her grave and the blessing by the vicar.

"Here it is," I say showing it to Mike pushing my thoughts abruptly to one side. "Does this look as if it will fit the door?"

"Could do," Mike says briskly. "Let's go see." Taking the key from me he walks hurriedly ahead of me back to the far cellar.

"Here let me give it a go," he says moving over to where his men are still standing by the opening in the wall. They stand aside expectantly as Mike inserts the key into the lock. "Well what do you know? It fits!" He turns the key decisively and puts his hand on the round black handle.

"Anyone there," calls a voice from the other end of the cellars. Abruptly Mike lets go of the door handle and turns towards me.

"That must be Ben Wright," he says reluctantly. "We'd best wait. I'm sure he'll be able to find out what's behind the door soon enough anyway."

A trim man in dark blue overalls appears through the doorframe, followed by a second man also in overalls. "Hi," he says extending a hand to Mike. "I'm Kirk Williams and this is Jason Brown. Ben Wright has subcontracted us to have a look. He's had to go out on another job. One of your guys out in the road told us where to find you. Hope you don't mind us walking in on you."

"Glad you're here," says Mike shaking hands but at the same time looking none too pleased.

"Not before time," I add. "We're just about to open the door. Even found the key to it would you believe," I say indicating the gaping hole in the wall with the thick set door behind. "Amazing find isn't it?" I'm fascinated despite myself. Drawn to discover just exactly what is beyond the door, to try and find out why it might have been bricked up in the first place. To unravel yet further the mysteries of the house.

"Right," says Kirk purposefully approaching the doorway. He's carrying a heavy bag of tools in one hand and a blue safety helmet fitted with a lamp in the other. "What have you found so far?"

"Well," says Mike and again I notice him hesitate. Was there going to be some kind of tension between the two teams I wonder.

"My men here have opened up the brickwork and as you can see there's a door beyond. Fee has miraculously found a key that fits. Maybe you and your colleague should take a look."

"Thanks," Kirk says with smile seemingly unaffected by Mike's touchiness. "Jason got your gear?"

They both check their lamps carefully and then don their helmets, fastening the straps carefully under their chins. "No need to take your kit at this stage," Kirk says turning to Jason. "Mine should be enough. Are you guys going to come with us?" he says turning to Mike and his men.

"Sure," Mike says looking surprised. "Give us a minute to get our headgear." The three men rummage in a large holdall in the corner of the cellar. Taking out their helmets they each fasten the straps.

"What about me?" I enquire. "Can I come with you?"

"Well," Mike says cautiously. "I suppose we shouldn't let you really. But we wouldn't be here if it wasn't for you. If you go fetch a helmet from one of the guys outside I'm sure Kirk will let you at least see what's behind the door. Right?"

"Okay but only just to have a look see initially. I'm afraid you can't get involved if we do manage to break into the tunnel," says Kirk guardedly. "We have absolutely no idea what we're going to find. It'll very likely be dangerous. In any case we'll have to get our protective gear from the van."

I move off like a shot and race up the wooden stairs. Running round to the front of the house I approach one of the Highways men. "Got a helmet I can borrow?" I gasp.

The man gives a grin and goes over to his van. "There's probably one in here that'll fit," he says amiably opening the back doors. "Here, try this one." He picks out a bright yellow safety helmet with a black strap.

Taking it eagerly I try it on. "Will it do?" I say showing him the fit.

"Yep, that's good. It looks to be tight enough. We carry a few spares for when we've got apprentices or work experience youngsters with us."

"Thanks, you're a star," I say flying off back round the side of the house. I move hastily to the trapdoor and make my way back down to join the men in the cellar. Kirk and Jason are disappearing through the doorway with Mike and his men close behind. I join them expectantly.

"Now this isn't what I would have anticipated," says Kirk shining one of the halogen lamps before him. "There's some stone steps spiralling down to the right, it's some kind of passageway. I rather thought we'd find ourselves in another cellar."

"Me too," says Mike. "Never seen anything quite like this."

"Nor me," added his ginger-haired colleague. "Wonder where it goes?"

"Wow," I say passing through the doorway and standing flabbergasted at the top of the steep pale coloured stone stairway descending to the right. Pulling my jacket closer round me I gaze in disbelief, the brightness of the lamp against the stone making me blink.

CHAPTER 35

"I'm coming down with you," I say breathlessly. "You've got to let me see where this leads. After all it is my house."

"Not sure that's a good idea," Kirk says looking to Mike Thompson. "Health and safety and all that. You're not trained to do this kind of thing."

"Look I've got my hard hat and I'll only come as far as it's safe for me to be. I promise you."

"What do you think Mike?" asks Kirk and I can see that any animosity if there is some is not on Kirk's side.

"Well it certainly is a very unusual find. You can't blame Fee for being excited. I think we all are," replies Mike. "Let's just see where these stairs lead and we'll take it from there."

"Okay," says Kirk, "let's go. I'll just find my mg monitor."

"What's an mg monitor?" I ask.

"It's a portable multigas detector which bleeps if there are any noxious gases like methane or ethane in the atmosphere. Although I wouldn't particularly expect to find any in a place like this but you have to check for it all the same."

He searches in his bag and takes out a small orange-coloured instrument with a digital display monitor at the top. "See, it has a vibrating detector movement as well as an instant alarm and it automatically logs what it finds. I never go anywhere without it."

"Right," he continues, "torches to the ready." He reaches again into his bag and takes out a couple of heavy duty black and yellow flashlights. "Got yours Mike?" he asks as he hands one to Jason.

Mike reaches into the large holdall and takes out four red, heavy duty torches passing one to each of his men and one to me.

"So," Kirk says, "are we all ready?" The guys nod and he leads the way down the steeply curved spiral staircase, the light from our flash lamps bouncing eerily off the stone. The slabs of stone lining the walls and angular steps are huge and the air is becoming surprisingly fresh. I wonder fleetingly where the air source is coming from.

Pulling my scarf more tightly round my neck I reach out to the wall with my left hand for support, shivering slightly I'm glad that I've got all those guys in front of me. I certainly wouldn't be coming down here on my own.

We descend about twenty steep winding steps and then as I turn the bend at the bottom I am dumbfounded to find myself stepping into a large tunnel stretching away in both directions. Standing stock still I gaze in astonishment at the shadowy passageway before me which I assume must run from west to east under the house.

One of Mike's guys has ventured a few metres down the tunnel his torch held out in front of him and in the beam of light shining on the pale walls I can see that the passage is solid and well built with an arched roof and walls and floor of stone.

"So this is the subterranean passage you heard rumours about Fee," says Mike excitedly, "the one running from the castle to the abbey." He looks at Kirk.

"And it could well be connected with the road subsiding," Kirk says. "It's all beginning to make sense."

"Now what?" I ask, still shocked by the unexpected find.

✤

"And then they made me go back up the stairs," I said indignantly to James and Judith. We were sitting in the kitchen later that day, seated round the table drinking coffee.

"Well they had to didn't they," said Judith laughing at my indignation. "They couldn't let you go traipsing off into the darkness now could they?"

"I suppose not," I said with a begrudging smile. "But boy was it frustrating. I had to just sit about upstairs waiting for them to emerge. I couldn't really get on with anything. I was just twiddling my thumbs and marching up and down in the study."

"So tell us all about what happened next," said James.

"Well Kirk and the others took the passageway to the east, under the road. They were gone for about an hour. Apparently the tunnel is quite solid. They didn't find any signs of collapse or any places where the stone has given way. From taking bearings Mike thinks the road subsidence is to the right-hand side above the tunnel. Anyway what it means is that the tunnel runs from the castle beneath the garden and courtyard under the dining room and then under the road leading to what was the old abbey"

"This is all unbelievable!" said James. "And what a historic find. It's just amazing to be party to something like this. What happened next?"

"Mike and his men went back outside. Said they were going to start work on the exposed surfaces round the cracks. Then when they've succeeded in stabilising things they can work on shoring up the swallow hole."

"Will it take long?" asked Judith.

"Well they said that it'll probably take a few days although things are not as bad as they could be because the tunnel itself is so solid. When they've shored up whatever they find under the ground they can start the repair work on the surface and then get on with reconstructing the road."

"And what about this so-called swallow hole? Have they worked out what caused it?" asked James.

"The rubble under the road is limestone or, as Mike said, it's actually called ashlar clunch. Strange name. Anyway swallow holes are often caused by localised pockets of soft sand. This sand sometimes gets saturated and washed away through the rest of the subsoil and bingo, you get a hole opening up which is what caused the subsidence in this instance."

"So it probably was the heavy rain last week which started it all off," said Judith. "What's happened to all the rain if it's not gone into the tunnel I wonder?"

"I don't know," I said. "Mike said they are looking at the possibility of a pothole being formed under the road, if so the water would collect in there. That's one of the things they'll be investigating tomorrow."

"So they'll drain away the water and fill in the pothole and that's it?" said James. "End of problem."

"I think that's what they're hoping," I replied. "They want to get the road opened up again as soon as possible."

"And what about the archaeologists?" asked Judith. "What's on their agenda?"

"Well Kirk and his colleague Jason are coming back tomorrow possibly with another couple of men. They want to check that the tunnel is safe along its whole length. They're going to do an extended exploration going in both directions to see what, if anything, they can find of archaeological interest."

"Did they give you any idea as to what kind of things they might find?" asked Judith.

"Pretty much anything they said. From bones to coins to pottery finds, absolutely anything."

"I can't wait," said Judith. "There must be something down there."

"Sure," I said, "they're both really quite excited. Kirk told me that there are rumoured to be underground passages all over the country most of which are usually discovered to be unfounded. And now this. He said neither of them has ever seen anything quite like it."

"I'm not surprised," said Judith. "It must be a bit of an unusual find."

"You know what's going to happen next don't you," said James as he topped up our mugs. "Tom is going to want to get down there and see all this for himself."

"Mike and the others thought of that. They said did I mind if they took the key with them. They're obviously worried about the County

Council being sued if someone should get in there and get hurt."

"Thank goodness for that," said Judith. "You know what Tom's track record is like. He's always getting into trouble one way or another. He's like a cat with nine lives. One of these days he's going to go one step too far."

"Yes," I said. "I did think of him when Mike said about the key. And the whole thing really is fascinating. I think I might have been tempted to have a look myself if they hadn't taken away the key, although it is real scary down there."

"So are they going to let you have it back?" asked James.

"I suppose so, when they're done. I hadn't really thought about that. It is my key and my door after all."

"Well they won't let you have it back until they're sure it's safe down there," said Judith with her usual logic. "Anyway, just think what all this must be costing us, the tax payer? What with all those security men, the Highways engineers and the archaeologists and all their machinery. Must be costing a fortune."

"Good point. I couldn't even begin to imagine the cost when you take all that into consideration," I said. "It just goes to show these kinds of things must happen all over the country and we, Joe public, are none the wiser. All this money is literally being poured down the drain you could say."

"Very funny," said James. "Seriously though it must be costing a terrific amount looking at all those excavators and pumps, the hoists and all that lifting equipment and so on. Frightening."

"By the way," he added. "Charles was asking if he could come over and take a look when Kirk and his mate go down next. Do you think that would be alright?"

"Don't know. I can certainly give him a bell. Would Charles be free to come over tomorrow do you think?"

"Maybe. Why don't you touch base with Kirk and if he gives the okay I'll give Charles a call."

"You know something," said Charles slowly. "It's really weird. I keep thinking about it. When I was with Kirk and Jason today we spent a lot of time examining the tunnel and, as Mike told you, the walls are really solid. The whole thing is very well built and there are no structural problems. They must've had the finest stone masons. But, and this is the weird bit, in one place we found some odd wall markings. Down on the right-hand side, probably about halfway across beneath the road. There's something funny about it."

"So what's funny?" asked James. We were relaxing in the sitting room in front of the fire with a glass of wine after a meal.

"Well the tunnel as a whole is very carefully and exactly constructed," replied Charles taking a sip of wine and settling back in his chair. "All the stone slabs are the same type and roughly the same size. It's all quite uniform. But when Kirk and I were closely examining the walls we noticed that there's a patch, quite a large patch, of stone which appears to have been in-filled. The slabs are smaller and they've obviously been put in place by someone who's not such an expert." He paused. "Now why would that be do you imagine?"

"Who knows?" I said. "Does it matter in any case? What you're really looking for are archaeological finds aren't you?"

"Yes I suppose," said Charles thoughtfully. "But there has to be a reason. Why would someone have messed around with what seems to be a perfectly sound tunnel?"

"Hm, I see what you mean," I said slowly. "Is there any way that you and Kirk could open up that piece of wall and see what's behind it?" I added.

"Maybe. It could just be a blind alley and take us nowhere. But on the other hand it might prove useful, you never know. I think I'll talk to them about it on Monday. It is their show after all."

"So what did Kirk's other two guys get up to?" I asked.

"The two guys, Andy and Karl I think they're called, they worked the tunnel the other way towards the castle."

"What did they come up with?" I asked.

"Well they made their way quite a long way westwards. As you would expect the tunnel sloped a bit at first where it goes under your garden. They didn't really find anything much. They picked up a couple of buckles and a few coins which they've taken back with them to date. And then they suddenly came to a dead end, an enormous pile of rubble, just like that. They're going to take another look after the weekend."

CHAPTER 36

"Right," said Charles calling me on my mobile at work. "I'm here with Kirk and his mate Jason at the house. We're just about to investigate the wall in the tunnel I told you about on Friday night."

"Oh great. I hope you get on alright. Do be careful won't you. I know you all know what you're doing but anything like that must carry risks."

"Don't worry," said Charles, "we'll all have our safety gear and there are three of us. Anyway we're only going to cut a section out of the wall at the top first to see what if anything is going on there."

"Just to let you know that I'm teaching most of the day today so you won't be able to get hold of me if you have any news. Maybe you can wait for James and myself at the house later on and fill us in on everything. This is all getting a bit nerve-wracking."

"I know. It just seems endless. All the trouble with the road subsidence and the aftermath. Anyway we'll try and make strides today. I've been allowed some time off from my department so I don't have to take leave. My boss is intrigued by all this and wants to get the inside low-down on what's found. It's not every day that you get the opportunity to get involved in something like this."

"No, sure. It's very good of him."

"Well this isn't a particularly busy time for us anyway, mid-November. So it suits all round."

"Okay Charles. See you later?"

"Yes fine. I can wait for you. I'm not in a hurry to get away tonight."

"Maybe we'll get a takeaway delivered. That way we can feed you and hear about all the action at the same time."

"Sounds good," said Charles. "See you. Have a good day."

※

"Can you remember exactly where that piece of wall was?" asked Charles as the three men made their way along the tunnel under the road, their way lit by the three overlapping arcs of light from their torches.

"I think so," said Kirk from behind. "Jason can you shine your torch along the right-hand side ahead of me and I'll hold mine close to the wall. It shouldn't be difficult. After all we found it the first time didn't we?"

"Yes," said Charles. He was carrying a holdall and dressed like Kirk in heavy dark coloured overalls with a hard hat and lamp. He could see that Kirk had his mg monitor jutting out of his breast pocket.

Jason and Kirk were each carrying a bag containing stone cutting tools and equipment. Jason was also holding several steel support poles rolled up in a cloth. "If we need more poles," said Jason, "I'll go back to the cellar and get some. I left some there ready just in case."

They inched forward slowly, each scrutinising the wall of the tunnel in the torchlight, the shadows dancing on the light coloured stone walls around them. The air was surprisingly mild and Charles could tell that there was a plentiful flow of air. He stopped and felt the stone wall beside him with his right hand, it felt smooth to the touch and he was aware of the quality of the stone masons who had hewn the rock and cut it to shape all that time ago. That made the rough patch they were looking for even more peculiar. Why would anyone be satisfied with shoddy workmanship like that when they were obviously very skilled? It didn't make sense.

He felt quite tense with an underlying sense of anticipation which was unusual for him. He was generally very laid back both at work and in his personal life. But today was different. This didn't seem like an ordinary job and he felt strangely wound up inside.

Mentally pulling himself together he moved to catch up with the others. He could see Jason was several metres ahead of Kirk shining his torch systematically along the right-hand side of the tunnel, the arched roof of the tunnel framing his colleagues in an oddly surreal manner.

Suddenly Kirk stopped. "Hey, I think we've got it!" he exclaimed. "Look, right here." He pointed to a rough patch of smaller stone blocks which stood out from the smooth slabs around them. "It's as we remembered it. There certainly is something very peculiar about this."

"Right on," said Charles. "Let's find out what's going on here."

They put down their bags as Jason retraced his steps. As he reached them he bent down to scrutinise the area they were looking at. "Yeah," he said. "There's definitely something different about this bit. You can see how the stonework is different. Shall we get going then?"

"Too right," said Kirk taking a halogen lamp from his bag and placing it on the opposite side of the tunnel alongside them. The lamp cast an eerily pale light and lit the three men up in their dark overalls, the shadowy tunnel looming in both directions.

Kirk took out a couple of cold chisels and two iron bars from his bag. "Jason, you work from there and I'll start here. We'll cut a section across the top like they did with the wall in the cellar and then we can see if there's any reason why this piece of stonework is different." He passed Jason a respiratory mask and put on his own, handing one to Charles.

"I'm here if you need me," said Charles standing to one side as he donned his mask.

"Nope we're fine at the moment but maybe later we'll be able to use another pair of hands." Kirk stood to his full height and used the chisel carefully, tapping with the iron bar to break up the layer of soft lime mortar holding the rough cut stones in place. Jason did the same about one metre to the right of him.

They worked methodically removing the mortar from between

the stones, the dust showering down on their dark overhauls. Together they managed to take out a section of stone about twenty centimetres deep.

Standing back to let the dust settle Kirk said expectantly, "Now what? What the heck are we going to find behind here?"

"Only one way to find out," said Jason moving back towards the cut away section in the wall. He peered behind the stone. "Blimey," he said straining his head, "there's a hole behind here, some kind of cavity. What on earth is this all this about?"

Kirk moved over quickly to take a look with Charles close behind. "Goodness me," exclaimed Charles. "What the hell is this? Why would there be a cavity behind the walls of the tunnel?"

"I think we need to take a look see," said Kirk standing back from the wall. "It's about time we took out the whole of this stretch. It'll take some doing but we'll just have to take our time. Can't use the demolition hammer here!"

"Course not. We don't want to damage or destroy things. But if we all take a hand," said Jason, "it shouldn't take too long. Shall we get going?"

"Okay," said Kirk. "How about you and I make a start and then Charles you can have a go."

"Hang on, I've got a flask of soup," said Charles removing his mask and reaching into his bag. "Shall we take a quick break first and then start work?"

"Good idea," said Kirk taking off his mask.

Charles took three plastic mugs from his bag and poured out steaming hot soup, passing one each to Kirk and Jason. "Only packet soup I'm afraid," he said wryly. "Tomato and vegetable. Still it'll fill a hole."

"Smells good to me," said Jason. "Tastes okay too," he said downing a few mouthfuls.

They stood there watchfully in the pale light, each unsure as to what they might find when they started work. The dark tunnel stretched away in both directions, their peculiar cocoon of light encapsulating them. Charles wondered to himself what else they might find in the passageway but decided to say nothing to the others mindful that they already had an important job in hand. Taking a sip from his mug he felt the warm soup giving him a welcome energy boost. All of his work was demanding but this job seemed to be quite draining. Probably because of all the trauma poor Fee had been going through he thought. It's a good job she has James for support.

"Right," said Kirk draining his mug and interrupting his thoughts. "Thanks Charles, nice one. Here Jason, let's get moving. We'll need our powercap respirators," he said taking off his helmet and placing it on the floor. He put his hand into his tool bag and brought out three lightweight respirator caps.

Jason took one of the black powercaps from Kirk and fitted it carefully before sliding down the visor. Charles and Kirk did the same. "These have got an eight hour life," said Jason. "And they should all be charged up so here goes."

Kirk handed him a chisel and Jason moved over to the wall. He began work dextrously cutting into the mortar and working away at the stones, Kirk at his side. Charles stood watching, his face impassive. He was pleasantly aware of the steady stream of cool air being filtered over his face.

Kirk and Jason worked on carefully, showering stone and mortar dust around them as they did so. Removing his powercap and laying it carefully on the floor of the tunnel Charles strolled slowly up the tunnel in the direction of the old abbey, taking his torch with him. "I won't go far," he said.

As Charles returned to the site of the excavation some while later he could see that both men were still working steadily. Piles of rubble lay on the ground beside and behind them.

"Find anything?" asked Jason.

"Not really," said Charles slowly. "Well, not sure I should say." He paused.

"I just went a bit further along the tunnel towards the abbey end," he continued, "and I found these. They were scattered along the floor."

He held up a gloved hand holding what looked like several pieces of tuberous root. Each between ten and twelve centimetres long they were gnarled and misshapen. Almost human-like in formation, they had oddly shaped tops resembling a head and stumpy tendrils that looked rather like waving arms or legs.

Kirk and Jason looked at them and then Kirk said, "If you're thinking what I'm thinking, those are mandrake roots."

"Yes," said Charles. "I rather think they are."

"So what are mandrake roots?" queried Jason.

"Mandragora belongs to the nightshade family and as such roots like these are hallucinogenic. They're also poisonous," said Charles. "Hence the gloves. I always carry some when I'm on site."

"And why would they be found down here?" asked Jason.

"Who knows," said Charles, "except they are usually associated with witchcraft. They're said to be endowed with numerous healing powers and more importantly were used by witches to protect themselves against demoniacal possession."

"And I thought we were just working in an old tunnel," said Jason laughing. "I didn't realise it was a witches' walkway! So have those roots been pinched to make them into those shapes?" he added. "They seem amazingly humanoid, if there's such a word."

"Yes," said Kirk. "In witchcraft their dream-inducing qualities are vital in many rituals and spells. Apparently the shaping of the root is an all important aspect of their powers. I've even seen them with carved faces and genitals."

"How odd," said Jason.

"Anyway we'd best get on," said Kirk. "Let's have a closer look at them when we get out of here. Do you want to put them in a specimen bag?" He bent over and pulled out a clear plastic bag, passing it to Charles who dropped the roots into the bag and sealed it with a plastic tie.

"Shall I have a go now?" asked Charles. "You two seem to be doing all the work."

Kirk handed him a chisel and an iron bar and Charles donned his powercap, working steadily away to remove the stones. He could see that the cavity was dug roughly into the ashlar clunch subsoil and was aware that the temperature behind the stones was a few degrees warmer than in the tunnel. "Amazing how the stone breathes and absorbs the water. It's just a bit moist on the other side," he said as he worked on.

And then he was down to about sixty centimetres from the floor of the hollowed out space. "Crikey," he gasped dropping the chisel and iron bar to the floor with a loud clatter. "I can see bones in here. What look like human bones."

Kirk jumped up from where he was sitting next to Jason on the other side of the tunnel with Jason a couple of seconds behind him.

"You what?" he asked incredulously. "Human bones? How many?"

"That I don't know," said Charles shocked. "But I can see what look like several skulls or parts of skulls at any rate."

CHAPTER 37

"Right," said James putting the telephone down. "I've ordered the takeway. The food is very good at the Blue Lagoon. It'll be here at eight so we've time for a beer beforehand."

"What can I get you?" I asked. "We've got some good beer. James makes sure of that. Brakspear or Shepherd Neame?"

"Great, I'll have Brakspeare I think. Thanks," said Charles.

"And I'll have the same," said James showing Charles into the sitting room. "I've lit a fire so when Fee comes through you can tell us all about your discoveries in the tunnel."

"Thanks," said Charles taking a seat on the sofa.

Bringing glasses of beer through from the kitchen I passed one to each of the guys and sat down with my lager. "So Charles, tell us what you found," I said, taking a mouthful.

"Well you're not going to believe quite what we think we've found," said Charles looking bemused.

"Go on," said James.

"Okay. I hope you're all ears. This is some story." He took a sip of beer and settled back in his seat. "Well we decided to do what you suggested the other day and take out some of the stones on that bit of wall that's different. It wasn't difficult. We had the right equipment.

Anyway we quickly realised that there was a cavity behind the wall, a cavity just under a metre deep."

"My goodness," I said. "How peculiar."

"Yes and it was even more bizarre than that. We found bones scattered on the ground. Human bones."

"Christ!" exclaimed James.

"Good God!" I said, stunned. "That is bizarre alright. So what did you do?"

"Well it's not a crime scene as far as we know," said Charles, "because the bones look old. Very old. And it's only potentially a crime scene if the bones are found in an unexpected place and they're less than say seventy years old. Then the police and coroner have to be called in."

"Why aren't they interested in bodies before that?" I asked.

"It's because if they pre-date seventy years there would be nobody to prosecute," said Charles. "There's no point in discovering a crime scene and spending a lot of money establishing the cause and then finding the police can't take it any further, whatever they may suspect."

"Why seventy years?"

"The timescale of seventy years is set because that's supposed to be the time span of so-called 'living memory.' Anything which happened before that couldn't properly be corroborated by anyone who is still living. Although of course people are living much longer these days so it might all change one day. Anyway for the moment it's seventy years."

"I see. I suppose that makes sense," I said.

"So what will you guys do with the bones?" James asked looking mystified.

"We're going to bag them up, try to keep them separate from each other because it looks as if there were quite a few bodies."

"How many are you talking about?" I asked feeling quite shaken to think of bones and a possible crime scene so close to the house.

"Oh I should say about six or more," said Charles. "You can tell the bones are old by the fact that they're quite hard and crusty. Also because they've been preserved in that cavity. Ashlar clunch is limestone which preserves bones very well. They're quite dense and heavy which is a sign of significant age. What's happened is that they've absorbed stone from the surrounding limestone which has given them a chalky encrustation. It's also the fact that only the larger bones have survived," Charles continued sitting forward and becoming quite animated. "The smaller bones, like those in fingers, would've disintegrated long ago. The bones we found are parts of the skulls which are obviously quite substantial and then there are femurs which are the longest bone in the body. Also various leg and arm bones, parts of rib cages, scapulas, pelvises and so on. Skull bones can fall apart over time but we've found several craniums and jawbones, enough to enable us to tell roughly how many bodies there were altogether."

"How gruesome," I said shuddering. "The things you have to get involved with. It doesn't bear thinking about. So what happens next?"

"Well Kirk and his guys will take the bags of bones back to their base and carry out a series of tests on them. They should be able to confirm how many bodies there were and their gender and age and so on. It will certainly take some time. We haven't moved anything yet. We're going to start bagging things up tomorrow."

"Did you find anything else in there with the bones?" James put in. "If there're human bodies they must've been wearing something."

"There were no signs of any clothing," said Charles. "Clothing would be one of the first things to disintegrate. But once we run the tests there may be fibres on the bones or in the dust particles. That'll help with dating the bodies."

"And what about teeth?" said James. "Or am I just getting into morbid detail?"

"There are some teeth," said Charles. "And you can tell a lot about age and diet etc with teeth. And then as you'd expect there are some other artefacts which we haven't collected up yet. There are some coins, what look like some purse hasps, some buttons and the like. All very interesting finds. I must say we've really got your friend to thank for all of this."

"Tom is known for being tenacious or you could say just plain nosey," I said. "I suppose its all part of his job. He's a media researcher and always looking for a story or an unusual lead."

"Well he did us all a big favour when he started getting curious about that wall in your cellar. Without him we'd never have gotten down into the tunnel and found the remains. The mystery would've stayed hidden, probably for ever."

"What will happen to the bones when you've elicited as much as you can about them?" I asked. "You can't just put them back where you found them."

"They'll be interred in a coffin, a small one, and probably buried in the churchyard. After all whoever they were it seems likely that they died in Whittlesham so they should rightly be buried here. That's if your vicar is okay with it."

"Oh Robert Delforth. He's our vicar and he'll be fine. He's a great guy," I said. "He'll want to do the right thing by them. Presumably you'll be able to tell whether they are male or female remains?" I added.

"Yes, you can tell gender by the pelvis bones and also by the skulls. A woman's pelvis is shallower and wider than a man's."

"And what about ethnicity? Can you tell anything about that?" asked James.

"Not really. Very little evidence relating to ethnicity can be seen in bones. Any ideas about measuring that sort of thing date from pre-war archaeology and have largely been discredited. However ethnicity can be checked by looking at teeth enamel. There are certain minerals which build up in young children and form a kind of signature which can be traced back to specific areas. But that doesn't prove ethnicity conclusively, it's only a lead as to where a person grew up."

"So we're not likely to find out much about that. I don't suppose Kirk's department have an unlimited amount of money to throw at this anyway," said James.

"No you're right there," said Charles. "They can really only do so much so I think ethnicity is not going to be the main interest. Trying to date the bones and establish as much as they can with the limited resources they have is going to be the order of the day I should imagine."

"Anyway have you guys got any theory as to why those bodies might have been hidden like that in the first place?" asked James. "It's all a bit weird isn't it?"

"No ideas really. We need to get a rough date first and move from there. It is very likely that there was some kind of foul play. Bodies don't just get hidden behind a wall in such an obscure place for no reason. But it's going to be very hard to get an answer on that one. We can get DNA evidence but that won't tell us anything. Not with the likely age that they are."

"Will this get in the papers?" I asked. "Is it a public interest story?"

"I don't know. We haven't got that far yet," said Charles. "It's all so unexpected. We'll just have to take things one step at a time. And it is Kirk and his team who're in charge after all. It's up to them to drive things and say what should or shouldn't be done. I'm just an intelligent bystander as they say."

"Well what a day you've had!" I said. "Amazing stuff. You must be exhausted."

"I am," said Charles. "Nine o'clock this morning seems a long time ago. We really had absolutely no idea what to expect. Kirk and Jason were completely shattered too. Chiselling the stone out by hand really takes it out of you."

"If you're up to it I'd like to hear a bit more over the meal but I think I'd better get the table ready right now," said James. "Fee, do you want to pour the wine and perhaps some water?"

"Oh yes, the delivery chap will be arriving any minute. Do you want to come through to the kitchen Charles?"

"Sure," said Charles getting up. "Shall I put the guard across the fire?"

"Please," I said as we moved into the study and through to the kitchen. "What a chain of events. And where is all this leading us I wonder?"

CHAPTER 38

From: Tom Jackson
To: Fee Hunter
Subject: Hi Fee

Hi Fee,

Judith told me about the finds. Amazing stuff! Bodies, bodies everywhere by the sound of it. This sounds like a story. 'I knew you'd say that' is what you're thinking.

But seriously if there is a story can I have it? You know my connections with *Archaeology Today*. I'm certain they'd go for it like a shot.

Will probably see you tomorrow anyway but I thought I'd sound you out. From a safe distance!

C U Tom

From: Fee Hunter
To: Tom Jackson
Subject: Hi Tom

Tom,
You know I can read you like a book! So it's no surprise you want the story. Of course you can have it. After all there probably wouldn't have been this find if it hadn't been for you.
Only thing. You'll have to promise to go carefully if Kirk lets you go into the tunnel. Judith will murder me if you get hurt.
See you.

Fee

From: Tom Jackson
To: Fee Hunter
Subject: Hi Fee

Hi Fee,
I may be a book but I hope I'm an interesting one! C U

Tom

"It all seems to be taking such an absolute age," I said to Judith. We were having a coffee in town, having just been on a spending spree as a distraction.

"It certainly is," said Judith. "But I don't suppose there's anything they can do to hurry it all up. These things do take time and they've got to get it right. There's no point in them rushing their research and analysis and then jumping to the wrong conclusions."

"I know. You're right as usual," I said taking a sip of coffee. "But what is it really all about? Bodies behind a wall and possibly ancient ones at that. Whatever can the explanation be?"

"Goodness only knows. And we may never know," said Judith evenly. "You've got to consider that."

"I suppose," I said thoughtfully. "Anyway the good thing is that the archaeology guys and Charles all know what they're doing. They're all very experienced by the sound of it. At least we haven't got a bunch of amateurs working on it."

"True. So think on the positive side. They're doing what they can. I'm sure they'll be in touch soon."

"Okay. I'll stop whingeing if you like. Let's take a look at what we've bought."

"Good idea," said Judith feeling on the floor for her bags. "This jumper for Tom, it feels really soft," she added holding it to her face. "And you like the colour? I know he likes dark colours."

"It's great. A mauvey purple I think you'd call it. It'll really suit him with his blonde hair. I'm sure he'll love it."

"And what about this skirt?" she said taking the skirt from its bag. "Tom always says I don't wear skirts enough."

"It's lovely. The black with the silver and cream circles looks really good on you. Especially with that black top you bought. You'll look amazing. I hope James like these shirts I've picked up for him. He said he wanted a few work shirts," I continued taking a peek into the bag. "Now this one, the soft grey one, he'll like that I'm sure. He can wear it for work but it's nice and casual as well."

"It certainly feels good," said Judith. "A sort of jersey mix I suppose. Anyway retail therapy is great at a time like this, isn't it?"

"Too right. How about some more? Are you up for it yet? I really want to try and find a jacket with a difference."

"Fine, I'm ready," said Judith. "Jackets here we come!"

Pale and ethereal, damp and forbidding the mist hung in the air as I stood in the garden later that day with Barnie waiting for him to empty his bladder. It was three in the afternoon yet the fog hadn't lifted all day, hanging in ever-shifting swathes round the trees at the bottom of the garden and through to the mound beyond. The association with the past was never as strong as it was in winter when I could see the stark outline of the castle mound through the darkly silhouetted layers of trees. The weather would have been the same all those years ago at this time of year when the castle was occupied. The mist hiding the enemy with its flowing swathes just as it did today.

How would they have felt knowing there was an enemy out there and not being able to see them? Even now I don't know what's hidden in the mist. A secret world, a timeless world where all stands still and all is unknown.

I shivered and as I did so a pale sun broke softly through the mist and hung on the horizon brightening the afternoon for a few outstretched moments. Just as it must have brought hope to the castle baron and his soldiers, cold but bright and reassuring that it was still out there somewhere even if hidden from sight for so long. The trees looked darker against the brightness of the sun, emphasising the broken tree line and the rising slope of the mound above the grassy moat.

I could envision the rough stone blocks of the castle walls with their turreted top rising steeply above the moat, the very same stones that now stood within my own house and that of other villagers. The castle would have been a lively, bustling, bawdy place, displaying humanity in all its forms. The scenes it must have witnessed. Life and death in every aspect, the kinder side of human nature against the realism of everyday toil and struggle, petty in-fighting and constant vigilance against the enemy. When would they strike? It must have been an ever-lasting mantra. Keep watch, keep watch, keep watch. Lookout, lookout, lookout.

And what would it have been like living in such a crowded place with no real space of your own? Holed up in a castle behind those massive walls with the sheer drop all round, the smells and the smoke, the constant mayhem and coming and goings of the soldiers. The women and children probably never venturing far from the towering fortress except maybe to gather firewood. It must have been very much an 'us and them' mentality, reinforcing the values of those in the castle as hostile towards those outside of the walls and vice versa. What a strange existence. What an insular life.

I shifted my position in the chill wind as the sun dropped abruptly behind the darkening cloud bank, the all-encompassing mist enveloping the valley and beyond. The menace of unseen threats looming once again.

The past is ever here I whispered. It's all around me.

CHAPTER 39

"Fee hi. This is Kirk Williams. We've got some findings to share with you. Are you around later this afternoon? Mike Thompson and I could come over and see you if that's convenient."

"Sure. That'd be good. I'm on tenterhooks here waiting to find out more. It seems to have taken for ever."

"I'm afraid these things do take time. Sorry about all the wait. It must have been very difficult for you. Anyway shall we say about two pm this afternoon then?"

"Fine."

"We'll be bringing a first draft of our report. We have to write things up officially for Ben Wright as you can imagine."

"Oh great. I'd really like to know everything you've been able to establish about the bodies. Who they were or at least what kind of people they were," I said. "Although I don't suppose you've been able to find out all that much."

"Well yes and no. We do have some likely possibilities as to who they might have been. And we have managed to cross-check our findings by using different techniques so we're pretty sure we know the approximate period when they were alive and their age and gender etc. Some interesting finds all round."

"You bet," I said. "Anyway see you later at two o'clock. I'll be waiting with bated breath."

※

"So Fee, it's all here," said Kirk handing me a bulky blue folder. "First draft anyway. We're still working on it and adding the finer details but we thought you'd like to be kept in the picture."

"Thanks," I said taking the folder eagerly. "Quite a weighty document isn't it? I thought it'd only be a couple of pages."

"When you start writing these things up," said Kirk, "they really get quite complex and can soon run to reams. However I think you'll find it all makes interesting reading."

"Do you think you could just give me a run-down on your findings and I'll read the whole report later?"

"Of course," replied Kirk looking at Mike Thompson. "Do you want to begin or shall I?"

"You go," said Mike. "After all your team has done most of the work on this."

"With your help," said Kirk. "Okay then. We had some input from the osteology team at Nottingham University. They're the local specialists when it comes to human bones. Anyway it seems that there are the remains of six bodies dating back to around the early 1500s, probably around 1530 before the Dissolution of the Monasteries. They're certainly medieval but they're in a better condition than they might have been because of the localised limestone cavity. As Charles probably told you limestone has the beneficial effect of preserving bones."

"So have you been able to ascertain how they died?"

"Well, not really," Kirk replied. "The bones are quite marked and pitted, probably gnawed by rats amongst other things. So it's going to be hard to tell the likely cause of death. We think it must be foul play, simply because of the way in which they were hidden. They can't have gotten there themselves!" He paused. "But what we do think is that they may have been monks," he added.

"Monks!" I gasped. "What makes you think that?"

"It's really about putting together all the evidence, stacking up what we found if you like. And it made us think that they could well have been monks. You see we found other items in there with them, the type of things a monk at that time might have had on their person. Unlike commoners who probably wouldn't have possessed such items. And also they were found very close to the old abbey of course."

"What sort of things did you find?" I asked.

"Well there were four or five cloak pins. We know the monks at the abbey were Cistercian and they would have been wearing a habit with a cloak over the top. The cloak pins we found are very simple but of the type monks would have used to fasten their cloak around them."

"Sounds a bit like a Sherlock Holmes mystery," I said wryly, "unravelling all the parts."

"It is in a way," put in Mike. "That's exactly how you have to work. Like a detective, but a detective with a difference because you're working in the distant past and therefore many of the clues will have disappeared by now."

"So what else did you find?"

"Quite a few bits and pieces actually. Some coins, some metal fastenings which could very well be purse hasps. Monks would have carried a few coins on them of course, to give to the poor and needy. We also found the blades of several knives," said Kirk. "A monk in those days would be carrying a knife with them most of the time, probably with a wooden handle which would've disintegrated by now. A knife would have been a well-used tool, essential both in the kitchen and the fields as well as for eating and such like." He looked at me and I realised that I probably looked gob-smacked. "Also we found several keys and a seal," he continued.

"What sort of seal?"

"It would appear be a monastic seal, made of lead. Not a personal item. A monastic seal served to legitimise documents. Each monastic house would have had a seal with which they signed their legal documents to prove where they had come from. Commoners wouldn't have possessed seals like that. So you see, when you take all of that into consideration it does seem quite likely that they were monks."

"But why? Why would they have been killed, if they were killed?" I asked.

"Now that is another story," said Kirk looking serious. "Monasteries were places where there was a lot of coming and going. As such they were very busy places. The senior monks would have been the Choir monks devoted to the Liturgy of the hours, but Lay brothers were also encouraged to join a monastic community and there would've been a fair number of them. They were the ones who provided the mainstay of support for running the workshops and the farms and kitchens to free up the Choir monks for their rituals, although they also would have had to do some manual labour themselves. Of course the Lay monks were generally less well educated and often illiterate," he added. "They would have lived and worked in a separate section of the monastery and only been allowed to participate in simplified forms of prayer. And as in so many corners of society there was corruption and abuse of power in many of the monasteries."

"Wow," I said, "I'd always been naïve enough to think that monks were monks and as such good people."

"Well they did do good works it's true. They did help the needy and put up travellers who were passing by. And they also developed very efficient infirmaries which they put to good use not only for themselves but also for the local people as well as travellers. But that's only one part of it," said Kirk. "Like any community they would have had their disputes, maybe meted out punishments and such like. Who knows what they really got up to? And of course corruption was rife. Maybe there was friction sometimes over what was going on in the monastery. There were all sorts of illicit practices going on. I don't suppose we'll ever really know for sure."

"Hm. So what was the main difference between the Choir monks and the Lay monks?"

"They took different vows in the first instance in respect of the proportion of work, study and formal prayer they would commit to. The Choir monks being committed to the Liturgy of the hours, meaning they had to pray at regular intervals. They prayed together eight times a day between midnight and seven in the evening. The Lay brothers on the other hand undertook most of the manual labour, cooked and cared for the sick and the poor and were only required to pray a couple of times each day."

"So there could well have been animosity sometimes between the two groups."

"Maybe. Maybe not. We're not going to be able to find out much about that kind of detail. All we do know is that Abbots were often absent from their monastic house, especially smaller ones like the abbey in Whittlesham and that could lead to all kinds of turmoil. Suffice it to say that trouble in the monastic orders would not have been at all unusual despite the good works that they manifestly undertook."

"Goodness me. All this makes me realise how ignorant I've been," I said.

"Anyway all that we can say is that it's very likely that they were monks and it's also very likely that we will never know for sure how they died," put in Mike. "But then, how would one expect to unravel the truth from something like this? We are talking about some events that took place nearly five hundred years ago after all."

"I suppose you're right," I said. "It is a heck of a long time ago. But I would have liked to have known more about what really happened."

"As far as the dead monks would have been concerned if they knew about our discovery they'd be pleased that we'd uncovered things thus far," said Kirk emphatically. "They wouldn't expect to be avenged."

"So Fee," said Tom. "Tell us the latest. What did the archaeology team find out?"

We were having a drink before a meal in The Royal Oak pub. Judith sitting opposite me in our usual oak seat, the fire crackling away in the background.

"Yes," added James. "I don't think I've heard all the news yet."

"Well there have been quite a few developments," I said sipping my wine. "About time too. I was getting fed up with waiting. Anyway Kirk and Mike came over to the house today and gave me their written report. Draft really. I've managed to have a read and it really is quite detailed. Some of it is a bit over my head. But they talked the whole thing over with me anyway so I can give you the gist in layman's terms."

"It seems that there were six bodies, all male and all quite young," I continued. "Around the age of sixteen to twenty. Using various techniques they dated them to around the 1500s, give or take fifty years or so. They confirmed that the bones look the way they do because they've been encased in an area of limestone, hence the encrustation they talked about."

"How could they tell the age of the men?" asked Judith.

"Partly by wear and tear on the bones. They can tell a fair bit from that apparently and also from the teeth. Even back in the 1500s flour was milled using grindstones. Some of the grit would end up in the bread and it gradually eroded people's teeth. The teeth they found were all in a reasonable state so they were able to conclude that they were of a certain age. Interestingly, what Kirk said was that life expectancy at that time was only around thirty five."

"Astonishing," said Tom. "I knew people had a much shorter life span than nowadays but I had no idea it was so short."

"Morbid," said Judith. "If we had the same life expectancy as they did, it would mean that we'd all be dead within a few years."

"Strange thought," I said.

"So what else did they tell you Fee?" said James taking a long draught of beer. "It does seem that they've been able to unravel quite a lot about the bodies themselves, if not who they might have been."

"When they examined the area behind the wall they discovered quite a few other relics apart from the bones. There were some coins and what looked like the hasps of what could be from a purse or suchlike. Also some keys, a few small ones and a couple of larger ones and some knives, just the blades. The handles had gone. And there were also some medieval cloak pins."

"That must be exciting, finding all those items as well. It must have helped the archaeology team to confirm the dating of the bones," put in Judith.

"I suppose you're right," said Tom. "Clever stick!"

"Just sheer logic, you know me," said Judith with a laugh. "Should we be ordering our meal now by the way? I'm sure Tom is his usual starving self."

"Let's just hear anything else Fee has to report," said James, "and then order. That's if you're not going to die on us Tom?"

"No I'm okay actually. I had a latish lunch anyway. Do tell the rest Fee."

"Not much more to tell. I'd like to read the full report again. You guys can have a look at it at the weekend if you like. There's a lot more detail in there as you can imagine."

"Oh there was one other thing," I added. "Kirk mentioned a seal. Charles is apparently going to take it and some of the other items to the Ashmolean in Oxford to try and get more information on them."

"That's interesting," said James. "A seal. There wouldn't have been too many of those around at that time. Seals would have been used by the wealthy and probably also the monasteries but not by the peasant folk. So that's an important clue."

"That's what Kirk said. He and Mike think that all the evidence stacks up to the likelihood of them being monks. Monks from the abbey. He talked of corruption being rife as well as possible rivalry. They hypothesized that the younger monks may have been trying to stop corrupt practices at the time."

"So what did the seal look like?" asked Judith. "Did they say?"

"Kirk said it's made of lead and oval in shape. He called it a vesica seal if I remember rightly. Apparently vesica seals are unusual because they contain two images. The top one probably depicts the monastery's patron saint and the lower one the prior or abbot at prayer. That way the Papal office could be sure where the communication received by the Vatican originated from."

"So," said Judith slowly, "what would one of the monks have been doing, carrying the seal in the first place? You'd think it would've been kept in a very secure place, after all it was a very important item."

"Maybe that's something to do with the corruption," said James.

"Could be," I said. "You never know."

"Yes," said Tom thoughtfully. "Food for thought. This is all coming together like a jigsaw puzzle. I'm going to love writing this story. I have a feeling it'll make me rich and famous!"

"I hope it'll make me rich too," said Judith giving Tom's hand a squeeze.

"Sure," he said squeezing her arm back. "Maybe I'll make an honest woman of you if I get lucky."

"I hope that's not a proposal," quipped back Judith. "If so it's not a very romantic one."

"Oh no, I promise if it happens I'll do it properly," said Tom with a smile. "I'll get down on my bended knee and just whip the ring out of my pocket. Anyway," he went on, "I think it's time to do the ordering now. My stomach is telling me to eat. I'll get the menus."

"You know Fee," said James, "this is all an amazing example of cause and effect, free will and determinism and all that. Right through from when you were driven to buy the house and then lured by some unknown force to have the cellar opened up, even though it was problematic, and then Tom being suspicious about the bricked up wall. It could so easily have been overlooked. And then the exceptionally heavy rain and all the subsequent events. It's hard to believe where we find ourselves."

"Free will and determinism," I murmured. "So everything is already written."

CHAPTER 40

"Hi Tom," I said opening the door. "I wasn't expecting you. Not that this isn't an unexpected pleasure."

"Hi Fee," said Tom stepping inside carrying his silver laptop. I closed the front door and showed him into the study where I was marking assignments.

"Oh, I'm sorry. I'm disturbing you," he said looking at my papers spread out on the large round table by the window.

"No not at all. I could do with a break. You know what it's like when you get your head down working. You forget about the time. How about a coffee?"

"That'd be great. I've been up since the crack of dawn. Writing," said Tom sitting himself down on the small sofa by the fireplace.

I fetched us a cup of black coffee each and joined him back in the study.

"I do like this room," said Tom looking about him. "With the deep red colour and the cream sofa. It goes really well with all your dark furniture."

"Thanks. I enjoy colour and putting things together. I suppose because it's something completely different from my work."

Tom opened his case. "Here," he said thrusting several sheets of paper into my hand. "What do you think? It's the beginnings of my article."

Grabbing the pieces of paper expectantly I sat down at the table to read, sipping my coffee as I did so.

Archaeology Today
Medieval mystery unravels
by Tom Jackson

Evidence of corruption in the monasteries in the 1500s has been exposed in the small village of Whittlesham in Buckinghamshire. Following unexpected road subsidence on the A422, local resident Fee Hunter contacted the Highways Department informing them that she had discovered a bricked up door in her recently re-opened cellars which might give them access under the road and help them to discover the cause of the subsidence.

Further investigation by the Highways Department, who also brought in the local Archaeology Team, resulted in the discovery of a stone staircase leading to a tunnel running under her house. It is believed that the tunnel originated in Norman times and led from the castle to the medieval abbey on the opposite side of the road to Ms Hunter's house. The solidly built subterranean passage would have been used by the baron of the castle as an escape route in times of need.

There have been subsequent developments at the site. Kirk Williams and Mike Thomson, from the Archaeology sub-contracting team and Highways Department, respectively, noticed the walls of the tunnel contained an area where the stones were of a different size and finished off in a rougher manner than the rest of the tunnel. On removal of the stones they found a cavity behind the wall which contained numerous bones and various medieval artefacts scattered on the floor. Several dating techniques were carried out and the bones and artefacts were dated back to the early to mid-1500s.

"This is good," I said looking up. "It reads very well indeed."

"Thank you," said Tom. "It did just kind of flow. It makes it somehow come alive when you're personally involved with events."

"I guess so," I said turning back to the article.

Further investigation by a fellow archaeologist at Oxford University, Charles Lawrie, who worked in collaboration with one of the Oxford study centres, uncovered evidence that the bodies were possibly those of six young monks who could have been disposed of by members of the monastic order. The order of monks at the abbey were Cistercian, which was a daughter house connected to Woburn Abbey dating back to 1397, Woburn Abbey being in turn a daughter house from Fountevrault Abbey at Perseigne in Normandy.

Reports of corruption in the monasteries contained in a book entitled *Aftermath – The Dissolution of the Monasteries Uncovered* were discovered at the study centre. It is thought that the bones belonged to six of the younger monks from the order. There are a number of possible reasons why they could have been disposed of. Could it have been a punishment? Or was the violence a result of some kind of internal dispute? Or could these young men have been trying to make moves to stop the corruption which dogged many of the abbeys at the time? Such corruption was often exacerbated by absent Abbots who left their abbey in the hands of senior monks who, in turn, were lured by burgeoning wealth into corrupt practices such as the taking of money for sham relics or the promise of special favour in the afterlife.

The archaeology team are having further tests carried out on the bones to try and establish whether there are any signs of violence which could indicate how the monks died. As Kirk Williams explained "Due to the extreme age of the bones, together with the evidence of gnaw marks from rodents, it may be difficult to determine the cause of death. We shall, however, endeavour to uncover the facts of this case as this is an extremely important find.

"Excellent and to the point," I said laying the sheets on the table.

"How much longer will the finished article be? Do you know?"

"Oh a fair bit longer. Probably at least three or four times the length. Say, two to two and a half thousand words."

"Great stuff. When's your deadline?"

"Well what with Christmas and stuff they're looking to publish in February or March next year. So I've got a bit of time. I'll need to get it to them by mid-January."

"Well you're certainly on the way. It's really good."

"Glad you feel I'm on track," said Tom finishing his coffee. "I shan't keep you. I'll let you get back to your work. I have to go to London now."

"What are you working on?"

"Well I'm writing a story on how areas of run-down London have been regenerated by councils and the community working together. There are some amazing examples of real ingenuity, some costing very little. It's very exciting. There are some wonderfully visual examples of how the joint effort has transformed the area. Basically I'm taking photos today, I've largely done the write-up."

"Sounds good," I said. "Anyway thanks for showing me the article. Keep me up to speed with it won't you."

"I sure will," Tom said as he stood up to go. "I'll email it to Judith and James when I've finished, see what they think."

CHAPTER 41

"So you've got the key to the cellar door?" asks Tom expectantly as we await Charles' arrival.

"Yes. Kirk left it with me on strict instructions that we'd only go down into the tunnel if either he or Charles were with us," I say cautiously. "I must say I'm rather nervous about going down there, it all sounds quite macabre to me."

Moving over to the cupboard in the study I open the top drawer and take out the ornately carved key. "Here it is," I say passing it to Tom.

"Heavy, isn't it?" says Tom eagerly. "I can't wait. I just want to get more of a feel for the atmosphere before I do any more work on my article."

"Well, Charles will be here any moment," I say closing the drawer, "and we're not going down into the cellars until he arrives," I add firmly. "I don't blame Judith for not wanting to come with us. I'm really not at all sure why I'm going down there."

"Oh you'll you glad when you do," says Tom. "Where has your spark gone girl? You used to be the driving force behind things. And now look at you, you've turned into some kind of shrinking violet!"

"Thanks," I say somewhat miffed. "Not sure how you'd like to have been through all the hassle I've had lately. Anyway let's wait in the kitchen. I don't trust you with that key. I'll make you a drink. That'll keep you quiet."

❦

We make our way down the spiral stone staircase, Charles leading the way with a torch followed by Tom and then myself.

"Crikey, this is amazing!" says Tom. He is carrying one of the portable halogen lamps and the light bounces back off the stone giving the effect of bright yellow neon lighting. "They must have been some stone masons to construct this so well."

I follow him gingerly down the winding staircase. At the bottom we turn to the right with Charles in front. Tom takes my arm and gives me a squeeze. "You'll be alright," he says gently. "Charles and I will look after you. I didn't mean it before about you being a wimp."

"I know. Thanks. By the way, what about rats?" I ask Charles. "Did you see any before?"

"No, we didn't," replies Charles turning back towards us. "Didn't hear anything either."

"Thank goodness," I say with a shudder.

"The tunnel is remarkably dry," Tom says reaching out and touching the stone with his right hand. "I'd have thought it would be quite damp."

"Stone actually breathes and absorbs the water," Charles replies, "so the walls will be quite dry. It's what you'd expect. There might be a bit of moisture on the other side but here where there's an air flow I wouldn't expect them to be damp."

"And how come it's not really cold down here?" I ask.

"The temperature never drops below freezing underground, not when you get below seven hundred millimetres. That's why building regulations require pipes and services to be laid below that depth," Charles says as he comes to a halt. "Here it is. Here's where we found the remains."

Tom places the halogen lamp directly in front of the opening in the wall. I hang back, noticing the heap of stones which has been moved to one side. The dust and rubble has been carefully brushed into a neat pile on the other.

Tom takes his camera from round his neck and moves over to the cavity. "Wow," he says, "this is awesome, actually seeing the place where the bodies were hidden all that time ago. Fee do come and have a look. Don't worry there are no bones here now."

He puts out his hand to me and I move reluctantly over to peer behind the layer of stone remaining at the bottom of the wall. All I can see are piles of dust along the length of the cavity.

"What do you mean no bones?" I ask. "Charles surely that dust there must be the remains of the smaller bones, the ones that disintegrated."

"You're right," Charles says with a dry smile. "There was no point in sweeping it all up when we bagged up the bones but maybe Kirk and his guys will come and do that before the bones are interred. I'll mention it to him when I give him a bell."

Tom flashes a few shots from different angles. "There's really not much to photograph but the atmosphere's great. That's what I wanted to experience for myself. That and the tunnel itself."

"Where did you find the mandrake roots you gave me by the way?" I ask Charles. "Was it near here?"

"No it was a bit further along," he says pointing into the blackness beyond. "What are you going to do with them?"

"I don't know. Probably send them to Paul McEwan at the Witchcraft museum. I don't want them."

"Don't send them until I've written my article," put in Tom. "I'd like to find out more about them. More about their witchcraft connotations. You did say they were more than likely connected with the occult didn't you Charles?"

"They sure are. Their roots have long been used in magic rituals. They would have been very important to your practising witches, Eliza and Rose. From what you've told me I suspect they must've belonged to them."

"Well that's even more reason for me to get rid of them," I say hastily. "You know I want nothing more to do with witchcraft. Tom you'd better get on with it so that I can parcel them up and post them to Cornwall."

"I can do some research today if you like," Tom says with a grin.

"You know me. Never let the grass grow under my feet. Especially if you can run to lunch."

"Okay. I'll do lunch but those roots have got to go. Soon. By the end of this week at the latest. How about you Charles? Can you stay for lunch?"

"Thanks but no. I've got to get back to Oxford. Got a meeting at two o'clock."

"Thanks for coming over. We really do appreciate it. I know how busy you are. Anyway," I say looking at Tom, "are you done here?"

"I suppose so," Tom replies somewhat reluctantly. "Not sure there's anything more to see."

"Not really. And what about the hole?" I ask turning to Charles. "You can't just leave it."

"I rather think Kirk will have the stones put back when he's finished. Although who is going to come down here in the future I really don't know," replies Charles. "Why would they?"

"Fee, come and have a look," says Tom as he taps away on his laptop.

I get up from the table where I'm putting the finishing touches to a lecture and move over to sit beside Tom on the sofa. "See, this is interesting stuff." He scrolls back up to the top of the page and starts reading.

> "All parts of the mandrake plant are poisonous. It was believed historically that death befell anyone who dug the root and pulled it screaming from the ground. For this reason dogs were often tied to the root and used to excavate it.
>
> It has been associated from ancient times with magic and is a valued aphrodisiac, fertility drug and a powerful anaesthetic. It was often kept by its owner in a wooden coffin shaped box, sometimes with a crucifix marked on the lid. Its association with both life and death make it important within magic rituals and it is a central part of moon rites and ceremonies.

Today it is used within the Craft as a powerful protection herb as well as within exorcisms, sex magic, to empower visions and help bring those visions into manifestation."

"Seems it has an awful lot of powers," says Tom. "You wouldn't believe it to look at those stumpy little roots."

"You're not going to get carried away with all that stuff are you?"

"Course not. But I just wanted to find out a bit more about it. That's all. Hey look at what it says here."

"Mandrake is the most magical of all plants and herbs. It is used as a talisman and, according to legend, if a mandrake root is sold or given away it will eventually find its way back to its original owner."

"Well what do you know?" says Tom. "Maybe that's the reason Charles stumbled across them. He was meant to find them and give them to you. They belong to you."

"Your fella is a blooming nuisance," I said to Judith later as we walked Barnie. I had decided to stick to the lanes to make the going easier for her. Holding her arm I guided her down the hill.

"No need to tell me," said Judith. "Never been known to keep his mouth shut, that one."

"That was all I needed to hear. Just when I think I'm getting on top of things And then he tells me those roots have made their own way back to me, that I won't be able to get rid of them. He's ghastly and that's all there is to it."

"Do you believe in all that?" Judith queried.

"I don't know what to believe," I said with a sigh. "What do you think? You're the level-headed one."

"Well," she said slowly. "I think what you believe is important. If you believe in that myth then maybe it will become true. And if you can really say that you don't believe it and you get rid of them then maybe things will be alright."

"So what you're saying is that I should go ahead and send them to Boscastle and be done with it?"

"Yes, I think that's going to be the best bet. You really don't want to keep them. What good would it do? And you've no use for them."

"You're right. I shall just ignore that stupid Tom. I'll do it when we get back," I said relieved to hear Judith's good sense.

As we approached the end of the lane I stopped to call Barnie who was looking through the gate at the cows leaning over towards him. "I shouldn't go there if I were you," I call to him laughing, "they're bigger than you."

Barnie turned to look at us and paused, then trotted back towards us. "At least the road has been re-opened," I said as we set off walking back up the lane.

"Thank goodness for that. Mum hated driving all the way round the diversion route," said Judith. "And I expect you did too."

"I certainly did. Anyway they seem to have made a good job of all the repairs. The road surface looks as good as new."

"Did they say there might be any recurrence, that is if we get more heavy rain?" asked Judith. "I suppose you need to be prepared for these things."

"Mike Thompson said he thought it was probably a one off," I said. "They've done a thorough repair job beneath the surface so he said there shouldn't be any possibility of another swallow hole. I only hope he's right."

I stopped as I pushed the peculiarly shaped mandrake roots into a jiffy bag, still in the plastic bag in which Charles had given them to me. They seemed to be looking at me, their oddly shaped heads cocked to one side, twisting as if craning to see what I was up to. They certainly looked human in a strange kind of way. I could see how the branches of the roots had been pinched a little below the tops to resemble a head and neck. As I looked I was aware that the upper and lower branches had been twisted off to form arms and legs, their stumpy bodies exuding what seemed to me to be smug self-satisfaction. It was uncanny. They were like real people.

Abruptly I shoved them into the bag and grabbed the sellotape, quickly sealing down the flap with several pieces of tape. Fixing a label on the front addressed to Paul McEwan in Boscastle I stuck a couple of stamps on and then turned the bag over and pressed a label on the back telling him that the parcel was from me.

"Right," I said to myself. "This is it. You're going in the post right now."

I picked up my keys and went out, shutting the door behind me. Walking to the post box at the far end of the village I tried not to dwell on the possible consequences. "This is ridiculous," I thought. "A couple of mouldy old roots unnerving me. I'll have something to say to that blooming Tom."

CHAPTER 42

Going outside to open the post box by the gate I was surprised to see a brown jiffy bag sticking through the mouth of the box. It can't be I thought hastily turning the key in the lock. The jiffy bag fell inside the box on top of my other mail as I opened the door.

It was one and the same. The jiffy bag I had addressed to Paul McEwan in Boscastle and posted the other day. Turning it over slowly I looked for the address label and realised that it must have come unstuck. So the post office had returned it to me I breathed. Incredible. I could see my sender label clearly showing on the back of the bag. Shakily I collected the other letters and took the package inside the house. I went and sat down in the kitchen wondering what to do next.

I dialled James' number but it went immediately into answerphone. I tried Judith's number but there was no reply. She and her mother must be out. I scrolled down my contacts and tried her mobile number but that was switched off and I didn't want to leave a message. I wasn't in the mood. I needed to take action and I needed to do it now.

I sat there my mind whirling. What if Tom's prediction was true? What if I wasn't going to be able to get rid of the mandrake roots? They had come to me in such a peculiar manner, almost as if it was meant to happen as Tom had said. Why else had Charles wandered off along the tunnel like that and just stumbled across them. They could have lain there forever but for the mischance of the hour. Some force must be at work, a force with a stronger will than myself.

Suddenly I thought of Llewellyn Price. I need to talk this over with him I thought, reaching for my mobile. I clicked on his number.

"Llewellyn. Hi it's me, Fee. Fee Hunter," I said breathlessly. "I need to talk to you."

"Hello Fee. Good to hear from you. Is there anything wrong?" he asked. "You sound worried."

"I am. There's something happening and I don't like it. Can you come over or should I come to your house? Sorry to be a nuisance."

"I'll come to you," said Llewellyn levelly. "I can come now if you like. I haven't got anything on that won't wait."

"Oh would you. That would be really good. I just need to talk to someone, see how to make sense of it all."

"I'll make a couple of phone calls and then I'll be right over. Say in about half an hour."

"Thanks Llewellyn. I do appreciate it." I rang off and took a deep breath. Using a knife I carefully slit open the sellotape on the jiffy bag and wincingly pulled out the clear plastic covering. Inside the mocking figures waved their stumpy misshapen arms at me and grinned.

※

"So you see there's something very funny going on here and I just don't know how to stop it," I said nervously to Llewellyn as we sat in the kitchen by the Aga each with a cup of steaming black coffee.

I put my hands round my mug and waited.

Llewellyn sat for a few moments, clearly surprised by my tale. "Well Fee I don't know what to make of it either," he said slowly. He paused. "Why don't you show me the roots?" he added.

Holding up the bag towards Llewellyn I could see him scrutinising them carefully.

The greyish brown tuberous roots were gnarled and scarred and quite old looking I thought, wondering whether they would eventually disintegrate and rot or whether they were preserved in some way. He sat there deep in thought. Barnie scratched at the door and I got up to let him in quickly, anxious not to disturb Llewellyn.

Llewellyn looked up, " I think," he said, "that we need to examine to what extent the mandrake roots might bring harm to you or even if they might be of help. After all you did say that they're used as a herb for protection."

"Yes, we did read that on the internet. But I don't want to have anything to do with witchcraft. I don't want to use them for protection or for anything else, I just want rid of them."

"It seems to me that just because something which is morally neutral in itself is used in witchcraft it does not necessarily make it bad. The roots may have absolutely no effect on you at all if you believe them to be just harmless pieces of plant," said Llewellyn.

"That's possible," I said feeling a little calmer now that Llewellyn was here and I had someone I could talk things through with, someone level-headed who could help me to work out what I should do. Strange I thought how much I've been turning to Robert Delforth and Llewellyn Price over the last year. Religion has always been rather at the edge of my life, now it seems to be giving me real support from different directions. They are two such very compassionate and helpful people.

"I could try sanctifying them for you," said Llewellyn thoughtfully. "That would mean that if you find them worrying or disturbing any vestiges of what they might have been used for in the past would no longer be there. It would render them harmless and you could either keep them or dispose of them."

"Maybe that's it," I said. "It seems to have worked with the exorcism you carried out. The house has been fine since then, as far as I know."

"Okay. Why don't I do that? If we can get them out of the bag, maybe with a glove, and just put them on a piece of paper. That might be best," said Llewellyn.

I fetched a pair of rubber gloves from the utility room and spread out some folded newspaper on a tray, tearing off some kitchen paper for them to lie on. Gingerly opening the plastic bag I used a gloved hand to remove the roots and placed them charily on the paper towel, their smug looking faces gazing up at me. "How's that?" I asked.

"Fine. Just give me time to prepare a suitable prayer," and Llewellyn and he sat quietly for a few minutes.

I looked on at the scene blankly, feeling like an onlooker. The table was bare except for the folded newspaper with the mandrake roots nestling in the kitchen paper. The house was absolutely still with not a sound outside, no cars passing in the road which was strange now that the road had re-opened. It was like a moment suspended in time.

How can this be happening to me I thought? All these strange occurrences. And now here I am sitting in my own kitchen with some tuberous roots waiting for them to blessed by the Methodist Superintendent who I'd never even heard of last year. If it wasn't happening to me I'd be thinking it was quite funny, ludicrous even. But this was happening to me and it wasn't funny. I resolved to find some way of thanking Llewellyn Price. He was really very kind and always there to help even though I wasn't exactly one of his parishioners.

"Right," he said, "I have it."

He put out his right hand and held it above the mandrake roots.

"Transforming God, who takes what is good in every situation and gives us the strength to stand against what is evil, help us to use this material in a wholesome way rather than a destructive way, as life-giving rather than taking away from life. In the name of Christ, Amen."

And then he sat there for a few moments. I looked at the mandrake tubers suspiciously but they looked unchanged to me, still bearing their human-like expressions. "So what now?" I asked. "What do I do with them?"

"Well you can either place them somewhere in the house and just leave them there, say in the cellar, or you may still wish to get rid of them."

"If I leave them in the cellar I'll always be wondering what they're up to," I said uncertainly. "I think I'll have to have another go at getting rid of them. Maybe not send them to Boscastle, they might get their power back by association with other magic artefacts."

"Perhaps you could place them in a rubbish bin, not yours but one in some kind of public place where they don't belong to anyone?" suggested Llewellyn "That way they'd be taken away with the rubbish and disposed of."

"Good idea. I'll take them with me tomorrow when I go to work and drop them into a bin somewhere. Hopefully that will be the last of them," I said relieved that a decision had been made. "I really want to thank you Llewellyn. You've been a great help, as usual."

"It's nothing. That's the nature of my work," he said with a smile getting up. "And now I'll be off, I do have a couple of other calls to make on my way home."

I showed him out and then went back into the kitchen. I put on a rubber glove and carefully picked up the roots and dropped them back in their plastic bag, sealing them with a twist-it tie. Then I put them back into the jiffy bag and put it into a carrier bag. Catching up my car keys I went out of the house and round to the car. I opened the boot and dropped the bag on the floor. Banging the boot shut I went back into the house and flopped on the sofa in the sitting room exhausted.

CHAPTER 43

"Ten bottles of wine!" I exclaim tightening my scarf and turning up the collar of my leather coat against the gusty night. "We're going to try ten wines? You didn't tell me that."

"Only a taste or so of each wine," says James laughing as we make our way up the dimly lit path to the church, the last whirls of crackly winter leaves chasing each other in the wind. "That's what it said on the flyer. It is a wine tasting evening after all."

"Well I'm not going to use the spittoon if there is one. It would feel like a criminal act. And in any case I don't know how to do it politely."

"No, I'm not sure I do. Just for the record I'm not going to waste my wine either," says James. "At least we're not driving so we don't have to worry about that."

"Anyway I think we deserve to have a good time tonight. After what we've been through over the last few months."

"Especially you," says James as we approach the church porch, the clumps of chestnut trees buffeting in the wind away to our right. "You've done very well to deal with it all. You've certainly showed a lot of strength."

"Well I've had a lot of help from so many people. You in particular. I really do appreciate it," I say giving his arm a squeeze. "Let's get inside out of this wind."

Stepping through the heavy wooden door I can see that the inner doors are open. Within the church is velvety red, decorated in readiness for Christmas. There are wreaths of ivy hanging from the pillars and garlands of red ribbon and holly with berries tied round the ends of the pews, at the far end, over to the left, a tall Christmas tree shimmering with silver lights. Handfuls of gold and silver baubles tied with lengths of sparkling ribbon adorn the higher reaches of the columns with white berried garlands of mistletoe looped round the ornately carved font. All about us is bathed in a soft red glow. It looks magical.

Looking up I can see that the colour is emanating from the thickset heaters incongruously perched high up on the rafters. "Wow, just look at this," I say in wonder, gazing all around.

"Amazing isn't it?" says James ushering me inside. "Shame that Judith and Tom can't be here tonight. You know how Tom likes his wine!"

"Yes, it is a shame. They would've enjoyed it. I think they've gone to a family do somewhere in London," I say. "How beautiful and welcoming the church looks. Great setting for a wine tasting."

"James, I'm not sure you know Nina Johnson," I add turning as a tall dark-haired woman approaches us. "Nina, this is James. Nina and David have organised the wine tasting tonight. To raise money for the church. Ostensibly," I say with a smile.

"Nice to meet you James. I think we've said hello before in passing," says Nina. "We're hoping to raise a fair bit for the church restoration fund. And we might as well enjoy ourselves whilst we do so."

"Too right," I say. "The decorations are brilliant Nina."

"Thanks. It was a joint effort and it does seem to have turned out rather well. The muted light from our rather ancient heaters does give everything a special glow."

"By the way, who's that lady over there?" I ask Nina as I notice a vivacious red haired woman dressed in a shapely black dress with a bright turquoise and cream scarf draped round her shoulders. She is standing near the altar talking enthusiastically to Robert Delforth the vicar.

"Oh, she's an old friend of his. From college apparently. She's staying with Robert for a few days. David and I are rather hoping she might turn out to be more that just a friend," she says softly. "Robert is such a dear person. He could do with someone special, especially someone like Olivia."

"Match-making now are we Nina?" I tease.

"Oh, you know what I mean," Nina replies. "We've only got his best interest at heart. I sometimes think he must be so lonely in that big old house, rattling around by himself. Anyway, do excuse me I must carry on with my meeting and greeting duties." And she moves over to welcome more villagers as they filter into the church.

There is a long row of trestle tables stretching down the middle of the church towards the altar with flickering candles in wine bottles carefully placed in the centre of the crisp white tablecloths. Plates of cheese, bread and biscuits are piled up along the length of the neatly laid table with tall wine glasses placed in front of each chair.

I follow James as we make our way towards Robert. "You must meet Olivia," says Robert stepping forward. "Olivia, this is Fee and this is James."

"Good to meet you both," says Olivia warmly, her tousled red hair tumbling about her shoulders as she shakes our hands. "Robert has told me about you both."

"Good things I hope. Are you here long?" I ask.

"Just for a few days. Maybe I'll be coming again soon," she says looking at Robert and I can see there is indeed a special kind of sparkle between them. Nina's right I think fleetingly. It would be wonderful to see Robert married or at least with a companion.

Nina's husband David is standing at the far end of the trestle tables near the altar beside a table covered with wine bottles. Each bottle enclosed carefully in silver foil. Clearing his throat he bangs on the table with a spoon.

"Attention please everyone. Do sit down. I'd like to welcome you to this wine tasting event, the first of many I hope, and to thank you all for coming. Briefly we're going to try ten wines. Three whites, two types of rose, followed by five reds. And I'm going to ask you to guess the grape and the price as we go, with a little help from me," he says genially.

"There's plenty of bread, cheese and biscuits to keep you going. And don't forget there's lots of water for you to drink." As he spoke Nina was moving down the table placing bottles of cold water down the centre of the extended table. "And you've each got a spittoon in front of you if you should need one," he continued indicating the tall red paper beakers next to the wine glasses. "Mind you, I'm not saying you should waste all this wine, but just in case….."

"Great atmosphere," I whisper to James.

"Sure," he replies.

"Okay, so the form is this," David continues, "Nina and I will pour you each some wine and we all have a go at tasting it. Before you do so I'll tell you how to use your mouth to get the most of both the flavour and the nose. Nose is the bouquet. And we'll also look at the legs. Legs means the way the wine hangs on the glass. You'll all be experts by the time you leave."

A brief round of applause follows as we all sit expectantly in our seats. David and Nina move expertly down either side of the table and pour wine into the glasses. Then David returns to the front and gives us the low-down on the first wine.

"This is going to be fun," I whisper to James and his friend Matt, who is sitting next to us with his Indonesian girlfriend Kade opposite.

"Sure is," Matt says. "Never been to a wine tasting before. Have you?"

"No," says James, "and I don't think Fee has either."

"No I haven't. Ten wines sounds like a heck of a lot of wine. But never mind, we can always carry each other home. Or even spend the night in church," I joke.

"This is great," James says quietly as we move onto the second red wine, "but I wonder if we should make a move now? I'm getting tired and I'd quite like for us to be on our own."

"I know what you mean. I am enjoying it here and the atmosphere is really good but I'm happy to get going. Like you I'm tired and we don't need any more wine," I reply taking his hand under the table.

"Shall we just say our goodbyes then and slip out?" says James.

"Fine. Let's go."

"You know I can't help thinking about all that's been going on, reflecting back on how we live in tandem with history. It's all inextricably part and parcel of where we are now," I say pensively as we lie on the floor together in the sitting room back at the house, Barnie stretched out beside us.

The dying fire has been rekindled and the coals are beginning to crackle and spit as they heat through. It feels warm and cosy with the lights low and the curtains drawn, the gusting winds of the night shut firmly out.

"I know. We can learn so much from the past if we take the trouble to trace things back, to see what's gone before. It can help us to know what to do now, what the implications might be," says James.

"So often we're concerned with the present and what's going to happen in the future," he adds, "that we forget the past. We don't make time for it. And then suddenly something hauls us back in time quite unexpectedly. Politicians learn from history all the time I'm sure and people like me, us boring old historians, we're all aware of the impact of the past. But we can all learn from it, every last one of us."

"So where does it leave us," I say languidly. "You and I have got a history now. We've been together over a year."

"Scarey. After all I only rang you to help you with the history of the village. And now look where we're at!"

"You helped me with more than the history of the village," I reply sitting up and leaning against the settee. "You know, I feel quite exhausted by all that's been happening. The way the past has been catching up with the present. I wonder if it will leave us alone for the time being now. I do hope so."

Getting up I poke the fire to shake the ashes through the grate adding, "I can't say I'm glad it all happened but I've certainly learned a lot from it. And I think it's brought us closer together."

"You're right Fee," James says putting his arm round my shoulders, "and the drama of the deaths in the monastery, that needed to be exposed. And it wouldn't have been if it wasn't for you. The dead might be anonymous but they have in some way been avenged."

"I suppose so. We can't go back and put anything right but at least their story has in part been told."

"So," says James looking at me as I lie back on the floor beside him. "Life's about living. Let's get on with it."

"To voices past, to us and to the future," I say with a mock toast, thinking of the wine tasting still taking place at the church.

As we lie there on the floor Barnie rolls over inviting me to stroke him and the fire crackles. I hear the soft drawn out crunch as a log falls slowly into the glowing embers and stretch out feeling relaxed and content.

"You know something?" I murmur suddenly brought back to the present.

"No, what?"

"I've got a feeling I left my handbag in the church."

"Oh bugger. Should you go and check?"

"Think so. Won't be a minute," I said, diving into the study.

"Oh drat. I must have. Do you mind coming back over there with me?" I call through to James.

"Of course not. Shall we go right now?"

We make our way back up the path to the church, the wind gusting heavily round us, the lights in the church dimmed. James opens the heavy outer door carefully and peers inside. Nina and David are busy putting the paper plates and red beakers into black sacks as they move down each side of the table and Jane Marsden, whom I recognise as one of the church wardens, is passing along behind them gathering up the white paper tablecloths which are now covered in spatters of red wine.

"Hi there," says Nina. "Did you forget something?"

"Yes, I think so. I seem to have left my handbag behind. I'll just have a look where we were sitting. It must be there, under the table I expect."

I cross over to the far side of the trestle tables and make my way down the aisle. Pulling back a couple of chairs I can see my bag nestling down there, fortunately not trampled upon. "Here it is," I say with some relief, thinking of credit cards and the like going missing and all the related hassle.

"Do you guys need a hand?" asks James moving to help Jane Marsden fold up the table cloths.

"Thanks, don't mind if you do," says David. "It's getting a bit late I think." He checks his watch. "Yes, as I thought, it's gone half past twelve."

James and I jump to it and assist with the tidying up and soon the church is in good order. "We'll leave the tables until the morning," says Nina. "But thanks for your help. Many hands make light work as they say," she adds with a smile.

"Okay then, we'll be going," I say giving Nina a hug. "Thank you both for organising all this. It's been absolutely great."

"Bye to you both," said David. "See you soon."

Clasping my handbag James and I make our way out of the church and back down the lane to the main road. The wind has somewhat abated but the air is still chill and the sky a velvety black. I notice that several of the street lamps have gone out and the road is unusually dark and deserted.

Suddenly I hear something coming along the road and before I can turn round I feel myself being vigorously swept up and carried along by a rush of moving air. Then, just as swiftly I find myself falling, falling, down, down. Abruptly I hit the grass verge.

"Whatever is going on?" I hear James saying as he peers anxiously down at me where I lie in the grass dazed and shaken.

"I really don't know," I gasp, "but I think some kind of horse and carriage just hit me. I could hear what sounded like jangling reins and the rumbling of wooden wheels. It was uncanny."

James looks taken aback. "There was nothing here," he says slowly looking about him. "I just saw you being thrust into the air and blown along, then dropped like a rag doll," he adds looking bemused. He sits down beside me and takes my hands in his.

"Are you thinking what I'm thinking?" I ask stunned by the fast-moving events. "I think I've been caught up in the past again. Is it never-ending?"

James looks at me sideways. "I'm beginning to realise that you're somehow connected inextricably with the past, voices past, people past, events past. And I'm not sure you're going to be able to change that...."